"[LeCraw's] storytelling is confident and well-crafted, as she juxtaposes scenes from the past with those of the present, vividly demonstrating how characters, situations, and conflicts persist through time." —*Bookreporter*

"Engrossing. . . . Set at the overlap between Updike and Cheever countries, on the Connecticut coast and Cape Cod."
—*The Free Lance-Star* (Fredericksburg, VA)

"LeCraw's characters are well-drawn and her writing fluid. . . . The back-and-forth through time of the narrative works amazingly well. And the heartbreaking progress of Callie's depression creates nail-biting suspense." —*Edmonton Journal*

"This exceptionally complex and accomplished novel does not read like the work of a beginning writer. With a strong underlying theme of longing woven throughout, LeCraw's work skillfully takes these characters through varying emotional journeys. An insightful piece, not just for beach or airplane reading. An author to watch."
—*Library Journal* (starred review)

"The kind of dark, thorny, complex novel I love. . . . *The Swimming Pool* is truly a knockout."
—Caroline Leavitt, author of *Girls in Trouble*

"Seasoned by a cast of refreshing-yet-familiar characters and set against the backdrop of summer life by the sea." —*Marie Claire*

"An insightful, compelling examination of love and betrayal. Powerful and page-turning." —*Winnipeg Free Press*

HOLLY LECRAW

THE SWIMMING POOL

Holly LeCraw was born and raised in Atlanta. She now lives outside Boston with her husband, journalist Peter Howe, and their three children. Her short fiction has appeared in various publications and has been nominated for a Pushcart Prize.

www.hollylecraw.com

ANCHOR BOOKS
A Division of Random House, Inc.
New York

HOLLY LECRAW

THE
SWIMMING
POOL

A NOVEL

For Peter

FIRST ANCHOR BOOKS EDITION, APRIL 2011

Copyright © 2010 by Holly LeCraw

All rights reserved. Published in the United States by
Anchor Books, a division of Random House, Inc., New York,
and in Canada by Random House of Canada Limited, Toronto.
Originally published in hardcover in the United States by Doubleday,
a division of Random House, Inc., New York, in 2010.

Anchor Books and colophon are registered trademarks of
Random House, Inc.

The Library of Congress has cataloged the Doubleday edition as follows:
LeCraw, Holly.
The swimming pool / by Holly LeCraw.—1st ed.
p. cm.
1. Married people—Fiction. 2. Adultery—Fiction. 3. Murder—Fiction.
4. Murder victims' families—Fiction. 5. Cape Cod (Mass.)—Fiction.
6. Psychological fiction. I. Title.
PS3612.E337S85 2009
813'.6—dc22 2009008314

Anchor ISBN: 978-0-307-47444-5

www.anchorbooks.com

Printed in the United States of America
10 9 8 7 6 5 4 3 2 1

Home is where one starts from. As we grow older

The world becomes stranger, the pattern more complicated

Of dead and living.

— T. S. ELIOT, "EAST COKER"

ONE
THE
BATHING
SUIT

Bodies, bodies. The beach was crowded, Marcella had not expected all these people everywhere—she had forgotten it was Saturday, forgotten, even, that it was June. Today, after Anthony's phone call, she had come here gulping for broad sky, a long horizon, a vast and indifferent emptiness; but instead the beach was alive with babies crying and children running and their parents yelling or laughing or just watching, with that look of contentment she faintly remembered from a long time ago—

She veered toward the tide line, away from the massed umbrellas and beach blankets, going through a swath of tiny shells. They crunched beneath her feet, but she did not alter her path.

Anthony had said, "I've got some news." His voice had been odd, solicitous and pained at the same time, and when he had said it, *news,* her throat had caught and she had thought again that she hated the phone. "Toni has gotten a job," he said. At the Cape. Where he and Toni were, and she was not. "A babysitting job."

"Babysitting! Our Antonia?" She laughed with crazy relief. *See, you worry for nothing—*

And then he told her where.

"*What?*" she whispered, her laughter gone, gone. "Anthony. You can't let her."

"Chella, what the hell am I supposed to say?" There was a pause and then he went on more quietly, grimly, "She found the job herself. She didn't tell me ahead of time. We like shows of initiative."

Marcella didn't keep in touch with anyone from Cape Cod. It was Anthony's place, it always had been, and when they divorced it had seemed natural to leave it too, entirely. She hadn't even known Callie McClatchey, Cecil's daughter, was married. Hadn't known Callie had not one but two children—Cecil's grandchildren, and Betsy's too, whom they would never see.

Anthony said, "The McClatchey girl does need someone to help her, I suppose—"

"Stop it. *Please.*"

"I'm sorry," he had said. "I'm sorry." And she had known he was. He was not a consciously cruel man.

She walked on, mechanically, down the beach. The shells were still crumbling beneath her feet. Why was it satisfying to be destructive? She resisted the impulse to stop, squat down, examine the wreckage her bare feet had wrought, here on *her* beach, only a few hours from the Cape, in Connecticut. She had come to this little town blindly, after the divorce. It was near the boarding school where Anthony had sent Toni, and even though Marcella had known it would not make much difference, she could not bear to stay in Boston, so far away. Now Toni was in college but Marcella was still here, and she still could walk this beach and, most days, have no one recognize her. Even with all these people, she could be alone.

She had not asked Anthony when Toni's job was starting. Already, even without details, her brain was barreling ahead, painting its pictures—it could be that right now Toni was holding the baby. A tiny girl, Anthony had said. Marcella remembered how an infant would turn its head toward a breast, even a stranger's, mouth gaping like a fish, seeking even when there was nothing there to find. She wondered how Toni would deal with that, and felt a brief smile on her face like sun. Toni would just hand the baby over, as quickly as she could. *Velocemente!* To Callie McClatchey. To Cecil's daughter. She looked like him—blond and blue-eyed, with an open, oval face. The brother was dark, favored Betsy. Marcella remembered him too, quite clearly. She couldn't think why. Did the baby perhaps take after him? Or in its tiny face, in the baby with whom she, Marcella, shared no blood, none at all, could one find Cecil again? Was Toni seeing him right now, not knowing whom she was seeing? And the smile fell away.

She had left the public beach by now, and though there were still people it was quieter. She headed down to the water, and the coolness on her feet, the gentle splashing of her steps, calmed her in spite of herself. Perhaps she would swim later. An ordinary thought—and she felt a timid swirl of resentment, because she had been having more of these small pleasures lately, coming upon them like green atolls in the endless gray sea of days, and she wondered now if she had left them behind again. Only yesterday—yesterday—she had eaten some of the first sugar corn from the farm stand down the road, let the butter trickle down her chin. Then she had devoured a whole pint of local strawberries, and for the first time in a long while had felt the small thrill that comes from being alone, and doing what one pleases. She had felt carefree, or at least able to pretend—

Just then a small figure charged by, splashing her, and she exclaimed in surprise. It was a little boy, about three years old, his belly childishly round but his limbs just beginning to lengthen. Even as he flashed past she could see the sweet, faint outlines of muscle in his shoulders, his calves. But then he stopped short, and she turned to see an inflatable ball, colored like a globe, floating away past the wave line.

She had to clear her throat. She hadn't spoken since that morning, on the phone. "Is that your ball, sweetheart?" If he had been her own she would have said *caro.* Dear one. Something she had always thought she would say, to a little boy who was hers.

He didn't answer, just regarded her with a steady gaze that seemed older than the rest of him. "I'll get it for you," she said.

She waded out and retrieved it, turned back. Up on the beach, she saw a couple who must have been his parents—they smiled at her, waved, but did not come closer, and she could see that they were letting their son have a tiny slice of independence, letting him talk to the nice lady by himself. She thought of what they saw when they looked at her: a tallish slim woman (she heard her grandmother, her *nonna*, long ago: *molta mingherlina—you are too thin, Marcellina*). Dark hair twisted up on her head, not much gray, not yet. Alone—did they wonder why? The mother was holding a baby. She shifted it up higher on her hip as Marcella watched.

The boy had not moved. "Here is your ball, darling," she said, and held it out with both hands. Still he didn't move, and she walked slowly toward him, afraid he might dart away. She had not looked at a child this closely for so long! His eyes were solemn, dark brown. "Would you like to catch?" she said, and he gave a hint of a nod. She threw the ball, and in a sudden burst he caught it, turned, and hurtled toward his parents. She waved to them and they waved back but the little boy did not look at her again, and then the young family continued down the beach.

She stood bereft in the water, and thought again of Anthony. He had never liked wistfulness, regret, longing for anything that had not come, that never would. If he could see her expression now, he would stop, one step too far away. His lean, handsome face would harden almost imperceptibly. There might also be a hint of old pain in his eyes, a look that would make her want to reach out to him—but she wouldn't. Because she was the one lacking, the one who had failed.

Their conversation had ended badly. She had wanted only to get off the phone. To be alone, to howl. Anthony, though, had wanted to chat; usually he was all business. Finally she said, "Anthony, please."

It had stopped him short. She did not say *caro*; why would she now? Still, today she felt that he noticed. She said, "I must go."

She knew he heard it, that he knew what she meant—*must*, right now, I cannot stay in control. "I'm sorry to have upset you," he said.

"It wasn't you," she managed to say. "I'm glad you told me."

"Otherwise it would have been a nasty shock," he said.

"Yes." Then she realized that he had said it as a test, that even now she was supposed to pretend otherwise. Even now, after seven years, Anthony could not have stood the mention of Cecil's name. "How hard this must be for you too," she said, and then was disgusted with herself. *Dio mio*, she thought, *still I say the wrong thing, always it is wrong—*

An old, familiar silence. Then a thought came to her, hitting her like a fist. "You won't tell her," Marcella had said.

"Of course not," Anthony had said, as though he had been waiting. "I will not tell her a single damn thing."

In a cramped upstairs closet of a two-hundred-year-old house in Mashantum, Massachusetts—on the bay, the bicep of Cape Cod— Jed McClatchey was hunting for his old wooden tennis racquet. He wanted to give it to his nephew, Jamie, who was three and whose first word, still his favorite, had been *ball.* Jed hadn't bothered to ask Callie if she approved. Once upon a time, he was sure, the answer would have been *no;* Jamie, like as not, would see beyond the racquet's sporting purpose to its other, weaponlike possibilities. But now Callie was exhausted and probably wouldn't care, and Billy, his father—who would have been all for it—was back in New York trying to make partner. When Jed felt the need for a coherent reason to be here on the Cape, jobless, for an entire summer, he told himself that he was just here to do some of the things Billy would have. Teach Jamie, direct him, show him how to hit balls. The man things.

For now, though, he was not finding the racquet. Maybe it wasn't in this closet—or even in the house. It was exactly the sort of thing his mother would have carted away to the Congregational church for their annual rummage sale. She had been unsentimental about mere things, an attitude he had admired. Her confidence had seemed to him absolute. *Sweetie, you don't need that anymore,* she would say, plucking from him the stained, beloved shirt or his first, too-small fielder's glove, and he would believe her, as he always did. As he had believed no one since.

But there was still plenty of junk left to paw through in the closet, which was full, in the way of summer houses, of odds and ends made sacred and immovable by the passage of time. He ducked his head back in, narrowly missing the low lintel of the door. There were enough faded shirts and high-water pants to outfit an army of home improvers. Outdated, water-swollen best sellers his parents had read at the beach. Dead tennis balls, useful if they had had a retriever, which they did not; wooden racquet press; still no racquet. Two lefty golf clubs he had once bought at the same rummage sale, wanting to make himself both a golfer and ambidextrous. A box fan, caked with dust, with a grille from the heedless bad old days that was wide enough for Jamie or, next summer, little Grace to stick a finger through. And if this was so, Jed wondered, why were there not more missing fingers in his generation, before people worried so much? Nevertheless he took the fan out of the closet, reminding himself to throw it away.

At the bottom of the closet, among the dust bunnies, was a half-crushed shirt box. It felt light, and he opened it expecting to find nothing or, at most, some old, ill-considered birthday gift. But instead, neatly folded, there was a woman's bathing suit.

He felt he was seeing it not only with his eyes but with his whole body. A one-piece, plunging neckline, dark blue with vertical white stripes. Almost clownish—but then he lifted it out of the box and held it up by the straps. Yes. He remembered. He popped out the firm cups of the bra, gingerly, with one finger, as if he were touching her actual breast. He remembered what he had seen, and a ghost of old desire swirled deep in his groin.

How old had he been?—that afternoon by the pool, *their* pool, when Marcella Atkinson had been stretched out in a lounge chair, alone at the corner of their patio? She had seemed separated from the rest of them, from the party that was going on, not only by the few feet that her chair was pulled away but also by her stillness and, Jed had sensed, her sadness. And her beauty. Her perfect legs and olive skin and dark upswept hair had not seemed to belong with the cheerful Yankees in their madras shorts and flowered dresses, grilling fat American burgers and drinking gin and tonics.

That had not been his mother's last summer. The memory was older than that, there'd been a chance for it to sink in; he had had a good long time to dream about Marcella Atkinson before everything, even the patterns of his idle thoughts, irrevocably changed. Before his mother had walked into their own house, back in Atlanta, and encountered a stranger, the last stranger she would ever meet.

"Jed?" He started. "Where are you?"

"Here."

"Jamie is asking about some tennis racquet." Callie was in the doorway, the little bundle of Grace on her shoulder. Her blond hair was uncombed and she was wearing an old white oxford-cloth shirt of their father's, a relic perhaps of this very closet, what she now called her milk-truck shirt. "What's that?"

"A bathing suit."

"Yes, I see." Callie came closer and squinted at it, as though she were nearsighted, which she was not. "That's not Mom's."

"I know. Weird."

"Some girlfriend of yours?" Jed made a face, his heart thumping, and wondered why he was not telling her about his teenage crush.

"What?" Callie said, misinterpreting. "It's a nice suit. Kind of sexy. Come on, whose is it?"

"I told you, I don't know. You want it?"

"God, no. God. I'm as big as a fucking house."

Even though Grace was only ten weeks old, and, accounting for her prematurity, barely a newborn, Jed instinctively cringed. "Cal."

She ignored him and said, "Maybe Toni will want it. Toni!" she called, and it was too late to stop her. He heard steps in the hall, and Jamie appeared, running. "I want the tennis ball racquet!" he declared.

"We'll find it," Toni Atkinson said, behind him. She pushed a strand of her dark-blond hair behind one ear and leaned artfully against the door frame, crossing one long tan leg over the other.

Jed refused to let her catch his eye and instead turned his back just in time, folding the suit small, small. "It's not here, bud," he said. "I'll keep looking. Maybe it's in the barn."

"Toni," Callie said, "we found this bathing suit—Jed, where is it?"

"It's not her kind of thing." He had gotten it back in the box and closed the lid, and now he stuck it in the closet as casually as he could, behind a pile of books. "Bunch of stuff here I should take up to the church," he continued, to no one in particular.

Toni cocked her head, raised an eyebrow. "Let me see it," she said. "Not my *thing*? What is my thing?"

She said this looking at Jed with perfect coy confidence, and it was true that only minutes before Jed would have taken this opening and run with it. Toni Atkinson was nineteen to his twenty-seven, a fellow adult, he wouldn't be doing anything wrong—he had already gone over it in his mind. He could have said now, for instance, that she was more given to string bikinis, which was true; but all of a sudden he did not particularly care to answer her. "Jed?" she said.

And yet he didn't want to arouse suspicion. Toni would be the type to sneak in here later and go into the closet and find the suit, and then—what? He looked straight at her and grinned, feeling an unfamiliar shame as he did so. "You don't need some old-lady bathing suit," he said. "Trust me."

"And I do?" Callie said.

It was not as strong a protest as he would have expected, but he acted as though she were in her old form. "Sure," Jed said. "Embrace it, Cal. Old lady mommy. Hip no more."

For a moment Callie looked like she was trying to come up with one of her normal snappy retorts, but then she just gave him a half-hearted smirk and sat down in the armchair next to the bed, her hand limply on Grace's back. Toni said, "Do you want me to take her?" and wordlessly, Callie handed her over. Jed knew these were matters he didn't really understand, but still he didn't like Callie's look of relief. Grace was so tiny still, wizened and unsmiling and light as a puppy; Jed had seen her in the hospital in Greenwich, when she had been in her little plastic box with cables strung all over, and he could not forget that sight. He felt that he or Callie should never put her down. He tried to ignore Callie stretching her now-empty arms to the ceiling, clearly relieved, turning her face to the light streaming through the old, small-paned window. Toni was already out the door. She liked to have Grace to herself, Jed had noticed.

But then Toni turned and said, in what was clearly an after-thought, "Hey, Jamie, big guy. Let's go look for that racquet. Maybe it's in the barn." She held out her free hand to him with a sweet smile, and then raised the same smile to Jed—Lady Madonna. He resisted rolling his eyes at her, instead smiled weakly back.

Jamie began to follow but then looked at Jed and Callie, reluctant. "I'll be there in a minute, pardner," Jed said.

"Be careful," Callie said. She smiled too but it was automatic; her eyes were opaque. "Be careful with that racquet."

Jamie screeched, "Mommy, we don't know where it *is*!"

"I know, sweetheart," she said, not looking at him. "I'm sure you'll find it." She settled her head back into the faded chintz. It had been their mother's favorite chair. She said, "I'll just stay here awhile." She did not look at Jed.

He heard Toni's and Jamie's footsteps go down the hall, then down the creaky back stairs to the kitchen. The screen door squeaked open, slapped shut. Callie was looking out the window, her gaze flat

against the trees. Jed eyed the closet door. It would be the most natural thing in the world to go get the bathing suit back out. To say, *Do
you know whose this is?* To say, *Why is it here?*

But instead he whispered, "Have a good rest, Cal." She gave him
the barest of nods.

He left the room then, but instead of following Toni and Jamie's
path down the hall, he made an abrupt turn, into his own room, and
shut the door. He sat down on the edge of his childhood bed and
stared at his empty hands. They tingled.

The ghost of memory, of the desire, shimmered again and then it
was no longer a ghost but alive and warm and vivid. He had been
keeping it at bay—why?—but now he could see and feel it all. An
ordinary day, an ordinary party, Marcella Atkinson perhaps slightly
more than ordinary at the edge of it. And then not at the edge but at
the center. His life had not been ordinary for a long time.

The party had been mostly people from the Nobscusset Tennis
Club, which was the grandiloquent name they had for the little col-
lection of clay courts in the woods half a mile away. There had been
kids in the pool and a few dads, but mostly the adults were dry and
dressed and drinking; Jed himself had been directed, by his mother,
to help entertain, and so he had been in the pool, throwing kids
around, letting them climb on him. He preferred doing that to having
the parents of his friends ask him about college and what he was
majoring in and all the rest of it, which was what would have happened if he had been making conversation over by the grill. He'd
known he would have ended up telling them he was pre-law, but he
wouldn't really have meant it, and he hated himself when he said
something just to sound impressive. He had just finished his freshman year, and he had hated, too, the idea that his life would take pre-
dictable turns.

Callie was there but she was mooning around waiting for their friends, specifically Ham Storer, to show up. He remembered that. And Toni was there—she must have been ten or eleven, and Jed had had the distinct impression that she was showing off for him, which he thought was funny because he himself had been showing off, just a little bit, for her mother. Maybe he'd stood in front of her to throw a ball, maybe, oh, he'd flexed a muscle once or twice. Marcella Atkinson had been sitting at the corner of the patio, alone. He tended to notice her when she was around, which was not often—she seemed to play tennis only under duress. If one of his friends had happened to ask him about her—and maybe they would have; surely he wasn't the only one noticing her—he probably would have said she was hot. Another thing to impress. But in his mind, he held her more gently. With more awe.

He was trying to ignore Toni and not be rude about it, and he ducked under water and swam to the deep end. When he surfaced, he found himself looking directly at Marcella. He was in a little space of quiet; he checked; the kids, including Toni, were now in a knot at the other end, playing Marco Polo. He propped himself against the deck with his elbow, and when he looked back, furtively, at Marcella Atkinson, she had sat up in her lounge chair, and was taking off her dress.

It was only a beach dress, of course. Her bathing suit was underneath. He wondered for the briefest of moments if she was going to swim, and then, for a moment that was even briefer, the dress caught around her hair and she twisted to free herself, and her bathing suit pulled back, and he saw her nipple, dark as an unblinking eye.

He had been almost nineteen. He had seen nipples before, whole breasts in fact. He was not a virgin, and he fancied himself an adult, but as the dark privacy of Marcella Atkinson's body flashed by him— almost instantly she twisted again, and the suit slipped back, and her breast was covered—he had realized he wasn't. He realized that normally he would have felt a throb of transgressive glee, a thrill of good luck, and that that would have been wrong. Because instead he wanted to run and protect her. To hide her, even though now there was nothing to hide. He gripped the edge of the concrete deck and resisted.

Instead, as he watched, she pulled the dress the rest of the way off. She sat back in the chair, unaware of what had happened, and looked down at the bundle of the dress in her lap, pensive, as if she did not know what to do with it. And then she looked straight up at him.

She had light-green, northern Italian eyes. They were startling against her skin, her dark hair. They were wide open and innocent with a guileless, heartbreaking longing, and he knew that somehow it had everything and yet nothing to do with him.

His old self—the self he had been until a minute before, the self he was jettisoning at that very moment—would have been disappointed to realize she wasn't looking at *him*. But this abrupt new self (he saw with the clarity of memory) knew he had seen something mysterious and fascinating: Marcella Atkinson's body, and Marcella herself. He thought of the girls he knew who seemed to offer him sunny manicured lanes instead of turning, twisting mysteries, and he knew his own life would not be ordinary, that it would instead be boundlessly rich. He was eighteen and things had always gone well for him, and while he knew that his good fortune so far had not involved much choice on his part, he thought that being an adult, in the land of choice, would only improve things. He stared at her for another long moment. He was all nerve endings. And then he knew suddenly that he had to get away.

He turned his back to her and heaved himself out of the water, took a towel from a nearby chair, covered himself. When he turned to her again, Marcella Atkinson was looking beyond him, into the trees, like she wanted to escape, and he knew she was no longer thinking of him at all. Somehow it didn't matter. But escape seemed exactly the thing and so he left without saying good-bye to anyone and went to the club. It was empty; everyone was at the party. He slammed balls against the backboard for an hour, sweating out his lust and wonder, effecting the change in himself. When he had gotten back home, the party was breaking up, and the Atkinsons were gone.

He sat now, rigid, on the edge of his bed. He knew Callie was still in the other room and that she was not really resting and that something was wrong. Through the open window he heard Toni's voice, indistinct but with an impatient edge, and he knew Jamie would come looking for Callie soon, and he would have to intercept him. And he knew that since that moment years ago, when life had seemed to lie exquisite before him, he had lost faith in any ability of his for agency or happiness.

And he knew also that Marcella Atkinson's bathing suit should not be there, in the upstairs closet of his parents' house. He knew that later, when the room was empty again, he would go back for it. He would hold it in his hands, and figure out what to do.

It was sultry, for June. Marcella opened the windows and let in the muggy breeze, and then sat at her dining room table working on a translation job that was not due for another month. Outside, all week, it was sunny and bright, and the garden bloomed without her. By Thursday, she had to admit she was completely done. She called her editor—who was happy, but not surprised, to hear that she was finished ahead of schedule—and then she was free. She told herself that she would spend Friday in the garden. It was the only way, besides her work, that she could lose herself.

But she woke the next morning to a gentle rainfall. She looked at the clock: far too early. She had never been a good sleeper, and was getting worse. Outside, the leaky gutter at the corner of the house dripped steadily. Was that what had woken her up? No, there had been screaming—she touched her throat. *She* had been screaming. In her dream. She had been screaming because no one was listening to her. There had been some kind of macabre party, a roomful of unconcerned faces, herself in the middle, seemingly invisible, mute.

But Cecil had been there. He had been—hurt? Was that what she had wanted people to see? The dream was already fading. She tried to ignore her leftover panic and remember instead the feel of Cecil's presence, warm and comforting, blanketing her like sleep itself. She pressed her arm over her closed eyes to block out the weak light and go back to nighttime. She knew it wouldn't work.

Until now, Cecil had left her alone for—how long? a year, two?—
at least at night, in her dreams. She remembered her *nonna* moaning
that Marcella's dead father or grandfather, or both, had visited her, as
if it had really been they, their restless spirits, and not the toilings of
her own unconscious. And Marcella's mother scoffing, derision on
her face masking her own pain: *There are no ghosts.* It was one of the
few points on which she had dared disagree with her mother-in-law.
No ghosts, she had said. *Only God.* She had been religious, her
mamma. She had believed that God gave you what you deserved.

Marcella lay in bed wondering what sorts of things her mother
had dreamed of. If she had ever cried out in her sleep, and why. But
the dead were retreating, and as she herself inexorably woke she was
forced to admit that the Cecil in her dream looked nothing like the
actual Cecil, that he had been a feeling rather than a man, and now
that she was awake she wasn't sure if her dream had been about anyone real at all.

Finally, she got out of bed and went over to the window to raise
the shades. Outside, her garden glowed in the milky light. There were
her blue geraniums, the last of the peonies, the white roses on the
arbor, luminous as stars. She stroked them with her eyes, again and
again, trying to soothe herself, although there was nothing to be upset
about—she did not deserve to be upset. She turned from the window,
wrapped herself in her old cotton dressing gown, and went down the
hall to the kitchen.

It was a bit brighter here, with the windows facing east. She filled
her kettle, set it on the stove, and turned on the burner, watching the
gas flame up blue. Her own little kitchen. Would her mother have
wanted such a thing? It probably never would have occurred to her,
and if she could see Marcella now she would think her solitude was
only a sign of failure. Marcella stood up a little straighter, resisting.
She tightened the front of her robe. It was bright pink, with a raucous
pattern of zinnias, something she herself never would have picked;

Toni had given it to her. Toni—who was not at work yet. Not yet at Cecil's house. Likely not yet even awake. She thought of Toni sleeping, her full long body beautiful and relaxed, dreaming her own dreams. Good ones. Marcella would will it so.

The kettle sang and she carefully poured the water over the grounds in her little French press, and the scent blossomed warmly in the pearl-gray light. *Yes, Mamma, this is my little pot for one.* She pressed the coffeepot's plunger firmly, watching the grounds swirling, and then poured her cup and stepped resolutely out to the porch. The air was close and wet, as thick as the early quiet. *Yes, alone, Mamma, Nonna. What do you think of that?*

In the crumbling palazzo in Florence where she had grown up, the revered ghosts had been the only men in the house, and her mother and grandmother had been conspicuously incomplete. They were together only for her, for Marcella. *If only, if only,* they frequently said, their bodies said, their very gestures—futile grasping hands, sighs, all speaking of unending lack. If only the men hadn't left them—one in war, the other in a car accident, two commonplace stories that struck them as spectacularly tragic. All the hope in the house had landed on her, on Marcella. Someday, she would find a man to complete her, and them; it had been her birthright, her only task. But sometimes Marcella imagined they looked at her with narrowed eyes, as if they doubted her capacity to succeed.

When she had met Anthony, then, right after her *mamma* died, she had felt weak with relief. He was so clearly the goal for which her mother and grandmother had prepared her—so handsome, so sure, so fearsomely complete in himself! Men, the di Pavarese men she had never known, had been wondrous creatures, and it had seemed that Anthony Atkinson could stand with them. Love had seemed not a matter of comfort, but something much more august.

The rain pattered more and more softly, and she knew it wouldn't last. No, she could not crawl back into bed and hide. There was already an edge of brightness in the sky. In the garden the ground would be lovely and soft, easy to work. This day, this Friday, was supposed to be her reward, after all. So why did she feel lost? She shifted in the creaking wicker chair, the cushion's dampness seeping through her robe, and clung to her warm mug like an anchor. Toni at Cecil's house. Today, all summer. The murk of her life that had settled to the bottom was being stirred up again. She wondered if Anthony thought the same thing. If he dreamed of it, and if he then dreamed some kind of comfort. If he needed that, in his sleep. *Don't cry, Marcellina. Don't be sad.* Long ago her tears had made him anxious, and then, later on, impatient. *What do you want me to do?* She hadn't known then that men could be frightened, that they could have weaknesses for which they needed to be forgiven, that they would expect things they themselves could not identify.

Cecil had seemed, at first, to need only her.

Even though the sky was continuing to lighten, a last gust of rain blew through her yard. The one peony bush she had forgotten to stake tossed in the breeze, its heavy balls of bloom bent to the ground. The weight would break the stems—she would have to cut them. She felt a moment of ridiculous loss and then stood suddenly, spilling her coffee. Enough. A vase of peonies on her table. She would go get the scissors.

MARCELLA WORKED OUTSIDE all day. The sun did come out, but the humidity from the night's rain, instead of burning off, intensified. Sweat rolled down her face. The salt ran into her eyes, stinging, and she reached up with her dirty glove to rub it out. Her face would be filthy by now. *So be it,* she thought. *That is what I am. A dirty woman!* Well.

Her garden was doing well, so well that she needed to move things around, give them a bit more air. It was the hardest work, the digging, the stomping on the edge of the shovel. She had just finished lifting the enormous root-ball of an astilbe that she had stupidly sited in full sun. Her back would hurt tomorrow; that would be good. Her *nonna* would have been horrified by such manual labor. Her *mamma* would have understood it. She felt a prickle of the old dilemma— whom should she please?—and then plunged her spade into the earth again.

By dinnertime she was covered in a fine layer of grime, her hair in muddy wisps around her face, dirt ground under her nails in spite of her leather gloves. It was after seven, and the mosquitoes were coming out. As she was putting away her tools, she decided she would go straight to the beach to swim; she'd be lazy and drive, instead of walk. If she got there soon there would be just enough time to swim to the seawall, her usual destination.

Once, she had sat on a seawall with Cecil, the one in Mashantum, at Howes Beach, where everyone went. Except that then it had been late September. No one else had been there, and the sky had been a deep, heartbreaking autumnal blue. That had been a stolen day—their first day. She had come down from Boston, looking for solitude, and instead found Cecil McClatchey, who had thought he was looking for the same thing. It had become a habit of hers, to swim to the seawall here and think of that other. She gave an impatient sigh.

It was later than she had realized—as she walked around the house to the garage, under the trees, she saw the light was almost gone. There was a car she didn't recognize parked in front of her house. She took another step and then froze: a man, his outline blurred in the gathering dusk, sat in one of the chairs on her small front porch. *It's not dark yet. Not dark. No one wants to hurt me.*

"Mrs. Atkinson?" the man said.

He rose and moved toward her, and she took a step back. "What do you want?"

"It's Jed. McClatchey. From Mashantum." He hesitated. "Cecil and Betsy's son."

She couldn't see his face. "You frightened me," she blurted.

"I'm sorry. I didn't want to do that," he said. "I knocked. I thought you were out."

"I was in the backyard." She went closer, through the grass, up the front walk. "You were waiting for me? Has something happened? Is Toni all right?"

"She's fine. As far as I know."

Her feet thudded up the wooden steps. "I'll turn the light on," she said, and looked at him again, enough to assure herself it really was Jed McClatchey. She hadn't seen him in years. So strange. Did he know? Could he? Had Cecil told his children in a fit of remorse? She was standing close to him now. She opened her front door and reached inside to flick on the switch.

He looked nothing like Cecil. She was blocking the door with her body, staring at him in the weak artificial light, but she didn't care. He was dark—dark eyes and hair, an angular face. Handsome. But so serious. "It really is me," he said. And something still boyish in his eyes told her: he did not know.

"Yes. It is you," she said. She held out her hand, then glanced at it, drew it back. "I'm sorry. I'm so dirty. I have been playing in the mud." He looked at her blankly. "The garden."

"Oh." He took her hand anyway.

His handshake was hard and firm. He had been a boy when she had last seen him—a young, young man when Cecil had died. He did not know that they shared a loss, his, truly, so much greater than hers—how odd that she had never given him her condolences. Impulsively, in spite of the dirt, she reached forward and hugged him, and although he accepted it stiffly, immediately she felt something electric and strange. She stepped back and said, "I'm sorry, but why, again—"

"I was passing through. On my way to the city."

"And Toni—?"

"She really is fine."

She nodded and forced a smile. "I don't have many visitors," she said. "I have forgotten how to behave. Do come inside."

She walked through her own front door, and after a moment he followed her. The door opened directly into the living room. She moved around, switching on lamps. "Please, sit down."

"Thank you," he said, but didn't move.

"Have you eaten? I'll make us a snack." *Dio mio,* she thought, *a snack. Don't babble.* She took a breath. "I'll just clean up first, quickly," she said. "Then I'll make us a drink. I'm not sure what I have—I'm afraid not much. I drink very rarely," she said. She turned to go down the hall, wincing. He would think she was chasing him away.

"Water is fine," he said behind her. "Thank you."

She could tell, from his grave tone, that he was still standing. She turned back to him. He was looking at her intently. In one hand he held a plastic grocery sack with something squarish inside. When he saw her look at the bag he glanced down at it himself. "Can I take that for you?" she said.

"No. Thank you." Slowly, he sat.

She detoured quickly to the bathroom, washed off all the most visible dirt, and slipped into the first clean thing she could find, an old linen dress. She brushed her hair and wound it again on top of her head: it would do. In the kitchen, she fixed two glasses of water, opened a box of crackers. Her fingers trembled as she unwrapped a wedge of cheese. *Stop. Stop.* She breathed, and then found the cheese knife and set it down, very slowly, with a tiny *clink* against the plate.

Carefully, she carried the tray back to the front room. It was a pretty space, cheery with the glow of lamplight. Look around. Calm. The flowered chairs, the arrangements of faience plates—she had done it all, made it cozy and welcoming. There were pictures of Toni, of relatives and friends; Jed wouldn't know how infrequently they spoke. The room was only hers. She felt the sweat still on her skin and wished she had taken a shower. Put the tray down, breathe deeply again, click on another lamp. The dusk outside had faded; the windowpanes were black. She sat down on the sofa. Jed was in the chair. He would not hurt her here, in her haven. Why would he hurt her? And she let herself look, full on, at Jed McClatchey.

Cecil had been blond, before she knew him, before his hair had thinned and grayed, and his face had had a roundness that she had loved, sweet and boyish. He had been tall and had had to guard against portliness; Jed was slighter. But when he leaned forward to pick up a cracker, the lamplight hit him in a certain way and the bones of his face seemed to briefly settle into one of Cecil's expressions—grave, almost angry, one she had rarely seen, except on that last night. "Do people ever tell you you look like your father?" she said.

"Not very often."

"No. But I saw it. Just for a moment."

Jed shifted in his chair and sat up with his glass. "People told me I looked like him after he died," he said. "Like that would make me feel better."

"I wish I could have come to the funeral." She pressed her lips together.

Jed looked at her piercingly. "Did you know my parents well? I don't remember—well, I don't remember you and Mr. Atkinson being around much."

"We were summer friends. So." She was light-headed, the world out of focus. "How is Mashantum? I haven't been there in years. I hear some news from Toni but she isn't so reliable."

"It's the same. I think. I haven't been there much myself. Until this summer. It doesn't change."

"Everything changes," she said. "Eventually."

"Well, it shouldn't." Unexpectedly, he smiled.

"Is Toni doing a good job? You can tell me."

"She's very good with the baby. But I don't think child care is her vocation. Put it that way."

"Yes, I know what you mean."

"Mrs. Atkinson—"

"Marcella."

"Marcella." He cleared his throat. "I found something, and I was wondering if it was yours."

"That's why you came?" She looked at the bag in his hands.

"It was a whim," he said. "That's what I'm doing this summer. I guess. Following whims."

She said brightly, not knowing where this social voice was coming from, "That can be rather dangerous."

"You're probably right," he said.

And then he was reaching into the bag and bringing something out, and she suppressed a little cry. "Why, I lost that—years ago."

Jed was holding the suit up by its thin straps. He stood, walked over, and dropped it in her lap. "Why was it in our house? I found it in a closet. In this box, wrapped in tissue paper."

"I must have left it at your pool. At a party."

"Why was it in a box?"

"I don't know." He was standing over her, too tall, too close; she could feel his presence like a mountain although she could not make herself look up at him. *I'm keeping it,* Cecil had said. *I've never done anything like this before. I have to have something of you.* She had watched him crumple it to his face, smell her in it. *My God, Chella, my God.*

But why in the world had he left it in a closet? Poor Cecil, guilty boy, wanting to be caught. "Why are you crying?" Jed said, clinically.

"It seems so long ago. Another life," she said—oh, she was good.

Disgusting. She breathed deeply, willed the tears to dry. "How did you know it was mine?" He didn't answer, and she was forced to look up. "Jed?"

Since he had walked into her house he had looked stern, unabashed. A man who wanted answers. But now there was a different look on his face. He backed away, sat down in his chair. No, his dark eyes were nothing like Cecil's. "I remembered you in it," he said.

"Really."

And to their deep surprise, they both laughed.

SHE CONVINCED HIM TO STAY for dinner. "I will just make a salad," she said. "It's what I would have anyway." Her dining room table was covered with her papers, and when she began to clear it off he said he didn't want to put her to any trouble. So they ate in the kitchen, across from each other at the little round table. She found placemats and cloth napkins, and when she opened her cabinet to get the salt and pepper, she saw a candlestick with a half-burned taper and decided to set that out too. *I am following whims.* When she struck the match, her hand trembled.

The question of why he was really there hung over them, embroidering itself in the air the more they avoided it. As they ate she wished again that she knew how to chat. Her grandmother had been able to take charge of any conversation, directing it exactly the way she wanted it to go while she pretended deference, coquettishness, and even now Marcella was trying to imitate her and failing. But as it turned out, Jed was no good at small talk either, only he did not seem to care.

"How is your sister?" Marcella managed. "And her babies?"

"Fine. I think."

"It is hard." Marcella saw herself putting on a wise, maternal face. "One is so sleepy. And all those chemicals are going *whiz-whiz,* making the milk, healing the body." She made her voice light. "I'm glad she has Toni to help her. And you. How long can you stay with her?"

Jed cleared his throat. "All summer. Or so."

"And your job?" Marcella said, before she could stop herself, like he was still a boy. "I mean—I am sorry. That is personal."

"No, I don't mind. I'm taking a leave. Callie needs me here. She—called a few weeks ago, and I decided."

"This is one of your whims," Marcella said.

"Yes."

A breeze blew through the open window over the sink, ruffling the curtain.

Marcella said, "It's not easy being a mother when your own mother is gone. I remember."

"How old were you when your mother died?"

"I was twenty," Marcella said.

"I was too."

"Yes." She wanted to say *I know, I know exactly.* Finally he gave her a polite little look: *Go on.* "Yes, well. They had sent me here for college. My mother died when I was a junior. And then my *nonna* died right after I was married. And that"—she shrugged—"was it."

"And your father?"

"He died before I was born."

"It's strange being all alone."

"Yes, it is. Would you like more salad?" She half-rose from her seat.

"No, thank you." She sank back down. "You feel—weightless," he continued. "When you're alone like that."

"Yes," she said slowly. "But not in a good way."

"No." He arranged his fork and knife carefully together on his empty plate. "Your mother must have been young when she died."

"She had a bad heart."

"So did my father." Jed looked up at her. "They think he died of a heart attack. That that caused the accident. But they're not sure."

"It is hard to be sure."

"That's a coroner's job, though."

She nodded; it was all she could do. The silence stretched. He kept looking at her, and she looked away. "Would you like some tea?" she said, into the void. "It's gotten cooler outside. Cool enough to drink something warm, do you think?"

"Yes, ma'am. Thank you."

She wasn't so sure about being a ma'am, but she remembered it was the Southern way. She took their plates to the counter and then busied herself finding mugs and tea bags and heating the water. Having her back to him for a moment was a relief, and she felt her face darkening, her mouth twisting, with the released effort of her politeness. Nancy Hale from the Cape had called her about Cecil, told her he had died alone in Atlanta, at night, in a one-car accident. It had been May; Betsy had died the previous November. She would never forget it, Nancy's patrician voice, the pity in it, pity for Cecil and the whole human race, really, that calm noblesse oblige. Marcella had not been able to speak, she had been afraid of what she would blurt. By then Anthony had moved out. She had been alone in the Wellesley house. She was lucky she heard the news at all. No one knew, of course, that she would care, that she would care so much. That after she hung up the phone, she would sink to the floor and wail.

Behind her, Jed said, "At first—before the autopsy came back—Callie and I thought he had killed himself. Crashed the car on purpose. He still could have. We'll never know."

She poured the water. She brought sugar and milk to the table and then their full mugs. She tried to calm her heart. Finally she said, "How could you think that?"

He waited until she was seated again. He was very lawyerly now, she thought; it was like he was taking a deposition. "They never solved it, you know. My mother's murder. They never found out who did it."

"Yes. I know. That makes it worse—doesn't it?"

The grim look was back on his face. "Did you know that my father was a suspect?"

She breathed in sharply. "I do not listen to gossip," she said.

"He was away the night she was killed. In North Carolina. The bed in his hotel room hadn't been slept in."

"Why not?" she said, without thinking.

Jed raised an eyebrow. "He said he couldn't sleep that night. That he had been out driving around."

Cecil on the unfamiliar black mountain roads, swerving back and forth. What had he been thinking about? Had he regretted his decision? Had he been wavering? Not that it mattered. Not in the end.

Jed said, "Does that make any sense to you? Because it doesn't to me."

Cecil had said, *Don't tell anyone, Chella. Please. I'm sorry to ask. But I can't do it to my children. Please.* And she had promised, not knowing she would never speak to him again. "They always look at the husband," she said now. "It's natural. Is it not? Even if he's not guilty. Even if there is no way he could be guilty."

"You believe that? About my father?"

Her heart thudded inside her chest. "Of course. I know it."

"How?" His face was hard.

"There is   I knew him. There is no way."

"They always say that. It's always a surprise. Everything always looks perfect."

"Jed, is that why you came here? To ask me this? My God!" Marcella got up and walked over to the stove, pointlessly turned the burner under the kettle back on. Her hand on the knob was shaking.

After a moment Jed said, "I'm sorry I upset you."

"Your own father! Do you ask everyone these questions?"

"No."

"Well, then, why to me? It is a strange thing to come here and do!" Her back was still to him, her face was safe, she could let it crumple. *Please, Chella.* The last thing he had asked of her—begged. But if his son wanted answers, why should she not give them to him, his son behind her living and breathing, tortured by sickening thoughts, instead of obeying Cecil, who had made his choices and left them all? Surely her obligation was over by now. How long did one have to keep promises to the dead?

"I'm sorry," Jed was saying. "You are right. I have been completely out of line. Thank you for the dinner."

She turned back to him. The already-hot water began to whistle again and she turned it off without looking. "Where are you staying?"

"I'll drive back tonight."

"That's ridiculous."

"It's only three hours. Give or take."

"But your sister thinks you are away for the weekend—"

"The friend got sick." He smiled a little.

"You will stay," she said. She could not believe she was commanding him. She was furious at Cecil, at his memory and what he had asked of her—so much. "You can sleep in Toni's room, or on the couch, if you'd rather. You must not be on the road so late." He opened his mouth to answer but she went on, her voice rising. "Do you really think your family needs to lose someone else?"

"Mrs. Atkinson—"

She swallowed. "Marcella," she said.

"It will be fine."

"Jed," she said, "why did you come here?"

"I don't know. I really don't know."

His eyes were so dark. They bored into her, down to her secrets. She looked straight back at him and said, "Please stay."

Callie had not expected it, but almost as soon as she gave birth to Grace she had thought of the Cape house, and longed to be there. She sat in neonatal intensive care with her tiny daughter and pictured the long vista from the kitchen, where everyone came in the back door, through the line of other narrow doorways, the low-ceilinged rooms like a string of boxes, one after the other, to the end of the house. Her father had always wanted to enlarge those doors, but they had never let him. He had been tall, taller than either Jed or Billy; he had always been laughing about short little Pilgrims, always bumping his head.

Every so often one of Grace's wires would get dislodged and set off an alarm, and a nurse would come, insultingly calm, and reset it while Callie waited, her mind suspended as if she were holding her breath. When the nurse finally walked away she could start her imaginary tour all over again. Kitchen to the dining room, there was the table with the cracked leaf, there was the hutch with the lobster platter; then the living room, there was the trunk she and Jed always said was full of pirate treasure; now up the steep stairs to her bedroom (her childhood bedroom, not the one she shared with Billy), now lie down on the blue and yellow quilt, look out the window at the thick leaves of the privet. She traveled the house over and over, slowly round and round, a spatial lullaby. If she concentrated on each step, each detail, she could drive away other thoughts, the ones that sneaked up, peeked leering around corners.

Meanwhile, Grace was endlessly asleep and could barely eat. *She'll wake up*, said Callie's least favorite nurse, *don't you worry*, as if scolding her for thinking only of trivialities—and maybe she was right: wasn't Grace alive, after all? Alive when she could have been dead? For the time being, though, there was a tube threaded through Grace's tiny nostril going down to her stomach. Multiple times a day Callie attached herself to the chugging breast pump, and later the nurse would simply pour the milk down the tube. One day Callie opened her mouth to say, *Isn't there something a little more high-tech? Something better?* But the stern nurse was again on duty and Callie, who normally was not afraid of anyone, kept her mouth shut. It had been a ward full of the desperately ill, infants so small they looked larval. Grace, breathing by herself, was boring. Callie knew this was yet another thing for which she should feel thankful. But instead she looked at all the wires around her and thought how easily they could wrap around a baby's throat, if a person wasn't careful. How hard the floor was, what it would do to a soft little skull, if a person slipped—

She clutched Grace more tightly, sat back down in the creaky hospital rocking chair. She waited for the nurse to move on so she could begin her lullaby again, but instead a new and clearer idea began to form in her mind, her heart: that although nothing had gone as it should, and she was in foreign Connecticut in a foreign hospital with not enough visitors, a wound across her stomach, holding a foreign child she had not pictured, who was not Jamie, an infant born too soon who lay in her arms like a changeling, whom she worried about only mechanically—that even though all these things were true, all would right itself in Mashantum.

She would go there, as soon as she could.

She knew she wasn't loving her daughter properly, she knew her feelings were all wrong; that would fix itself in Mashantum. Growing up, Mashantum had been far from Atlanta; now she lived here up north but Mashantum was still far, far in the best way—removed, unchanging. The pink rambler roses would bloom as they always had, the bees would thrum in the privet, and all would be well. Soon, soon, she would be at the house itself, she would walk through it and be bathed in the light and the smells and the very dust that were the essence of who she was. Her father's tennis visor would be hanging from a peg in the hall. She would see the linen closet shelves labeled in her mother's hand. She would walk barefoot through the porch, along the cool brick floor, and the screen door would slap shut behind her and then she would walk across the lawn, under the wild, over-grown arbor, to the pool.

It would be dusk. The pool would be perfectly still and clear. The leaves would rustle and the blue hydrangeas would glow in the deep-ening light and she would feel herself uncurling, relaxing, expanding back into the best, happiest places, the ones that had been invaded and ravaged and that now lay fallow and dark. The wall that had bricked up happiness, that had somehow built itself during the nights in the hospital as she fitfully dozed, the barrier of leaden fear that felt like nothing, like pure absence, would melt away.

Her mother had loved that pool. She saw her mother, swimming back and forth in her daily laps, her determination not hard or brutal but strong, calm, constant. And like her mother Callie would plunge into the water and be engulfed, and then her head would break the surface, she would breathe deep, she would be herself again. She dreamed it, rocking in her chair. She knew it would be true.

But then she had come to the Cape and nothing changed. Her parents were still not here. And because nothing changed, it was all worse. Although Grace nursed constantly now, she was not growing fast enough. This could only be Callie's own fault. As for herself,

Callie craved only sleep. But if she slept she would dream, the new dreams where she broke Grace's little limbs or bit off her tiny fingers. She would lie in bed exhausted but then her mind would start to revolve until it was a black blur she could not control, and she did not know if she was awake or asleep and she knew that the baby would wake any minute anyway and the minutes would slow down again until they were endless. She knew nothing would ever change.

Jamie walked and talked, he was not to be ignored, but even he seemed to be always hovering several feet from her, untouchable. Her love for Grace was an island far away. She could see it hazy in the distance but could not reach it.

But she was not alone. She had Toni—ha. She had Billy, on the weekends, Billy who loved her simply and wholeheartedly. She had let herself fall in love with him in the first place because he seemed like someone whom tragedy would never touch. And it hadn't: Grace was okay, he would remind her, looking baffled. She was fine, and wasn't modern medicine incredible? Weren't they lucky?

Yes, she would agree, they were.

But she also had Jed. Jed whom she needed most. She had called him, and he had come.

She stood in the sunny kitchen of the house where she had spent every summer of her life, trying to remember what she was supposed to do. She was good at pretending; she could fool anyone. There had been an order, but it had fallen apart. Jed had left but he would be back soon, Jed who knew her best, Jed whom, maybe, she could not fool after all. Jed was the only one who could put it back together.

V

Marcella put Jed in Toni's room for the night. It was mostly pink, with a satin bedcover and fluffy pink and purple pillows. But it was too neat and spare; it seemed to him to ooze wistfulness. "Do you have everything you need?" Marcella said, from the door. "I'll get you another pillow."

"Really," Jed said, "I'm fine. You don't—" But Marcella had disappeared, and in a moment came back with two more pillows, in plain white cases. "Well. Thank you." He went to the doorway to take them from her.

"Good night."

"Good night," Jed replied, but she was already turning away.

As soon as she had gone into her room across the hall and closed the door, he ducked down the hall to the bathroom. He tried to make as little noise as possible, to touch nothing—which of course was ridiculous; but he felt like he was breaking and entering. He resisted the impulse to examine the contents of her medicine cabinet and instead helped himself to only a minuscule dot of toothpaste, used his finger for a brush, and rinsed his mouth by drinking straight from the faucet.

Back in Toni's room, he slid between the pink sheets and turned out the light. The moon shone through the window next to the bed. He lifted up his hand; the light was so bright his fingers cast otherworldly shadows. He was wide awake.

The day he'd found the bathing suit, he'd paid more attention to Toni than usual. He'd known he was doing a terrible thing, as her eyes grew warmer and her laughter louder, but he was on a mission, and he nudged the conversation until the prize fell in his lap like an apple: the name of the town where Marcella Atkinson lived.

He told Callie he was going to see an old college friend that weekend, in Manhattan. "I knew you'd get bored here," she said shortly.

"I'm not bored. Nick Satterthwaite isn't going to quit bugging me until I visit him. I might as well get it over with."

"Fine."

"Cal, I won't leave till Friday afternoon. Billy and I will pass each other on the highway—"

"Just go. Have fun."

He hadn't explained any further and if Callie seemed surprised she was no more surprised than he, huddled around the little flame of his weird secret, furiously protecting it, even though he was not exactly sure what the secret was.

And now here he was lying in Toni's bed, Marcella Atkinson just feet away, through a couple of thin walls. He was on a strange little vacation. A vacation from a vacation—no one would wake him up tomorrow. He was like a dad himself these days, getting up with Jamie or Grace at first light, because he would hear them and he couldn't go back to sleep anyway. He understood, he thought, a little, how Callie felt, how tired she was. He, too, always wanted a little more sleep, was always operating on a slight deficit. He did not resent it, but he did wonder if Callie fully appreciated him. And it was odd, more than odd, that she had not scolded him about leaving work, about being irresponsible. Odder still that his taking a whole summer off really had been her idea, although if he had put it to her that way she would not have agreed. And since she hadn't brought it up, he wouldn't either.

Sleep. Now was his chance. Before he closed his eyes, he looked out the window at the moon, already high, clearly visible above the trees. Its light poured down. It was not quite full, and he wondered if it was waxing or waning. He could never remember which way it went.

CALLIE HAD CALLED HIM IN EARLY JUNE, at his office. It must have been about ten. He had been about to go get himself yet another cup of coffee; he had been at his desk since seven, which was not unusual. "Jeddy?" she had said, as soon as he picked up. He hadn't noticed anything unusual in her voice, although it must have been there, he had just not wanted to hear it. She had said, "I'm going to Mashantum tomorrow."

"That's great," he had said. "For how long?"

"All summer."

"Oh." He had put down his pen. "Billy can get that kind of time off?"

"He's not coming. That is, he's installing us. Me and the kids and the nanny. He's going to come on weekends. He's promised he won't work any Saturdays," she said defensively.

"You have a *nanny*?"

She told him about Toni Atkinson, the fact of her only—her hours, when she was starting—and he sensed her determination. She said, "I thought maybe you could come up."

"I do have a job."

"I know." She cleared her throat. "I know. Just—sometime."

"Well, I've already used a lot of time," he said, trying to soften his voice. He had spent more than a week in Connecticut after Grace was born, shuttling Callie back and forth to the hospital. "I guess I could talk to HR," he said. "Callie—you need to go for the *whole* summer? Without Billy?"

"*Yes*. I just *do*. I miss her," she said, and she started to cry. "I miss her."

She had been so weepy since the baby was born. Had she been like this with Jamie? Jed couldn't remember. He sighed. "I know," he said.

"She's so beautiful, Jeddy."

"She—?"

"Gracie."

"Yes. Yes, she is. She's beautiful, Cal." He hesitated. "Mom would have thought so too," he said. Callie didn't answer. "Look, I'll try to set something up. Okay?" He rubbed his eyes. Coffee wouldn't help, but if he didn't have it, it would be worse.

"Okay." Her voice quavered but there was a hardness in it too, and he pictured her face working at the other end. She must have fought and won, because next thing she said, "All right, Jed," like she was closing a deal.

Although he had been swamped that day, like all days, as soon as he hung up with Callie he had called Billy. He'd met Billy in law school; he had introduced him to Callie. Billy was an Atlanta boy too. It had never occurred to Jed that Billy would want to go after a big-deal job in New York, but that was what he had done, a year after graduation, and taken Callie and Jamie up to Greenwich with him. Jamie had just been starting to walk then. Jed remembered him reaching up for his two forefingers, insisting on endless stiff-legged circuits around Callie and Billy's little house in Virginia Highlands. And Jed had complied, surprising even himself with his patience.

He had told Billy he shouldn't take Callie away. "It's just for a few years," Billy had said. "Then I can come back here and be the big New York hotshot."

"You won't come back," Jed had said.

"Sure, we will! What are you talking about?" Billy had cried, but in his normally merry eyes there had been an apprehension Jed hadn't seen before, and he had known Billy was lying, known that he was simply trying to put miles between his new family and the McClatchey sorrow. As if that would work.

But now, on the phone, Billy was saying, "I can't talk any sense into her." There was nothing merry in his tone. "She is absolutely determined. I told her I can't be there. I don't know what to do."

Jed eyed the open file folders on his desk. He said, "You could be there if you wanted to."

"Sure. And the nice men in suits could foreclose on the house and repossess the cars. Don't give me that liberated-man bullshit," he muttered, and Jed wondered if Billy was going to start crying too.

"Is she okay?"

"She's fine. A little strung out. Full of energy though. She's amazing. No sleep, but she's zooming around with Jamie, running in the mornings, all that." Billy's voice swelled with pride and Jed felt a bit mollified: Billy worshipped her, he really did. "Look, bro," Billy continued, "I don't want her to go. I don't want her to take the kids."

"You told her that."

"Yeah, I told her that." He sighed again. "*Shit,* Jed. I'm sorry I brought her up here. I am. But—"

"You're there now."

"Nothin' you can do," Billy said. Jed knew Billy wanted him to agree, about the simple linearity of life and a man's obligation in it. But he didn't answer. "Jed?"

"I'll talk to her," he had said.

Jed had hung up fully intending to call Callie again and talk her down. He'd promise her another weekend, he'd try to get away in August. August—when it was sweltering in Atlanta but already cooling down in Mashantum, when the beach was still warm during the day but you had to use a blanket at night, and you lay in bed under that blanket knowing it meant summer was almost over. Over. August. Two months away.

He picked up the handset again, but instead of punching a free line, his finger hovered over the buttons. Then, slowly, he set the phone back into its cradle. He gathered the papers on his desk into a neater pile and folded his hands on top of them and sat there without moving for several minutes.

He had been a good soldier, a good little orphan boy who had graduated from college in spite of it all, gone to law school, gave no one pause about his state of mind. There had been no either-or: he had just done it. And now there was nothing wrong with his profession or with his job, except that he did not remember ever having picked them. The people working alongside him for the days that stretched into nights seemed to be doing it because they wanted something, very badly. It could even be—he was fairly sure about this—that in some cases the things they wanted had nothing to do with the law; but maybe a partnership seemed as good a stand-in as anything.

But he wanted nothing. His job was a stand-in for nothing. He simply existed in it and lately it seemed to have less and less to actually do with him. This was true of any number of things—his job, his apartment, the women he dated, all of whom he eventually just quit calling. The last one had beaten him to the punch. *I can't be with you,* she had said, *because you're not with me. I don't know where you are.* He didn't really care, but he knew most men would have.

But as he sat at his desk and stared at his phone he knew that finally there was something he wanted. He wanted to go to Mashantum. And he knew, too, that when he had been talking to Callie, his nerve endings had been quivering, like an animal's before a storm. Something in her voice was wrong. He needed to be with her. Now.

Afterward, he was not quite sure how much of this he had said out loud. He had gone to see his boss that same afternoon, and the man, give him credit, had tried to be kind: *This is an excellent firm,* he had said, *you can't afford to quit, it will be a permanent black mark, Jed*—but Jed heard the fatherly tone in his voice and it was a supreme effort not to turn his back and leave right then, slamming the door behind him. He seemed to be regressing. He knew that this man, along with everyone in Atlanta, had seen the McClatchey name in the paper, on the news, over and over, years before, and that they still remembered. He had always known this, of course, and been bothered, but now he felt full-blown disgust. He hated the pity and knew it would always follow him. Hatred for his own father bubbled in the back of Jed's throat. He could not have spoken if he had wanted to and so he let the man go on, being magnanimous: Jed would be given a leave. As long as necessary (what was necessary?), unpaid, but with benefits. Jed let him spin off into details, until he finally wound down and stopped, and Jed realized it was his turn to speak. "Thank you," he said.

But he felt no gratitude. Belatedly, he held out his hand and the other man took it in both of his own, like a preacher at the end of a service, and Jed suppressed what he knew would have been a maniacal laugh: go in peace to love and serve, yes, indeed! His boss was looking at him sympathetically, and Jed extracted his hand. It immediately curled, on its own, into a fist. He hadn't seen that particular look, so undisguised, in a while. He hated that look. He wished he would never see it again.

He had gone straight back to his office then, ignoring his secretary's inquiring stare, and closed the door. Under the coat hook was a small mirror. He rarely used it, but there was no coat hanging there that day to block it, and he found himself looking into his own eyes. They had been furious, his face twisted, unfamiliar.

And then he had been looking into a different mirror. He had been tying his tie. It was the morning of his father's funeral, one episode emerging distinct, acute, from the blur of that day. He was standing at the mirror in his childhood bedroom, and Callie was coming in without knocking. She was saying, "Your tie's stained."

He was saying, "All my ties look like crap."

"Why don't I get you one of Dad's?"

"No." He was thinking, in the weird third person that had begun to descend on him at odd times, *His hands were at his own throat,* and his fingers stiffened and lost their place. "Damnit."

After a moment's hesitation, Callie said, "Here," and she stepped forward and began to tie it for him. He had known she would do this and he held still. She had often tied their father's tie, or at least straightened it. Their father had been a man who liked to be tended to; maybe she was looking for Cecil in him even now. *Well,* Jed thought grimly, *she won't find him.*

But he in turn eyed his sister's black dress, her black stockings and shoes. He knew he was searching for their mother, and from certain angles he could see her but not enough, and then she was gone and he saw only Callie, straightbacked and stern, deep circles under her eyes. Callie would ignore any goddamn pathos and instead tie the ties, turn the wheels, keep this operation together by sheer willpower. She would not acknowledge their difference, would not mention again that she had wanted him to wear their father's tie and he had refused, that he blamed and hated their father and she did not. "I know what you're thinking," Callie said.

He didn't answer.

"Well, you're right," she said. "This is the same fucking dress."

Then he felt it, what he had been expecting for days, for months. Rage descended on him, and for one black, eternal moment he was engulfed, smothered, but then he ripped it off and kicked it away like some filthy garment. He would not, could not, put it back on. If he did, he would lose himself in it, and he refused to lose one more thing. Ever.

He held his chin up for Callie and looked at a patch of light on the wall. A sunny day. His mother's funeral had been rainy. Could muse on the unfairness of that. Wouldn't.

Her voice broke in. "Jeddy," she said. "I can't do this."

Her hands had gone away but he had known she didn't mean his tie. He had reached up and tightened the knot. Their elemental disagreement had hung in the air, but they had needed each other even more than they had needed to agree.

"You won't have to," he had said, and offered his arm, and she had taken it. "After today," he had said, "you will never have to do this again."

Jed woke to the warm, bitter smell of coffee. For a moment he didn't know where he was, and then he saw all the pink around him and remembered. Once he had finally drifted off, his sleep had seemed deep and long, but the clock on the bedside table said seven-thirty, which made him feel unexpectedly virtuous. The poignancy of the underused room was diminished in the morning light. He lay in bed a moment before getting up, feeling both embarrassed that he had actually stayed the night and somehow peaceful. He liked the idea that no one knew where he was.

Now he slipped out of bed and put on his clothes from the day before. He didn't want to use the silver brush displayed on the dresser, and instead combed his hair with his fingers. He glanced in the mirror and decided he was passable. A quick trip to the bathroom, and he would go. What in the world, after all, did he have left to say to Marcella Atkinson?

But when he went to the kitchen to say good-bye he stopped in the doorway. She was standing at the counter, her back to him, her elbows pumping slowly up and down, and he realized she was rolling dough. She was wearing white shorts and a plain white T-shirt, and her hair was twisted up at the back of her head. There were a few tendrils curling at her neck.

He didn't want her to be startled when she turned around, but this moment to look at her undisturbed seemed like a gift, and so he took it. She was barefoot. Her feet on the wooden floor were narrow, with a high, delicate arch. Her legs were slender—he'd noticed that already, but in this morning light they were not like a young girl's legs—the skin was different, looser, not taut and smooth. He didn't care. With her hair curling in the heat and the little song she was humming she was like a girl.

He cleared his throat.

"Oh," she said, and turned, and the smile she gave him was happy and a little shy. "I hope you don't mind," she said. "I'm making strudel. I hardly ever have someone to cook for."

"It smells good," he said, thinking, *She's not chasing me away.* He hadn't really expected that, but it would have been more intelligible to him.

Coffee was poured, he refused cream. The first batch of strudel came out of the oven and she sat him down at the table and gave him a piece. "I didn't know anyone really made strudel," he said.

"My grandmother used to make it. Or, rather, have it made. She had a Milanese cook, and Milan, you know, is not so far from Austria." She looked down at her own plate in mock disapproval. "This isn't real strudel. I do not have time for all those layers and layers of pastry. The real thing is very delicate. Although I suppose I do," she said, and laughed. "I suppose I have nothing but time."

A bell went off and she went to the oven and took out another tray. As she bent to reach he could see the swell of her knee, the tender stretch of her thigh above it. She was the sort of woman who would get thinner as she aged. She would be gray-haired and elegant. "I don't know why I wanted to bake," she said. "I'm heating up the kitchen, and it's going to be a hot day anyway." The kettle on the stove sang and he watched her carefully pour water into a little French press coffeepot. "There."

"I'm sorry. I drank up all your coffee."

"No, no. The pot is just too small."

She sat across from him with her mug. She ate nothing herself. Her ease had been dissipating, it seemed, as she had talked, and now the silence descended. He looked at her slender hands encircling her mug. Not old, not young. "Are you a good cook?" he said.

"Yes." She met his gaze, and they both smiled. She shrugged a little and said, "I see no reason to lie."

But the silence came on again as he ate and a childish fear descended on him, that she had made the pastry to somehow make him go away, that any minute now she was going to put two or three pieces in a paper sack, still warm, and send him through the door like a lost boy, out into the wood, temporarily provisioned but still doomed. He forgot that he had been so eager to leave. He chewed very slowly.

"I was thinking we might go to the beach," Marcella said. "It's just so hot. For June." Jed's mouth was full and so he could get away with only nodding. He tried not to look too surprised. "Did you bring a bathing suit? Did you pack for wherever you were pretending to go?" She did not smile.

"Not really. But there's a suit in the back of my car."

"I don't go that often during the day. I go later on, for a walk. When it's cooler. But I can't think what else to do on a day like today. Of course," she said, fiddling with the handle of her mug, "you might rather go home. To your own beach. It's a nice beach. I remember."

Jed said, "What is a day like today?"

"I don't know," Marcella said. She did not meet his eyes.

MARCELLA DROVE THEM to the residents-only lot, and after Jed had taken the chairs out of the trunk before she could reach them, and the bag with the towels and books too, she laughed at her empty-handedness and then led the way down the narrow path to the beach. The trail was covered in fine gray sand and where it slipped in the sides of her sandals it was already hot. It was high tide, and the beach was crowded; they found a spot between two large extended families, encamped with portable cribs and ice chests and elaborate folding chairs with attached umbrellas. Beneath her sunglasses Marcella was blushing with embarrassment. Why hadn't she checked the tide chart? Why had she brought him here, to bake on a Saturday among screaming children, when he could have done that as well in Mashantum? "At least the tide is going out," she said.

"Is it? When was it high?"

"I'm not sure," she admitted. She busied herself arranging her chair.

The night before, she had woken feeling that someone else had done it, woken her, that someone was in the room. But there was no one. Still, the house seemed alive to her, humming. She got out of bed and floated down the hall in her long nightgown to Toni's room.

He had been there, asleep, on his back. The sheet was pulled up to his waist and his clothes were in a heap next to the bed, and with a catch to her breath she wondered if he was nude, and at the same time smiled at the little-boy slovenliness. He had not pulled down the shade of the window next to the bed, and moonlight was pouring through, so bright that the shadow of the crossed muntins fell on his chest. She had stood in the doorway and studied him for a long time. His body first but then his face, over and over, making a circuit of chin, mouth, cheekbones, forehead. She had seen Cecil in him earlier that evening but now she looked and looked and could find no trace. She had been amazed that he was only, purely himself. She had almost expected the force of her attention to rouse him, but it hadn't.

And then she had awoken early, like it was the first day of school, and made him pastry, and then dragged him here. What had she been thinking? She had not been thinking, only acting. She was not so lonely and desperate that she would do anything for company. But probably that was what he thought. Well, that was safe enough, although her vanity was getting in the way, a feeling she'd forgotten about—she did not want to seem pitiful. She thought of his face the night before, how hard it had been. But underneath, pleading. Yes. When he had asked the question.

That, she thought, was why she had wanted to keep him here. She had not decided how to answer the question. If.

She realized she had been sitting with her book open on her knees, not turning the pages, for a long time. At the beach blanket next to them, a toddler was having a tantrum: his sandwich had fallen in the sand, and in his wrath he kicked over his sister's castle. The wails rose to a crescendo and the harried mother rolled her eyes ruefully at Marcella. But in her daze it took Marcella too long to muster a sympathetic smile, and the mother turned away, rebuffed.

She looked down at Jed, beside her. He was lying on his stomach on a towel, his face turned away. His brown back gleamed. Such an expanse of skin. She made herself say, "I'm going for a swim."

He turned his head and looked at her. Not Cecil's face, and not a boy's, but a man's: she was surprised yet again. He kept changing. "This is nice," he offered. "It's a nice beach."

"It's hot and crowded. I'm sorry."

"No, Mrs.—Marcella—"

"You were kind to come," she said, and put down her book and sunglasses and hat and fled.

The water was cold and familiar and she walked out chest-deep, past the waves and the children on floats and the teenagers throwing Frisbees to the calm, cold depths. She sighted the seawall, down the beach, and put down her head and began to swim. She loved the water. She loved the idea of the ocean stretching past her, thousands of miles of cool darkness, like a cushion, and on the other side Europe, Italy, the idea of home if not the reality. She fell into the groove of her stroke, felt her hips and shoulders rolling as if to a slow, steady drumbeat. In the water her body took over. If she kept moving, she would come to no harm.

She swam for a long time, not all the way to the seawall but close, and then turned back. Halfway there, she felt someone swimming beside her. She did not break her stroke but looked next to her as she breathed, and saw Jed's brown arms in a shower of water. She could feel his pace uneven beside her and realized he was holding himself back to stay with her.

She stopped when she thought she was almost there, and sure enough when she stood up, breathing hard, she could see the blue sign marking the path to the parking lot. Jed had come up too, and was panting beside her. With his hair dark and wet against his head and the sun sharpening the wet planes of his face, his handsomeness seemed almost two-dimensional. She felt more relaxed than she had before. "You're a good swimmer," she said.

"Not as good as you."

"I felt you slowing yourself down."

"That's because my stroke is uneven. I don't have the right rhythm."

"Do you love the ocean?"

"Not love," he said. "I like looking at it."

She said, "They say that looking at the ocean is calming because the horizon is clear. It's something left from the ancient days—we are always on guard for the enemy, but if we have a clear horizon we can be truly peaceful."

"You can't see what's under the water, though," he said. "You can't see what's coming." He lay down in the water on his back, and stroked away from her, looking up at the sky.

"No," she said, although he couldn't hear her. "I suppose not."

At lunchtime they left the beach and Marcella took him to the farm stand to get sandwiches. "It's a Connecticut farm stand," she told him. She remembered her social voice. "It's chichi."

They had ceased to discuss when he would leave. Marcella wanted to ask him every moment; she had to stop herself. She would not, of course, beg him to stay but she needed to prepare herself for his leaving, try to figure out ahead of time how empty it would feel, why she would care, how she had become a different creature from the day before, when she had been content in her garden, alone. He had brought her closer to Cecil. He had pushed her farther away.

The woman at the wooden sandwich counter asked what they wanted and began to cut bread from a large brown loaf. "These are as good as you would make?" Jed said.

"Oh, better."

"I don't believe it."

Marcella heard Cecil, or maybe it was just the South, in his voice: the trained, automatic charm. She knew that was what it was, she would take it at face value. She would remember the task at hand. A sandwich was good. He could take the bag in his car with him, go. "When you eat this on the road, be careful," she said. "Don't let everything drip into your lap and make a mess. Especially the tomatoes. Look at those tomatoes!" Jed looked at her sidelong but said nothing. She had to dismiss him, it was for the best. "I need to get a few things," she said. "I'll meet you at the register."

She crossed to the other side of the room, where fruit was arranged in shallow baskets. The farm stand was built of weathered, unfinished wood, and the windows were open holes, their plywood covers propped away, awninglike, from the building. The wind blowing through them was hotter than ever. Marcella felt the dried salt and sand on her like a second skin. The colors of the produce shone against the wood. Blueberries were piled high in their green cardboard boxes. She would make something. A pie. A whole pie for herself. Too much. *Damnit.*

"Marcella."

She flinched. Jed was next to her, close. "I came to tell you I'm leaving," he said. "I know your house is just down the road. I'll walk back. I'm sorry I bothered you. I really am."

"Your sandwich," Marcella breathed, idiotically.

"I've got them. Here." He handed her a wax-papered cylinder. "Don't pay for it. I mean, I already did."

"I don't want you to go," Marcella said, in a rush. "I wasn't trying to make you."

"Are you sure about that?" he said, and he smiled, and his face changed completely.

He had not moved away, he was close enough that she could see the skim of salt at his hairline. "I know a nice place to go to eat these," she said. "A pretty place. You could see it before you go." She felt she was luring him to a trap.

She took him to a plot of conservation land, with a short path from the dusty pull-off and a picnic table at the end. Although they were less than a mile from the beach, there was no hint of the ocean; beyond them stretched rolling fields. "I've never seen anyone else here," she said. "I don't think anyone knows about it."

"It's beautiful. It's getting hotter, though."

"Yes. I think the wind has changed."

They ate in silence for a while and Marcella was trying not to apologize again, about the heat, the sun, how exposed they were, when Jed said, abruptly, "I feel like I have a million things to say to you. Only I can't start. If I start I'll never stop."

"What are they? What things?"

"I don't know yet." He turned to her.

She said, "I really barely know you, Jed," but her hand almost reached up, of its own accord, to stroke his cheek. She felt them, her fingers with their own intentions, but then the expression on his face changed and he drew back, and she thought it was because of what she had said and then realized she was shaking her head. *No. No no no.* Something had made it move, some different, deep impulse for what was right. Thank God. She should be grateful. But instead she folded her arms on the table in front of her and buried her head inside, to make it stop.

"I'm sorry," he said. "I don't know what I'm doing."

"Jed, you must listen." She raised her head and held it very high, her back very straight, and looked out at the gold and green fields, wind blowing over them like a live thing. Her *nonna* had told her the dead could come to you on the wind. If she was not strong, if she was not honorable, she would make herself so now. "You asked me if I thought your father had killed your mother," she said. "No, no, a thousand times no. I know this." She took a breath. "I know this because on the night your mother died, your father was with me."

Jed had begun paying attention to the *Atlanta Journal-Constitution* at age thirteen or so, in the manner of a boy who already knows that someday he will face college interviewers. He formed rudimentary opinions about various Supreme Court decisions, Middle Eastern politics, and Northern Ireland. He read about wildfires in the West and hurricanes in Florida.

But by the time he was done with the national and international news he was in a hurry to get to sports and the comics, and so he rarely read the Metro section. He was not interested in new local highways or the shenanigans of the Atlanta City Council. It didn't occur to him that "current events" were also the sickening, ordinary tragedies: the coked-up teenager shaking every bit of sense, forever, out of his girlfriend's baby; the bankrupt father strangling his own children in the back of the family van; the man staking out his own wife, crouching in his own shrubbery, leaving the neighbors to say, *They seemed nice. Kept to themselves.* And always, *You don't think it can happen on your own street.*

When Betsy McClatchey was murdered, Cecil McClatchey was away, overnight, on a business trip. Jed and Callie, who went to the same college, were fetched by an aunt and uncle, and when they got home and finally saw their father, he looked utterly shattered. He cried at the funeral, and before, and after. Jed had never seen his father sob. He had been out of town, there had been a simple burglary, it had gone awry. That was that.

But then a maid at his hotel claimed his bed had not been slept in. His father said he had had trouble sleeping that night, had been driving around, and then he had come back and lain down on top of the covers. The cops thought he was hiding something. Asheville was not so far from Atlanta, and Cecil had been staying south of there; it was possible, just, to drive to Atlanta and back overnight. They did not say this to Jed, instead asking him questions that were little more than insinuations: *There's nothing else you want to tell us?* And finally once, point-blank, *Any chance your father could have a lady friend?* He had laughed out loud. His father? His broken, unadventurous father? "Of course not," he had said. He had nothing else to tell them, and his father had never changed his story. There was never an indictment or a trial, there was no evidence whatsoever, except for that unslept-in bed.

But as the investigation died down into the lull that would end with his father's death, Jed found himself doing a strange thing. He found himself reading the paper again, and going to the local news first. He found himself hunting for stories of heartbreaking crime, and then, when he found them, as he always did, looking for clues and motives and orderly outlines. Someone owed money, someone did drugs. Someone had been abused and turned to crime themselves: elementary psychology. He absorbed all this data with a frantic hunger. He learned it was usually the men, even family men, with heretofore unblemished lives. They made an insane decision, they became convinced of its necessity, they followed through. Jed built himself a house of horrors, brick by brick, and entered it and lived there. Then his father died, a car crash late at night, no other cars involved. It was probably a heart attack, there was no note, but . . . and the door to the house slammed shut, with him inside.

MARCELLA AND JED DROVE BACK to the house in silence. When they walked up the front steps and into the little living room Jed was struck by how familiar it felt, as if he had spent his life there, not just one day. He felt, again, that if he were made to leave it would be a kind of exile. He knew he should be very angry at Marcella, maybe he was— he had a right to be scathing; but he was too tired to muster up such behavior. He looked at her and thought again that she was lovely, even though now she looked gray and twisted-out, something in her collapsed. He was surprised his father had been able to see her love- liness. Jed was not convinced that he had. Probably his father had seen only the typical side of her beauty—the legs and breasts and cheek- bones. He would not have seen it all, her sadness, her thoughts. He would have seen only the things that were different from Jed's mother.

Jed felt a wave of nausea. He heard Marcella say, "Are you all right?"

The sick feeling passed but still he felt only disgust for himself, for the sweat and sunscreen dried on his body, the salt in his hair. "I'm taking a shower," he said to Marcella's stricken face, and marched down the hall.

In the bathroom all Marcella's things, like in the living room, seemed preternaturally familiar. In the shower he took the first bottle of shampoo he saw and squeezed some out, and a flowery scent rose up to him. Something else also, maybe citrus. The scent was cloying and he knew without hesitation that this was not her usual brand. The store had been out, she had bought this instead, she found the fragrance overpowering too. He rubbed some into his hair anyway, just as she did. His mind skimmed blindly over the surface of a deep black ocean. He wanted to stay there forever, the water wearing him down into nothing, a boulder reduced to sand.

But when he was finished he dried off, wrapped the towel around himself, and walked back to his room. He did not see Marcella. He put on the same old shorts again and combed his wet hair with his fingers. He had left his bathing suit hanging in the shower; he would have to get it. There were only his shirt and his flip-flops left. He had never traveled so light. He stood in the center of the room, paralyzed, until exhaustion overtook him and he lay down on the unmade twin bed, on Toni's pink sheets.

And somehow the house and the room reversed itself and became the strangest place he had ever been, and lying there feeling utterly lost he thought of his father and Marcella. He had sat next to her at the picnic table with the hot wind blowing and watched her mouth forming words, and gradually had realized that out of all the other feelings he could not identify there was one he could, a feeling of being bested. His own father. Jesus.

It was a middle-age thing, this affair, a male thing, Marcella had said. *Someday you will understand—*

I will never do that, he had said.

No, Marcella had said. *I hope not.*

He knew that here, finally, was his father's alibi. He could never have hoped for such incontrovertible proof of his innocence. There had been no midnight drive to Atlanta and back, his father cold and calculating at the wheel. That picture came easily, and Jed realized it had been there, fully formed but hidden, all along. But it was pure fantasy. He was not the son of a murderer. The prison door was open. He could leave.

But it was odd: he had grown used to it.

He wanted only to go back years before that false vision, to throw himself into his father's arms, to be lifted high, to be whirled above green grass at twilight, with the lit windows of his own house glowing across the lawn. He wanted only not to despise him. Jed buried his head in the pink pillow, wet already from his hair so his tears made no difference, and cried himself to sleep.

HE WOKE AGAIN to the smell of food. Outside it was still light, but by the angle of the sun he judged it to be past seven o'clock. Lying in bed, his mind still fuzzy, he thought: *It's a sign we're given that we're alive, that in spite of everything we can be hungry.* He swung his legs over the side of the bed. He had a headache, like a child's after a tantrum, but once he was upright it began to fade.

He put on his shirt and went to the bathroom, where he drank cup after cup of water, clearing the thickness from his throat. Then he walked down the hall to the kitchen and stood, as he had that morning, in the doorway, watching Marcella, her back to him again, her right arm sliding up and down, this time with a knife. He sensed that she knew he was there, but she did not turn around. The knife thunked against the cutting board. He went in and sat at the table. "What are you doing?" he said.

"Making dinner. Garbage pasta. That means I throw everything in." Her elbow moved steadily. "Peppers and zucchini. Basil from the garden."

He said nothing. *Chopchopchop.* She picked up the cutting board and slid a mound of peppers into the skillet on the stove beside her. They sizzled as they went in. He watched her go to work on a yellow crookneck squash. "I used to cook all the time for Anthony," she said. "I tried everything from the magazines. At first he thought it was wonderful but eventually we fought about that too." Her knife flashed up and down. "I spent too much money, it took too much time, why did I have to get so fancy. He just wanted a regular meal, damnit." She brushed quickly at her eyes with her other hand. "*Dio mio.* I am not trying for sympathy. I was just thinking about—oh, shut up. Shut up," she said, not talking anymore to him.

He got up and went over to the counter. Her eyes were red and swollen. She had taken a shower too, at some point; he smelled the too-sweet shampoo, and the twist of her hair was still wet. "Don't worry," he said, and finally she looked at him.

"Don't worry!" she said, and laughed. "Jed, go home. Ah!" she cried, in frustration, and wiped angrily at her eyes again.

Jed handed her a kitchen towel. She hid her face for a moment, and sighed harshly. Then she folded the towel and placed it on the other side of the stove. Jed watched her hands. When she finally looked up at him he held her eyes steadily, gently. It seemed the kindest, the only, thing he could do. After a moment she looked away, but her face was calmer. "Do you have another knife?" he said, and she opened a drawer and handed him one.

They chopped side by side, pushing the vegetables into piles. When he was done he took the big pot sitting on the counter and began filling it with water for the pasta. "Jed," Marcella said again, "go home."

"Don't worry."

"*Worry* again! *Worry* is not the word!"

"Marcella," he said. He set the pot in the sink, stepped closer, and took her shoulders in his hands. "Please." He wanted desperately to calm her. It seemed the only task that mattered.

"Jed, what do you think you need to do for me? Nothing! Nothing! Less than nothing!"

"I'm not thinking. I'm too tired to think," he said. She opened her mouth again and he said, "Please."

He was still holding her shoulders. He realized it was the first time he had touched her. After a moment he slid his hands down her arms and held her hands in front of her. He shook his head slowly, slowly, and said again, "I'm not thinking."

She whispered, "This is wrong."

"Everything is wrong," he said, and bent down to her, and she did not turn away.

TWO
THE
SWIMMING
POOL

The party was over, the guests had left, Betsy had gone to bed early, and the kids had escaped somewhere with their friends. Drinking on the beach somewhere probably. This thought didn't worry Cecil McClatchey, but instead made him feel content. His children out being kids, having a carefree summer—it made him feel he had succeeded as a father, that he had given them the setting and the means to not worry about anything, at least for now. It was what his own adolescence had been like, he didn't remember any particular angst like people sometimes talked about—he had always been popular and happy and things had always worked out. As they were working out now.

He was sitting in the living room with not enough lights on and he didn't know why. He got up and poured himself another scotch, neat, at the little table they laughingly called the bar, and then walked through the dark kitchen and the attached screen porch down the flagstone path to the pool.

Now that it was fully dark, the bugs weren't as bad as they had been when the party was breaking up, at dusk. The surface of the pool shimmered a little with the reflection of a distant streetlight, but he couldn't see the moon. Betsy had cleared everything away and there was no evidence that a party had taken place, not even a crumpled napkin on the ground; the empty lounge chairs and the table with the big open umbrella felt like a stage set to him, waiting for the actors to arrive.

Marcella Atkinson had sat in that chair, over there. God, she was a good-looking woman, but he wasn't the only one who thought that, surely, it was an ordinary fact by now that Marcella Atkinson was extraordinarily attractive. That is, he had seen her for years now. He was used to it. Wondered also for years how she could be married to Anthony. A handsome guy, sure, but utterly—what? Correct. Never broke a rule. Cecil would like to get him drunk, if that were possible. He was a type that couldn't exist in Atlanta, where people didn't take themselves so goddamn seriously.

It was a fluke that Cecil was here, that he had the Mashantum house at all. He had come up to Massachusetts one summer in college, maybe after freshman year?—had to have been, he hadn't met Betsy yet. He'd had a friend from some town outside Boston, unusual at Vanderbilt. Jim Morris, he remembered old Jim, and Cecil had taken a notion to visit. He'd been restless, back at home after that first year of freedom. He'd wanted something exotic, and Boston had seemed that way to him.

His Uncle Talbot was his mother's brother. He'd showed up infrequently in Atlanta; he had an apartment there but it seemed like he'd been up here most of the time. Went to Harvard. Uncle Talbot was exotic himself—everyone always said he was artistic, although it was unclear what he actually did for a living. Queer probably, but as Cecil remembered he seemed mostly to want to be alone. Although if you went to see him—if, say, you and your college pal showed up at his doorstep—he was kind and courtly and even seemed glad you were there. He had been Cecil's mother's favorite brother.

And then Cecil and Betsy had met and gotten married and they had gone to Nantucket for their honeymoon—Betsy had said, sensible as always, *Why go to the Caribbean in May? America is pretty in*

May—and the North had seemed exotic to both of them. That word again. Up north was still America, but it was a more serious place. New England, they felt, knew itself more thoroughly, it was where history had started, and he appreciated history, tradition, as much as the next person. So they had gone to Nantucket, and then after the ferry ride back to Hyannis they had come over here, to Mashantum, self-conscious and proud because they were married, adults now, going to visit another adult, the quintessential adult, Uncle Talbot. Betsy had charmed him. She had loved the house, loved the arbor, the one right over there, covered in purple wisteria—the only time they'd ever seen the damn thing bloom. She'd exclaimed over it all, because she was in love with the Cape, in love with Cecil and he with her; they were both in love with these little cottages covered with old roses, the kind of places they had thought couldn't really exist, that existed now only for them, two twenty-two-year-olds finally no longer virgins who fancied themselves adults—

and damned if a year later when Uncle Talbot dropped dead he hadn't left them the place. And money to take care of it, but the tricky bastard had set it up so the money went with the house; they couldn't sell it and take all the money and buy something at, say, Hilton Head or Pawleys or St. Simons, or even a house to live in in Atlanta; the money would have gone to Harvard then. And Betsy had wanted to keep the place. *Let's try it,* she had said.

So here they were. His children loved it, he could see that, and Betsy too—she was glad to get away from Atlanta for a while each year, she said it was interesting to be where there were different perspectives (that meant more liberals) and where everyone didn't know all your cousins and go to church with your grandmother. Betsy had actually said that, she could be funny that way, surprising him, she was old Atlanta herself but also adventurous—more adventurous in a way than Cecil, although he was the one who had these longings surface periodically, desires that had no name and that would gradually disappear when he reminded himself about the prudence and success and happiness of his life. He had been trained to be grateful. Been trained to pray, and even if he didn't do it that much he knew damn well that God was there, that not appreciating what you had was an affront to the Man Himself.

No, they all loved it here, in this funny little house with the chopped-up rooms. He mentioned renovation now and again, but Betsy and the kids wouldn't let him change anything. It was far too late for any kind of change.

He drained the last of his scotch and watched the water. His own private ocean. A normal beach house, you'd be able to see the water, or at least hear it—here, though, it was a mile away, it was like you were just in the country, maybe that was what old Talbot had been thinking when he put in the pool, that a person needed a piece of water to contemplate. Marcella Atkinson had been staring at the water. Stretched out in that chair over there.

He wondered how she would answer all these thoughts of his. She had ended up in a foreign place too; had she planned it? Not that the Cape, for him, was really like another country, like Marcella Atkinson leaving Italy and coming here. Hell, maybe he just wished he were someplace *more* foreign. Maybe he just wanted Marcella Atkinson to tell him what it was like to start a new life in a new place, to leave all that was familiar behind. If that was what she had done. He didn't know *her* story at all. Most likely never would.

He stood to go inside and as he did a breeze rustled through the trees and a lone leaf came fluttering down from the maples and landed on the surface of the pool. The water had been eerily smooth, so still it was almost invisible, but now the ripples went out in rings and the water was suddenly solid and alive.

It was late Sunday afternoon when Jed got back to Mashantum. Callie was in the kitchen with Grace. Jed thought she looked a little better rested. He needed to focus on that. On Callie. On Grace, on the kitchen, on the sun streaming through the window. He had to shut off his confusion, his memory, the raw desire he could barely manage to swallow. "Back so soon?" Callie said.

He told himself there was no edge to her voice. "Where is everybody?"

"Well, half of us are right here. The *men* are at the beach. Grace and I just got up from a nap, right, Gracie?" She looked into the baby's little face, nestled in the crook of her arm, and smiled brightly. But the brightness was an artificial glare, and it seemed to Jed that her gaze was not going out to Grace but inward.

"Was it a good night?" he said.

"Decent. She was up—well, I don't remember. Three times? That was so long ago. And we just had a nap so we won't worry about it, hmmm?" Grace yawned adorably, and Callie said, "You want her?"

As soon as Jed took her, the baby's face brightened. "How's my girl?" he crooned. Tiny little Grace, little cub—she would help him not to think. "Look at you," he said. "You're trying, aren't you? Look. It's a proto-smile."

Even though Grace had been in the world for ten weeks she

could not be expected to act like a regular two-month-old, and she had not yet begun to smile. Jed didn't care, but he knew Callie wanted it, she needed a reward. Now she glanced at Jed and the baby skeptically.

"Oh, honey," Jed said, "easy there." Grace had got an arm loose from her blanket and had flung it out and startled, flailing to catch herself. He held her up on his shoulder. "I've got you, I've got you," he murmured. He looked up at Callie. "She was doing that falling thing," he said.

Callie said, "It's a reflex."

Jed held the baby tightly and walked her up and down the sunny kitchen. The light wasn't kind to the scarred linoleum and chipped Formica, but he was grateful for the reality of it, the dinged white table and the old gray counters, the green glass pitcher with the tags of tea bags hanging over, clipped with a clothespin the way his mother used to do, the ancient kettle singing with the water.

"So, how was it?" Callie said, her back to him.

"Fine." Grace was beginning to wiggle on his shoulder. He brought her in closer to his face and suddenly he could smell his own hand, cradling her head: Marcella. She was on his fingers. He stopped dead in the middle of the kitchen floor and the desire he had been fighting broke through and hit him like a gale. Automatically he clutched Grace tighter, so much that she began to whimper. He loosened his grip. *Yes, yes, you're right, I will infect you if I'm not careful, infect you with this sickness or badness or insanity or whatever it is . . .* "I think she's hungry," he said.

"Not again. Not possible." Callie took the baby and held her out in front of her, one hand cradling the baby's head, the other holding her tiny body. "What-am-I-going-to-do-with-you-I-just-fed-you—"

"Plug her in, Cal. The girl's got to grow."

"You think it's so easy," Callie said, but she gave him an oddly grateful look, and sat down in one of the kitchen chairs. Jed looked away while she arranged herself. It was strange to boss her around and have her listen. He recited aloud the lie he had rehearsed in his mind: his friend sick with a twenty-four-hour bug, possibly forty-eight, he hadn't hung around to find out, he'd just left and wandered around—

"I *hate* being alone in Manhattan," Callie said.

"Well. I sort of met someone."

"Where? At a bar or something?" Jed shrugged. "Oh, *God*, Jeddy, not again."

"It was . . ." He couldn't help it, a smile was spreading across his face. "It was pretty good."

"*Jesus.* Does she have a name?"

He hesitated, all creativity leaving him. "Marcie."

"Marcie? Please. Is she from New Jersey?"

"Connecticut."

"Are you going to see her again?"

He felt the smile fading. "I don't know."

"Look at the long face!" Callie detached Grace and put her up on her shoulder, *pat-pat-pat.*

By the time Billy and Jamie came back from the beach Callie seemed almost jovial.

"*Marcie?*" Billy hooted. "Is she a blue-eyeshadow chick? A mall rat? How old is this girl, anyway?"

"Old enough."

"*Marcie.* Not a good Waspy girl. Not a Southern belle!" And he patted Callie's rear end. She was standing at the sink now, peeling carrots. As soon as Billy's hand dropped, Jed saw her take one small step away from him, not looking up, her hand with the peeler not stopping. Billy did not seem to notice.

Jed considered his brother-in-law. He appreciated his easy smile, his teasing, in much the way he imagined Callie once had: Billy was a balm to them, uncomplicated and cheerful. An Italian Southerner:

who could be more gregarious? Only now it wasn't working as well. He had betrayed them by taking Callie away, he was betraying them still with this weekend arrangement, but for once, all Jed wanted was for him to leave.

"And I notice that it's Sunday," Billy was saying. "Notice that you met this girl on a Friday night, and you did not see fit to return until *Sunday.* I can assume that you got to know each other *well.* That you are now, in a manner of speaking, *close*—"

Jed let him rattle on. Callie, nursing Grace again, sat with a half-smile on her face. He was grateful it was Sunday and the long, slow week stretched out in front of them. Tonight the midsummer sun would sink slowly, the shadows stretching longer and longer, there would be the feeling of infinite time he remembered from childhood. The summer never ending. Only now—now he suddenly cared what day it was. Sunday night, he had just gotten home, and when could he leave again?

THEN THERE WAS THE PROBLEM of Toni. She appeared Monday morning, long legs in short shorts, breasts swaying under her T-shirt, saying *look at me,* a challenge in her eyes as if she already knew what was going on.

Jed was sitting at the kitchen table eating cereal and Jamie was sitting with him, steering his toy backhoe and bulldozer around an imaginary construction site, periodically driving one of the trucks over his buttered English muffin. Jed had given up telling him not to. When Toni opened the screen door, Jamie eyed her warily. He was not always happy when she showed up.

Toni helped herself to coffee from the pot on the counter. "How was your weekend?" she asked—demanded, it seemed to Jed. "Didn't you go to New York?"

"Yeah. It was good." He was trying not to look at her legs, trying not to compare, and after a few moments some blessed screen came down and her body seemed only hers and Marcella was locked safely away in a golden tower in his mind.

"Jed? Hello? What did you do?"

"Uncle Jed came back," Jamie said possessively.

"I know that, silly. Look, he's sitting right there."

Barely, Jed thought. Toni made a funny face and Jamie relented and laughed.

"He met a girl," Callie said, appearing in the doorway with Grace. "That's what he did this weekend."

Surprise flickered across Toni's face for the merest of moments before the hauteur returned. She looked languidly in Jed's direction but then focused on Grace. "Little baby," she crooned, and Callie, without hesitation, handed her over.

Toni didn't ask any more questions but after a moment Callie said, "A Jersey girl. Marcie."

Jed was surprised Callie was rubbing it in. It was just as well, it would explain if he was suddenly cool to Toni, which of course he now would be. But it was as though Callie were speaking without really paying attention. "She's not from Jersey," he said.

"What's Jersey?" Jamie said.

"It's a state, little buddy—"

"Like Massachusetts," Toni broke in. "Where we are now. We can do the states puzzle after your breakfast. I'll show you."

"No."

"Jamie," Callie said wearily.

Listening to this, Jed decided he was safe. He reached for the box of cereal. "Hey, after I eat something, want to go to the beach, buddy? Cal, maybe you can take a nap."

"It's nine in the morning. How could I nap?"

Toni was still swaying with the baby. Her back was to Jed. It seemed to him she was moving her hips a little too much. "Maybe she'll fall asleep," Toni said. "Aren't you supposed to sleep when the baby sleeps? You said the books say that."

"The books! The books are full of—" In one step Callie was up and at Toni's side. "Just give her to me. Give her to me!" Toni, her eyes wide, handed her the baby and Callie peered, unsmiling, into Grace's face. "No, she's not sleepy. Forget it. No such luck. I probably have to feed her again. Jesus," she said, and turned heel and left the kitchen. They heard her bedroom door shut.

"Mommy's mad," Jamie said.

"She's not mad, bud. She's tired," Jed answered.

"She's mad at baby Grace," Jamie said, both satisfaction and apprehension in his voice.

"You can't be mad at a baby," Toni said, sitting down with them at the table. "Mommy loves baby Grace. You just have to take special care of a baby."

"You have to take special care of *me*," Jamie said gravely.

"We do," Jed said.

"We will," Toni said, almost at the same moment. Her eyes flickered to Jed's and then away. She rose, went over to the coffeemaker, and refilled her mug. She did not offer any to Jed. "So, do you like her?"

"Yes."

"Like who?"

"A girl, buddy."

"It will happen when you're older," Toni said. "If you're lucky." She looked over her shoulder, her flirtation a defiance. "Right, Uncle Jed?"

And suddenly Toni's mother was back again, the barriers he had set up dissolved, she was on the tip of his tongue—his tongue, God, her mouth, his mouth on her body, her body in her bed, miles away, where he was not, and all he could think was *how long? how long?*

———

WHEN HE LEFT, Marcella felt as if her life had fallen apart—the order of it, what little structure it had had. That was Sunday. On Monday morning she woke and the sun was shining and she felt a little calmer, like the engines of life had begun running again, but after she ate her breakfast and went outside and knelt down to dig, the aimlessness descended on her, making her almost dizzy. She had blue salvia to plant, eight packs of six, she had bought it last week and had to get it into the ground, she had meant to do it over the weekend— but instead she sat back on her heels and looked blindly at the border. She needed to decide where the little plants should go but her mind was like an untethered boat. *Jed,* she thought. *Jed.* She drifted.

Finally she rose and went back into the house, down the hall to her bedroom, and stood looking at her unmade bed. It did not make sense to her that it was empty. She could almost see, feel, the imprint of his naked body.

He had kissed her softly at first, in the kitchen, questioning. She had sensed the question was not entirely for her. She had been trembling, she had let him kiss her, but then she had thought, *I mustn't just let it happen. I must choose.* And she had drawn back. Just a little.

His eyes had been burning at her. He had said, once more, "Please."

She could see only his eyes. She saw no other part of his face, his body, nothing that looked like Cecil, nothing at all. His eyes had been brilliant.

She had prepared herself to be consumed but—*no, I do not have to disappear.* She had looked back at him, not shrinking away, and then his mouth was wild on her, he said *please,* and *please* again, and she had kissed him back, *shhh,* she had known for certain he was no longer speaking entirely to her, and then she had not thought anymore.

She looked at the bed again now and desire washed over her and left her shivering. He had held himself over her, his arms straight and hard. And then lowered himself and she was only skin. His mouth on her nipple and the heat blooming like some volcanic flower, and then the petals curving, curving and arching until she was being turned inside out. *Please* and *please* and finally *yes*.

She had a task. A task. She shook herself, and went back outside.

She knelt again at the edge of the flower bed. Old voices were trying to come back, old habits: *I am dirty, disgusting, a woman with no morals, a pitiful weak creature,* she thought—but did not feel. She had thought she was on a path back to a life of goals and normalcy, a life where she was not exiled, suspended. She had been creeping, creeping forward. And then Jed McClatchey had appeared on her porch. He had just appeared, and she had let him in. And now she was waiting for something different.

She wanted him.

She had wanted Cecil too, she had wanted Anthony, long ago, but both of them had gone along with wanting something else, with a kind of life. But Jed—she wanted to bury herself in him, never move, for as long as—what? As long as he needed her? It was not that simple. No, she was not sure what this equation was, not sure what the solution would be. She knew there would be a solution, knew it was finite. She was amazed that this idea of finitude already gave her pain. She could think only about now. She hated now, because he wasn't with her.

She turned back to her plants and lifted them, one by one, out of their crinkling plastic grid. She laid them on the ground and dug their new little holes and pushed the plants in and buried their roots safely in the darkness. She let all the words in her brain slip down her fingers into the black crumbling soil.

MARCIE. HE WANTED TO LAUGH. He wanted to laugh, and laugh, and laugh. He hadn't wanted to leave, that Sunday, but he had made himself, thinking that he couldn't take much more, that he might go crazy with the feel of her skin and the look of her body. He left her still in bed. He had buried his face in her neck, he had twined himself around her, and he had said, "I'm coming back."

"Good." Her eyes had been sleepy, soft, but then her brow had creased.

"Don't worry," he said.

"You keep saying that."

"I don't want you to think I'm going to hurt you." Her look now was downcast. He misinterpreted. "And we are not hurting anyone else," he said. "There's no one to hurt." She knew he was talking about Cecil.

So, back in Mashantum, Jed went to the beach. He held his niece, his nephew, took Jamie to the playground, made him peanut butter crackers. He watched movies into the night with Callie when the baby fussed and they were too tired to talk and he worried about her being alone. She sent him off by himself because they had Toni and what was she paying her for, anyway? And so he would go running, would run until his side cramped and he could barely see for the sweat and exhaustion but he wouldn't stop because it was a long way back home, and if he was in agony he knew it would end and it seemed right, anyway. The agony.

On Friday he made himself wait until Billy had been there more than an hour. His sister and her husband laughed at him and told him to go, go, and their laughter, together, made him happy and he did not remember until he was in the car alone how desperate he was.

When she came, it was with a long keening wail that took him out of himself, clinging only to her, and as she fell through endless space he had no choice but to fall with her.

Jed was out in the front yard with Jamie one morning soon after the Fourth of July when a strange car pulled into the driveway, crunching along the pea stone. Jed was facing east and the sun was directly in his eyes for a moment and then he could see that it was Anthony Atkinson, dropping off Toni, which Anthony had not done before.

Toni slammed the passenger door, waved through the window at her father, and sauntered over. She was wearing very short cutoffs and a purple halter top that hid only what was absolutely necessary. The day was already hot, and a fine sheen of perspiration completed her outfit. "My car died last night," she said.

"It's *dead*?" Jamie said.

"Well, not really, cutie. That means it's not working."

"Oh." Jamie seemed to consider this, accept it, and move on. "I'm hot. I wanna go inside," he announced, and he turned and took off for the door. Toni was after him before Jed had a chance to move, but not before he saw that Anthony wasn't pulling away, but instead was getting out of the car. He'd left it running—hopefully this meant he would not stay long.

Anthony walked toward him with his hand outstretched. "Haven't seen you much this summer, Jed."

Anthony had always made Jed think of gray, the gray of steel, smooth and opaque, gray neither light nor dark but instead cagey, indeterminate, the color of a brewing storm that might or might not blow over. His hair was dark silver, receding only a little, and precisely cut. He was of medium height and build and had always struck Jed as a person about whom there was nothing extra—no excess pounds, no wasted movements or superfluous words. His regular-featured, patrician face might have been bland if the look in his eyes had not been so sharp, missing nothing, or if his brow had not been a bit hawklike. It was the face of a man who rarely hesitated.

Jed shook his hand and was surprised to find that it was warm, normal flesh, not ice or metal or a live grenade. He tried to look Marcella's former husband and cuckold in the face without flinching. "I'm keeping busy playing uncle," he said.

"Well, take a break. That's what you've got Toni for. How about some tennis this afternoon?"

"Well—"

"During the kids' naps. I remember the days," he said, giving Jed a smile that was less chilly and more awkward than Jed would have expected. *He knows,* Jed thought, *he knows*—one of three people now, including himself. Knew that his father had been unfaithful. Did not know that Jed knew. Did not know a lot of things. Jed felt that his face was frozen. There was simply no safe expression for it to assume. "Let the women watch the fort for a while," Anthony said, and Jed saw he was trapped.

When Jed was back inside, Callie raised a droll eyebrow. "He'll cream you, Jeddy. You haven't played in ages." She looked at Toni. "Was this your idea?"

"Of course not," Toni said. She was blushing. "He thought of it. I swear. He probably just wants you to get out more."

"Thanks," Jed said. "I'd like to believe that."

"What does *that* mean?"

Jed made himself smile, banish Marcella from his mind. "Nothing."

THE NOBSCUSSET TENNIS CLUB had been founded fifty years before by Bayard Hall, a Bostonian with an unshakable loyalty to hard work, community spirit, cocktails, and sport. As the story went, he and his three sons had spent an entire July clearing out a patch of woods behind their house and installing six clay courts, which, by the time Jed started taking lessons, had been augmented by a small, sandy parking lot, a spigot that served as a water fountain, and a shack, known as Hall Hall, full of tennis balls, clay rakes, tarps, lime, a line-marking contraption, and the clipboards on which members registered for tournaments. Now, as he biked up the long, unpaved driveway, Jed noted some new, manicured flower beds as well as a Porta Potti, obviously a recent concession to comfort. He wondered if the male holdouts were still wandering off into the trees when nature called, highly visible in their whites.

He was bracing himself for greetings from people who didn't yet know he was here for the summer, but lessons were over for the day and only a couple of courts were in use. He parked his bike in the rack and went over to a bench to stretch. The place was bright and quiet, the only sounds the *pock* of the balls and the occasional brief conversations between players switching sides. He saw Larry Stowell, no doubt sweating extravagantly, playing a man Jed didn't know, and Nancy Hale and three other sinewy, gray-haired women playing doubles. They would notice him at some point, but hopefully by then he would be deep into his game with Anthony Atkinson.

He bent his head down as close to his knee as he could get, and as he felt the tension in his hamstring he realized the bench he was leaning on was new, the kind made from recycled plastic bags. It had a memorial plaque on the back: BITSY HALL / A LONGTIME AND BELOVED MEMBER OF THIS CLUB. Old Mr. Hall's wife. So she'd died too. He glanced around and realized that all the benches were new; come to think of it, had there been benches at all before? Had anyone sat down, ever? He gave a quick stretch to his other leg and then, walking as unobtrusively as he could—it was all he could do not to slink between the trees like some movie Indian—he made a quick tour. There were six benches altogether, and it was as he suspected. There was not a plaque for either of his parents. He had no doubt that, seven years ago, his parents' friends had discussed the idea among themselves and then decided never to bring it up, and instead made quiet donations to the Village Improvement Society, which would do some good without upsetting anyone.

The last bench, for Gardner White, was in front of the shack. He stood there in the shade near the water fountain, a small patch of real estate that had once seemed very large. He'd waited here in line, racquet in hand, summer after summer, for his lessons to start; even before that, he had played in the mud at the base of the spigot, waiting for Callie's lesson to end or even, he supposed, for his parents to finish a match. The woods around him had been hot and green and alive, the thrill of their mystery, he saw now, entirely benign.

"You kept up with your game?"

Jed started. Anthony was right behind him, in a white polo shirt and shorts that looked pressed.

"Sorry," Anthony said. "Didn't mean to sneak up on you." He held out his hand again as though they hadn't seen each other just hours before, and Jed had no choice but to take it. His handshake was the same, one decisive motion.

"I—no. I haven't played much recently." As soon as Anthony let go, Jed turned and took a drink from the spigot, as if that had been his original purpose all along. As usual—he remembered too late—the pressure was abruptly strong and water spattered his chin. He wiped it with the bottom of his shirt.

Anthony's eyes flicked down, then back up. "In Atlanta I suppose you can play outdoors year-round," he said.

This sounded to Jed like a veiled rebuke. "The weather is pretty nice," he said. "But I've been busy with work." He did a few knee bends. He wished he'd finished stretching. "Which court, do you know?"

Anthony said, "Toni tells me you quit."

"No, sir. Leave of absence." He would just let that hang.

Anthony gave a curt nod that could have meant anything. "Court three." He turned around and walked back to the court's entrance, and Jed followed. "After you." But when Jed was halfway through the tall gate, Anthony took his arm. "Jed. I just want to say. I always think of your mother when I'm here. She was a hell of a player."

The sun was in his eyes and he couldn't see the exact expression on Anthony's face. He imagined he looked generically pained. "Thank you, sir."

Anthony let go, stepped back. "And your father, of course. Your father too." He nodded again. "Shall we hit a little?" Anthony closed the gate behind them.

Jed's game plan was not to think too much. He was only going to feel his body and try to remember what he had learned years ago, right here. He began to walk to the sunny side but Anthony was already halfway there and so he let him go, without comment. He watched as Anthony pulled a ball from his pocket, tossed it, heard the *pock* as the ball came smoothly over the net, and here was his racquet swinging back on the lever of his arm and he hit it back. He was going to think with his muscles. His racquet connected again, and again. See, he did not have to think. He should have come here before now.

The sun was bright and warm and the day was quiet and Anthony's white figure shone against the trees behind him as hundreds of other players' had. As Jed's father's had, surely on this very court. *Pock.*

Anthony was being either solicitous or condescending and was hitting to Jed like a machine, the balls landing in the same foot-square patch of court every time, until Jed hit him a particularly wobbly return. Anthony lunged for it, hitting deep into Jed's backhand. Jed ran for it and swept his arm back, one-handed. That was what old Bayard Hall had always demanded: two-handed was *verboten*! It was for *sissies*! Jed remembered him at the sidelines, lean and white-haired, and behind him Jed's father, half a grin on his face as Mr. Hall barked out his commentary, waving around his perpetual cup of refreshment. Sometimes that cup made its first appearance at ten in the morning, but no one had ever heard Mr. Hall slur his words—and the ball shot neatly over the net, clearing it by two inches, and landed just beyond Anthony's reach. "Sorry," he called.

Anthony didn't answer, just pulled another ball out of his pocket.

Yes, Jed's father had thought Mr. Hall was a hoot. Here was the ball, *pock*. Actually *hoot* would have been his mother's word but his father would have agreed—he had been amused by people, he had loved them, the crazier the better—he tried to remember if he had ever seen his father play Anthony. He had had the impression that his father had not liked Anthony, but what had he actually said? Asshole Anthony? No, that was completely adolescent. Anthony had had a general reputation for chasing kids off the court when he wanted to play, of being, perhaps, too much a stickler for rules, even at Nob-scusset, where things were done just so—*pock*—no, he did not remember his father ever playing Anthony. Although it probably had happened once or twice. But everyone had liked Cecil McClatchey: Jed's friends, their fathers. It had probably always been that way.

For a moment a blond, laughing child danced through Jed's mind and then he realized it was his father, known only from old, old pictures. *Hey, come out and play!* and then the ball was coming and he saw it would fall once again in the center of his forehand, and he clenched his shoulders with a sudden savage force and hit with topspin that sent the ball past Anthony's surprised reach. It kissed the corner and bounced out untouched.

"Maybe we'd better begin," Anthony called.

Anthony won the toss, and proceeded to quickly rack up three games. This wouldn't have happened a few years ago, certainly not seven years ago, the summer Jed's father was having an affair with Anthony's wife, and Jed had been clueless and directionless and effortlessly in shape. He served and double-faulted, *damnit. Concentrate* and he aced the next one. "Nice," Anthony said. *Don't be fucking patronizing.* If he paid attention, if he played his own game, he would be all right. More than all right. He was getting looser. He could feel it. He was fighting back. He kept fighting and surprising both of them and then it was 3-all. Yes, surprising, here came the ball, it was going to land no less than two feet from the alley, just like all of Anthony's other shots, piece of cake, *don't think.*

Anthony was catching up, he was ramping up his game. Good. They came to deuce again and again but finally with another shot to the left corner Jed won the seventh game.

He walked back to the fence and his water bottle. He felt a moment of exhilaration before a voice that did not seem to be his wondered, *Does it matter?* Of course it did. He took a long drink. Of course it did. Otherwise there was no point.

Anthony had known. Marcella had told Jed that. He had known that Jed's father was fucking his wife and so now he was facing Jed knowing that his father had been an adulterer.

Jed turned, went back to wait for Anthony's serve.

It came again to the middle of his forehand. Anthony did not seem to be looking for Jed's particular vulnerabilities; he'd rather Anthony be cunning, wily. Dishonest, even. Had his father wanted to beat Anthony, humiliate him? *Stop it don't think.* Or had he thought he'd already done that, and so let him win? Ridiculous. All of it.

Focus. It did not matter who he was or where he was or who he was playing. He used to want to win and he wanted to win now, and he thought, felt, only his arms and legs and grip old Mr. Hall *don't think just play!* and it was his old body and he took the first set, 6–4.

They met briefly at the net. "That's some good shooting," Anthony said, and smiled. Of course the man could smile. He was just a man. "You're not in such bad shape."

Anthony was standing too close. Maybe just a half inch. Something felt wrong. Or maybe it was Jed, he didn't want to be close to anyone, he had forgotten how to carry on a conversation. And then, it was not even a thought, her name was just there: *Marcella.* "Thank you," he said. He walked to the other side and was again looking into the sun.

For a moment he was blinded and everything blurred into a gold and green and clay-colored mass, and maybe because he couldn't see Anthony's face or the court at all, because the white light of the sun dazzled him, he could not wipe his mind clear and she came to him again, lovely and foreign in this place where he needed to win. *Marcella* and she flowed into him. The ball came at him and he bashed it across the net. He had not realized he was working so hard to keep her out of his mind and now he concentrated in a different way *Marcella Marcella* he had been touching her and now that he had let her in he wanted to roar with the power of it. His father had been a big man, not a consistent player but he could summon up some power.

Power.

He saw his father serving and his mother up at the net, in one of those skirts that were so weirdly little-girlish, her legs muscular, a little veiny. They'd been in sync in a purely physical way. Even that last summer. His parents would have stood near each other, his father would have watched his mother crouched and ready, he would have known where she was going to go before she moved. If his mind had not been full of Marcella. *Marcella*—but she was receding now, she had given him only a temporary, illusory power, he could not keep her.

He kept hitting but he felt ragged. His eyes were adjusted now but it seemed like late light, August light, even though it was only July, high summer. It felt like everything was about to end. All depended upon the ball descending and hitting the center of his racquet but the stretch of his arm and the wrenching of his sinews weren't enough this time.

"Should we take a break?" Anthony called.

"No. Thanks."

He crouched, waiting, and the ball rose out of Anthony's hand, and Jed wished he could crouch and sway there forever, the bright lime dot of the ball hanging, unmoving. But then of course it began to fall and it disappeared for a moment into the blur of Anthony Atkinson's racquet and Jed thought how, really, every move was inevitable. How he knew that the ball was going to land deep into his forehand and if he ran he could catch it. And he wondered if his father had ever felt this powerlessness grip his spine. If he'd felt the bright air heavy and pressing. As he lunged, too late, Jed felt himself land on the side of his foot and stumble. He let himself fall.

Out of the corner of his eye Jed saw Anthony race around the net as though there were a true emergency—but then he was walking toward him slowly, casually. "Are you all right?"

He'd landed the wrong way on his ankle. He tried to remember if he had felt a pop. "Yeah, I'm fine," he said. He held the ankle: it didn't hurt to touch it. He'd only tripped, there was a scrape along his shin. "It was just stupid," he said, and took Anthony's proffered hand. But as he stood and put weight on it he made a face, though he felt no pain.

"You don't look all right to me," Anthony said.

By now the few people on the other courts had stopped to watch. Jed tested the ankle and flinched again and realized, *I want to get out of here. Enough.* Larry Stowell lumbered over, and Jed thought for a moment that Larry was about to heave him over his shoulder and carry him. "You all right, buddy?" Larry barked.

"Fine. Really." Jed limped over to the bench next to the fence. There was still time to recover and have it look legit. He rotated his foot. There was no pain. He sat down on the bench anyway.

"Not swelling," Larry said, and poked the ankle with a thick finger. Jed remembered to wince. Nancy Hale had joined them, and she said, "Larry, be *careful*. Hello there, Jed."

Anthony stepped just slightly in front of Larry, blocking him. "That's good," he said. "Probably not even a sprain."

"Can you move it?" Larry said.

Jed was getting annoyed, as though Larry were his own brain, the part he was arguing with right now. *Give me one good reason not to lie. Give me one good reason not to get the hell out of here.* He looked up at the people standing around him and felt like a child surrounded by accusing adults he had once trusted who had now betrayed him, although he knew that wasn't fair.

And then he finally heard it. He heard the thought that had been drumming in his head ever since he'd gotten to the Cape, and that had begun to build to a crescendo as soon as he had biked down Nobscusset's shady dirt driveway only an hour before. The problem was not unfamiliar flowers or benches or plaques but a larger, an infinite, violation: *What is wrong I am here this is familiar but Mom and Dad where are they not coming back why not—oh.* The idiotic incomprehension, the foul stream running in a deep crevasse (deeper even than his thoughts of Marcella), the entire line of question and response, was so swift and compressed that it was not separate sentences but all of a piece, like a heartbeat. It had been there for days, weeks. Years. But he hadn't been able to hear it until now. Now that he was in this place of clay and sweat and shifting leaf-filtered light from his childhood. Now that he knew more. Now that he knew that his father had not been an astonishing person of superhuman evil—that idea had been an anti-fantasy, a diversionary tactic. Instead, he now knew that his father had not done it. That he had been merely a weak, ordinary man. That he was, instead, merely dead.

He stood and limped around in a small circle.

"I don't know, Jed," Anthony said. Nancy sent Larry off for a cold pack and Anthony looked at Jed, eyebrow arched in amusement at her officiousness. Jed pretended not to see. He looked down at his foot thoughtfully. "You had me running, there," Anthony said.

Jed looked up. "Seems like you were going pretty easy on me," he answered, and saw something flick across Anthony's face—not an expression, rather the absence of one, a quick, willed blankness.

"I'll give you a ride," Anthony said, turning away toward the parking lot.

"Oh, no, that's okay."

Anthony turned back to look at him. "You can't ride that bike," he said, with the merest hint of a question in his voice.

Jed suddenly didn't care if Anthony knew he was faking. That would matter no more than anything else. "No," he said, shrugging. "I guess not."

At the house, Toni squealed when she saw him limping and insisted on bringing a tower of pillows for his foot. She fussed in the kitchen getting more ice and putting it in a bag and then a towel and crushing it with a rolling pin. Jed lay back on the sofa, his exhaustion suddenly real. He felt the match had lasted for hours and hours. He wished he had limped, convincingly or not, straight to his room. He watched Anthony watch his daughter. Sweet Jesus. "Hey, Toni, I'm okay," he said. "Really." He tried to keep the annoyance out of his voice. "I mean, thanks."

Anthony said abruptly, "I'll be going now."

"We'll play again soon," Jed said. His vanished father, on the court, tall and smiling. "And I'll beat you for real."

Anthony smiled, his eyes opaque. "We'll see about that."

TONI ASKED HER FATHER THAT NIGHT, "Is Jed a good tennis player?"

"He's fine."

"I thought you said he beat you."

"He won the first set."

"But you're good, Dad—"

"He seemed pretty determined."

"Were you letting him win?"

"Why would I do that?"

She tilted her head at him. "To be nice?"

His heart twisted with a love that was almost like pain. She was distracting him from his resolve—which had to do with *her*, after all: always it was Toni he thought of first. He had a horror of spoiling her. Of literally ruining her. "Do you really think he would want that?" he said brusquely.

Her look grew thoughtful, and he realized that he had just pushed her into exactly the wrong direction. That she was right now burrowing her way into what she thought she knew of Jed McClatchey's mind and heart—a place where, he knew with sudden certainty, she spent far too much time already. "Antonia," he said. He closed his book on his finger, to keep his place.

"Uh-oh."

"Listen to me. Jed McClatchey is far too old for you. Don't get any ideas."

She drew back in exaggerated offense. But she was blushing. "I don't know what you're talking about."

"This is not a joke." Anthony paused. "Has he—"

"Nothing's *happening*. All right?"

He put the book down, lost his place altogether, and leaned toward her, his hands on his knees. "Toni. Please. He's been through far too much."

"What kind of a reason—"

"He has lost a great deal, and he's not over it. He may never be." Anthony opened his mouth, closed it. Took a breath. "Besides being far too old."

"I'm in *college,* Daddy!"

Anthony made himself pick up the book. "I'm finished now, Antonia. You're smart. Think about it. It's not something you want."

His heart was pounding now. He had to say just enough. Hope that he could find the right formula, that it would innoculate his girl. With growing horror, he had been hearing the way Toni spoke of Jed, and he had asked Jed to play today so he could meet it head-on, see what he was dealing with. Anthony knew he was not the most astute reader of faces, but even he could see that Jed McClatchey was brittle. He did have those Southern manners, that overlay of geniality that went a long way toward masking anything unpleasant—God, to think that Toni was being charmed by the same act that had drawn Marcella in, years before, with Cecil! But the son was not the same, not anymore. Anthony could not allow this truth to cause him grief; it was simply a fact. Behind Jed's reflexive affability he sensed a pit of anger that might be bottomless. He had seen it in his eyes on the court. Seen it in the smashing serves.

Or maybe he was seeing nothing. Maybe he was seeing himself. He had been crazy to let Toni work there.

Of course he had wanted Jed to win, of course he had wanted to beat him. Whenever Jed was winning he felt relief, whenever he was losing Anthony had felt his old furious triumphant disdain. Or maybe it was the other way around. It had been a risky thing, going face-to-face for so long, and too often seeing Cecil across the net instead of Jed. Anthony was not sure of himself, of what he would say or do. There was very little he was sure of anymore.

When Anthony had met Marcella, she had been alone. Literally alone, standing at the sidelines of a party, although she should have been surrounded. The cut of her clothes, the elegance of her posture, the way her hair was pulled back from her face in a topknot like a child's—all were just slightly foreign, unfamiliar, not of the squalid American dormitory basement. Better.

When he walked over to her she didn't notice him in the beery darkness until he was close, closer than he normally got to someone he didn't know; when she looked up, startled, her eyes were surprisingly light under her sweeping dark brows. "Hello, I'm Anthony," he said, but the music was pounding, and she shook her head: she couldn't hear. He leaned in. Her scent was foreign too. It was an adult's, a woman's. "Do you want to go outside?" he said, so close to her ear that if he had pursed his lips they would have touched it.

She followed him out a nearby door to an empty patio. It was April, unseasonably warm for a New England spring. "Oh, my God," she said, and sank down on the brick wall as if she were exhausted. He heard her musical accent—which he couldn't yet place—and her words as if they really were a prayer. She turned her big eyes to him. "Thank you for bringing me outside," she said.

Bringing. The word had chimed. He had brought her. She had been waiting.

Anthony Forbes Atkinson was not in the habit of thinking any girl was out of his league, and he didn't think it now. But he had habits and patterns and a well-established level of comfort with a certain type of girl, and normally he would not have made overtures to Marcella di Pavarese. As it turned out, though, Marcella had been brought to the party by a friend of a friend, someone Anthony had known, in fact, since childhood. He found this detail affirming, and asked where she was from. *"Firenze,"* she said. "I am from Florence. Italy."

He watched her lips as she spoke and knew, with an empathy that was strange to him, that English felt odd to her. "Are you visiting for the semester?" There was only another month of school. Maybe he shouldn't be talking to her at all.

"No," she said. "I'm a junior. I am here for four years—for all of university." He nodded, carefully keeping his face impassive. But his rush of relief and the sudden, unfamiliar sense of vulnerability were completely unexpected. She smiled at him, again with that questioning, almost beseeching look in her eyes. *Thank you for bringing me.* And he smiled back.

Anthony was not given to rash decisions. He had known immediately, however, that he wanted Marcella, and no one else. His family was caught off guard; when he had first told his mother about Marcella she said, *Exotic was* not *what I had in mind.* But he dismissed this friction. Surely his mother knew how neatly tribal expectation and his own desires had always dovetailed. He was sometimes proud of this fact, but every now and then he thought he had nothing to be proud of at all. At some point that he did not even remember, he had received the family marching orders, but he had never had to bend his will or discipline away any errant proclivities or aspirations in order to follow them. He felt no sense of rebellion. Neither, however, did he feel he had to make any excuses for one unusual choice. It was an act that would, he knew, burnish the rest of his straightforward, unadorned life.

They were married, after graduation, at his parents' house in

Chestnut Hill. Marcella surely would have been surprised to know it, but one of the main things he remembered about that day was the long row of peonies just outside the reception tent. It had been a breezy day, and the big white blooms had been tossing at the end of their long bending stems, almost dancing, the white petals blowing like confetti. He had plucked them from her long dark hair. Marcella thought he didn't see details like that, certainly that he cared nothing for flowers. But he remembered those peonies because when he had seen them he had thought the life he was about to enter with her was going to be like that—heedless and abundant.

She had stuck close to his side. Although it was June, she had been shivering in her short-sleeved gown, and he had rubbed her arms to keep them warm. Touched her, claimed her. When they had still been in school she had sometimes seemed elusive, her thoughts far away, unreadable; Anthony, however, was not the sort of person who asked people what they were thinking, and he didn't ask her. But now things would be different. Neither of them would hold themselves away from the other. As if to confirm this change, she leaned up to him and whispered, "I can't believe you are mine, *caro*. I'm not sure it is true."

He smiled at her. Picked out another white petal from her hair. "You still look cold," he murmured back. "Do you want my jacket?"

"Of course not," she said. "You look too handsome. I don't want to spoil it." He remembered that too. He remembered how much he had wanted her. Right then, always. How he had wanted the damn reception to be over.

He had felt a nagging worry that she had so few guests of her own at the wedding—or rather, was conscious of his mother's vexation. She continued to be suspicious of the girl with no relations, even though Anthony had told her that her mother was dead and her grandmother too old (and massive, as Marcella said) to travel. "So she's completely alone," his mother had said, sitting ramrod straight at her desk, going over the guest list.

"No," Anthony had answered. "She has me." And his mother had raised one eyebrow.

Now his parents were over near the towering white cake, his mother's hand extended to a guest, Anthony knew, like a cold, slim board. Of course now Anthony's friends were Marcella's. And then his brother Charles appeared, and was kissing Marcella on the cheek. "My lovely sister-in-law," he said, not to her exactly, but to the group at large. "Lucky! Ant is *lucky* to land you." He gave Marcella a quick once-over that was supposed to be a joke. "Not sure how he did it," Charles said. Even today, Anthony was quite sure that Charles meant what he said, that it was dumb luck. He and his siblings had grown up competing most fiercely with one another. Even today, Charles wasn't going to let him think he had won.

"Aren't you ever going to let go of her?" his other brother, Amory, said.

"She's cold," Anthony had said, resisting the temptation to raise his voice and say that she was his wife, damnit. His *wife*! Marcella leaned into him, agreeing.

"You're supposed to say *never*!" Amory had shouted, and there was more laughter. Anthony felt himself going stiff as he always did, stiff as his mother's outstretched hand. He pulled Marcella to him even more tightly, until she was almost off balance, and he knew it must look ridiculous—but then he glanced down at her and her gaze back at him was adoring, almost amazed. She was his. He was sure, then, for just a moment, that he had won, after all.

His conviction held, for a while. The rest of his life was smooth and uneventful, as he had always thought it should, would, be, and Marcella was its jewel. Three years after they married, she became pregnant. He had assumed this stage, too, would come, but he had not anticipated that he would want her more than ever; he didn't think that was possible. But the sight of her round with their child made him nearly frantic with desire. He had not anticipated, either, that pregnancy would make her so happy. That finally the changes he had dreamed of, without wanting to name them, would begin—that she would soothe him with only her presence, that she would not seem as if she were still waiting for something, that she would no longer retreat into herself and make him feel he was lacking.

He loved her so much then that he thought he could never love anyone more.

In the hospital, his concern was only for Marcella. He had never been moved by babies, and although this baby would be his child and his heir and all the rest of it, she was going to be Marcella's concern, really, not his; it was the way things developed, progressed. They would have this child and then another and another and he would be in the background, the paterfamilias, writing the checks. The world was not going to stop.

Then a nurse handed him the impossibly light bundle, and he looked down into the new face, the skin that had just begun to touch air. Milky bewildered eyes looked back at him. This person had not existed. And then, suddenly, she had.

He stood there with the ridiculous blue booties on his feet, his feet planted on the gleaming white hospital floor, astonished. But wasn't this the result, in so many ways, of that hectic yearning he had felt for Marcella? Of course it was going to burst its bounds and make this new, exultant love. He almost laughed but then he didn't, because he didn't want to frighten her. His daughter. "Darling," Marcella said, from her bed.

He looked up at her and it seemed that any lingering doubts he had ever had about her as a wife, as *his*, were ridiculous, light as chaff, now blowing away.

"Come here, *amore mio*. Come here, *bambina*."

He went and sat on the bed, next to Marcella, the three of them close. He settled the baby into Marcella's arms but kept his own around her too. He did not know how to say any of the things he had just thought. "I suppose she needs a name," he said softly.

They had already settled on Marion Giulia for a girl, after their mothers, and after considerable pressure from Anthony, who felt that names should be as legible as a newspaper in declaring one's heritage, one's identity. Marcella had had more romantic ideas, typical for her; she had come up with names that no Atkinson or di Pavarese had ever held before, and he hadn't seen the logic in that. But now he would tell her she had been right. Why had he ever thought they should look to the past? Their child needed her own name, only hers—

"I think we should name her Antonia," Marcella said. She beamed at him.

He looked back at his wife with wonder. "What a gift," he whispered. He meant the name, of course. Marcella herself. Their daughter, their life.

But there was also a moment, half a moment, a thought he immediately discounted but never forgot, when he felt that Toni was his, only his. That *she* was the gift, that Marcella, under some spell, had rashly given her away, and he had snatched her up, claimed her, with a shameful greed.

Much later, when he realized that he had lost Marcella, it seemed all the more fitting that he *kept* Toni. He supposed it was part of his essential deficiency that he could adore only one person at a time. When they divorced, he insisted Toni begin boarding school, because the old Atkinson customs seemed safest for his daughter and himself. He did know this move further devastated Marcella, and he was not entirely sorry. He let himself feel that small bit of revenge.

But he didn't tell her that actually revenge had nothing to do with it, that, instead, he'd sent Toni away to shield her from himself. He still wondered if that had been the right solution. Did he protect his child with his presence or his absence? His own flaws had proved to be bottomless. So how could he trust the world?

V

Jed had felt a tension in the air since morning. It was Thursday. He was trying not to think *tomorrow, tomorrow,* trying not to have the scent of his lust rise from him like a cloud, but it didn't work because when they were alone making lunch Callie finally said, "Are you leaving this weekend?"

"That was my plan."

"That's three weeks in a row."

"I guess so."

"You should bring her here sometime. Or no—wait—you're probably fucking madly all weekend long, you'd rather not."

"Cal, please."

"Aren't you?" Callie said, and he hesitated. He couldn't help it. He had to figure out why what they did could not be described as fucking wildly all weekend. "See? And for God's sake, don't say"—she simpered—"it's not like that."

Callie had never sounded jealous about his girls before. He should have acted surprised but he didn't. "I don't know," he said. "Cal—it's really confusing."

He might have told her everything then. It was a moment when things were poised to abruptly become different. It would have been a huge relief. But he truly did not know which would be kinder, to tell her or not. He searched her face for a sign; there was none. He could feel the brief clarity of his resolve dissipating. There was a long moment and he wondered what she was deciding, and then she looked at him and gave him the same smile she gave Grace, bright and blank, and he returned it, and said nothing.

Meanwhile Callie thought, *It's not working.* She already hated this Marcie, despised her as a mortal enemy, but though she had begun this conversation ready to do battle she had already forgotten what it was she wanted to win. She couldn't keep him here, she couldn't keep anyone. Everyone was leaving, the house was empty. "Never mind," she said, "I'm sorry," but she said it so softly he didn't hear her. *Sorry sorry sorry*, she thought. *Sorry sorry sorry.*

THE WEEKS WERE LONG. When Jed called her, Marcella wanted to take his low voice and cradle it to her like a tangible thing, a child, and when they had hung up she wanted to call him back but she knew she had nothing to say. Neither of them did; between them it was all physical, actual, skin to touch and warmth to feel. If they could have sung each other wordless songs, perhaps. Hummed sweet endless tunes. That was what the calls amounted to, as much of each other's presence as they could suck out of their voices.

The blue salvia she had planted grew slowly, as it always did. But it was green and she knew it would get as tall as her knees, that when the indigo spikes finally lengthened and bloomed they would last until frost. A long time from now. She knew he would not be with her by then, and wondered, sadly, how it would happen.

It was strange and awful, but after the phone calls she sometimes thought of Cecil. She was parsing him, them, in her mind. Oddly, it felt safer now. She refused to consider why. She refused to think that Cecil's own son could cushion her from grief. But, for the first time in a long while, she was able to think of Cecil's face without pain. She was able to step back from his image in her mind and scrutinize it, like a painting in a gallery. A painting, almost, of a stranger.

THE SUMMER THAT TONI WAS TEN, Marcella had her fourth miscarriage. It was early August, just at the beginning of the wane of the short Cape Cod summer. The night before had been cool, and the next morning, as Marcella stood in the kitchen doorway feeling the crispness, looking out at the low mist covering the ground, sipping a cup of weak tea—see, she had already been taking care, oh, how she had tried to take care!—she felt a small yet reverberating *snap*, as though the line of time had broken. Later that day, she began to bleed.

She had not learned to distance herself. She never would. She had believed another baby was finally coming to her, to them, a completion of her family, a confirmation and blessing. She had felt its weight in her arms. She had believed that this time would be different.

It had been a Friday, and Anthony was coming down from Boston that night. For the first time in as long as she could remember, she pined for him to arrive. She knew even as she pictured him coming through the door, herself falling into his arms, that she was foolish, but she clung to this image for those first few hours. She had to save this grief for someone if she was going to keep it from Toni. And although Marcella knew that Toni was savvy and hyperobservant, she could not bear, on this day especially, to think of her daughter as anything other than a child who needed to be protected.

She was making dinner when she heard Anthony's car grinding up the pebbled driveway. As she heard his door slam she felt herself tensing, everything ready to burst through. From long experience, though, she was able to wait.

"Hello, sweetheart," she said. "How was the drive?"

"Awful. Idiots everywhere. The idiots come out on Friday nights."
He kissed her cheek, and then went to the refrigerator and took out a
bottle of tonic. "You're not dressed." They had been invited to the
Martins' that night, for cocktails.

"I don't want to go."

"Well, why not?" He took an ice tray out of the freezer, and even
though she was watching him do it, when he twisted the ice out the
sudden report made her jump. She felt her ready tears, terrible but
also so warm and alive. She waited for him to put the tray back and to
close the door, and then she told him.

He met her gaze as she spoke but his expression was flat, his eyes
flat, seemingly nothing in them at all, as though she had not even spoken. He looked down into his highball glass and poked the ice cubes
with one finger. Then he put the glass down and leaned over the
counter. He looked as if he were trying to push the whole thing off its
foundation. She watched, waiting for him to come to her, waiting that
was painful. She felt her tears, her self that had been ready to rush to
him, begin to shrink and dry.

All at once he brought his hand down flat onto the counter with a
crack. The ice in his glass jumped and the stack of silverware Marcella had set out for the table crashed over, and she felt a noise come
out of her, a yelp of fear and sorrow. He looked at her and she saw it,
the split second of contempt, before he banished it and came to her
and held her. "Chella, Chella," he said, "I'm sorry." She could feel his
cheek on the top of her head. He kissed her hair. His hand was
stroking her face. "I'm sorry." *For what?* she thought. For scaring her?
For her? him? them? She stood there wooden, her pain entirely
her own.

She went to bed before dinner and stayed there all the next day.
She heard Toni and Anthony laughing downstairs and felt bleaker
than ever, convinced they didn't need her. In the late afternoon,

Anthony came up and asked if the doctor had told her to stay in bed. "No," she said.

"Maybe you'd feel better if you got up for a while." She heard, *Don't lie around moping.*

"Did you want the baby?" she whispered. The golden sun was pouring in through her western window. She hated it. She wanted it to be rainy, dark, winter; she wanted to be alone. "Did you?"

"Of course I did! Of course." He sighed and she heard him struggling, adjusting. Making a good effort. Trying to talk to her, his wife. "I tried not to think about it much, Chella. It was too early." He sighed again and sat on the edge of the bed. "I'm not like you."

"What am I like?"

He ignored her question. "I look at what we've got. I look at what's *here.*" She heard his voice breaking. "I look at all the goddamn reality around me. I don't dream it away."

She curled up in a ball facing away from the window, from him.

"Toni and I are going to play doubles." He waited. She waited. She waited until he had shut the door and his footsteps died away down the narrow back stairs. She heard the barn door creak outside and the light spatter of gravel as they wheeled their bikes down the driveway. She waited until the noises had faded away and then she closed her eyes and let herself fall into sleep that was like an addiction, where she held a warm faceless bundle in her arms and was perfectly at peace.

THE DOCTOR HAD SAID she didn't need to do anything unusual unless the bleeding got worse, but it tapered to a trickle, another loss. They were invited to the McClatcheys' for Sunday afternoon and Marcella made herself go, mainly because Toni had come into bed with her that morning and said, *Are you getting up today, Mommy?*

with that uniquely ten-year-old combination of concern and judgment, and Marcella felt a sudden, urgent stab of possessiveness. She
would not leave Toni alone with Anthony, charming her, winning
her over, for another whole day. And it was so rare for Toni to say
"Mommy" anymore.

While Marcella was getting dressed, Toni came upstairs to her
room again. She was wearing a new pink shorts set Marcella had
recently bought for her, and around her neck Marcella saw the string
ties of her new, and only, bikini. Toni took in what Marcella was wearing and said, "It's a *pool* party, Mom."

Marcella had put on slacks and a collared shirt, with a sweater
tied around her shoulders. The hint of fall had receded and summer
had returned in force, but she wanted to be swaddled, hidden. She
would have wrapped herself in a blanket and gone dressed like that if
she could. She said, "I don't know if the adults will swim, darling."

"It's *hot*. They *will*." Toni's determined tone was nothing new, but
Marcella had the distinct feeling that she cared more than usual, that
she wanted her mother to display some phantom lightheartedness.
Just like Anthony.

Marcella glanced at her reflection in the mirror as if it were
another person's. She tried to tilt her head gaily. "Well, what shall I
wear?"

Toni rolled her eyes. "A *bathing* suit."

"Your favorite one?" she said. Toni smiled. She had once or twice
grudgingly told Marcella, with a shade of her old preschooler adora-
tion, that she looked good in a particular striped navy-and-white one-
piece.

"Well," Marcella said, "I'll get right on it." She fluttered her
hands, shooing her daughter away, and Toni grinned again, gratified
by this little bit of power. But as soon as the door closed behind her,
Marcella's eyes filled with tears. Her baby Antonia was gone, gone.

Could she possibly know now how Marcella loved her, how she wanted to fall prostrate at her feet, keep her entirely for herself? But instead Marcella knew that every day she lost a little more of Toni, just as her own mother had lost her. Another child would have eased her desperation. She could have loved them all, much better than she was able to love now. It was a long moment before she finally bent to open her dresser drawer.

The Atkinsons had been to the McClatcheys' only once before, for an annual meeting of the tennis club. Cecil and Betsy seemed like relaxed, unpretentious people, with their Southern accents and ready smiles, who nevertheless intimidated Marcella, Betsy especially. She wanted very much for Betsy McClatchey to like her. She was a sturdy woman with dark hair touched with gray, ten years Marcella's senior. She was a good tennis player, as Marcella was not, and had lovely manners, and always smiled at Marcella quite kindly, as if they shared a secret. But Marcella suspected she smiled at everyone that way, and could think of nothing to say to her. Betsy McClatchey, she thought, was a woman who had very few moments of self-doubt.

When they arrived at the party there were fifteen or twenty adults there, and kids in the pool. Betsy was passing around hors d'oeuvres, and kissed Marcella on the cheek, but then glided away. "Shrimp on fried grits cakes!" Annette Doyle exclaimed. "Imagine! Betsy is so creative!" Marcella had a feeling this was a criticism, but wasn't sure, and anyway she felt too tired to parse the comments of someone like Annette Doyle. "This must taste like home," Annette continued. "Aren't grits like polenta?"

Marcella swallowed her mouthful of shrimp. "A bit," she said. She knew quite well she was supposed to say more. She could think of nothing. There was a pause and then Annette waved to someone over her shoulder. "Hi!" she called. "Someone I haven't seen in *ages*," she said brightly. "Excuse me!"

"Of course," Marcella said, and watched Annette Doyle make her escape.

Toni was already in the pool and Anthony was talking to a group of men near the grill. She saw him eyeing her like a faraway bodyguard, but he did not join her. She went over and sat down in an empty lounge chair at the less-occupied end of the patio, and finally, after a few minutes, Anthony came over to ask what she would like to drink.

"Nothing, darling." She wanted to laugh—not at him but with him, at his ever-dutiful manners. She wanted him to pull a chair near hers and sit and be lonely with her. If people thought her odd and aloof, well, she and Anthony could be that way together.

"Nothing? You're sure?" He seemed to be daring her to get upset. She had not been drinking at all when she was pregnant.

"Yes," she said. "Darling, go talk to your friends." If he could not read her, she did not have the energy to help him. He reached down and squeezed her shoulder, as if she were a sort of teammate, one he felt obligated to support. Suddenly she did not want him to go. "Look at Toni," she whispered.

"What about her?"

"How big she is. How beautiful." Toni had just climbed up the steps of the other end of the pool and was standing, one hip thrown out and her head to the side, twisting the water out of her long honey-blond hair. The outlines of her funny little breast-buds were visible under the triangles of her bikini top.

Marcella looked up at her husband. The pride on his face was so fierce it frightened her. "I don't know why you want more," he said. "You always want more." He turned and walked away.

Marcella leaned her head back on the chaise. She wanted to go to sleep. She wanted to take the car and go home, but she could not bear Anthony's anger, nor any eyes or questions as she left the party. She glanced behind her, at a shaded hedge of blue mophead hydrangeas, and actually considered creeping through them into the neighboring yard and then making her way home on foot. She knew she was conspicuous, alone in the chair, that people would continue to assume she was standoffish and haughty. Then she saw that Cecil McClatchey was headed for her, two silver cups in his hands.

She straightened her back and swung one leg to the ground but by then Cecil was beside her saying, "No, no, don't get up for me, I'm coming to *you!*" He dragged another chair close to hers. She flinched at the noise it made scraping over the flagstones, but he seemed not to notice, and sat down and handed her one of the cups. "I brought you a mint julep. House specialty. Ever had one? I put in extra mint, just for you. Yankee mint from the yard here. But I think it will be all right."

The silver tumbler was sweating and almost painfully cold in her hand. She held it up to her hot face. "Ahh," she said.

"You're supposed to drink it."

"Oh. Of course." She heard herself laugh. She didn't care for hard liquor, but she took a sip anyway. The bourbon burned down her throat.

"You don't like it," Cecil McClatchey said instantly.

"No, I do. It wasn't what I was expecting. I always thought this drink was—how do you say it?—a sort of punch."

Cecil laughed. "Punch is for the little ol' ladies at church," he said.

As Cecil chatted beside her she surreptitiously examined him. He was a tall man, now with a little roll around his middle; he was balding, and his face had softened, but he had a strong chin and kind eyes. She imagined that he had been handsome in a gangly sort of way twenty-five years before, when he and Betsy must have met, perhaps with that thin, almost starved-looking face that young men sometimes have when they are all energy, and life hasn't layered on deposits of laziness or bitterness or disappointment. Not that Cecil McClatchey looked as if he had had to bear up under much misfortune. "You going in?" he said, and gestured toward the pool.

"It's tempting," she lied. "It is so hot today."

"We'll have to get rid of the teenagers." He grinned. "My crazy uncle put this thing in forty years ago. All the Yankees disapprove. Like ol' Anthony over there," he said, and winked. "Why, the beach is just down the road, and it's *free*."

Marcella smiled back timidly. She felt any skills she had ever had at flirtation were atrophied beyond help.

"You drink up," Cecil said, "and I'll be back to check on you."

The way he said it made her suddenly feel he knew what had happened to her—he sounded solicitous, as if she had a disease. But how could he know? She glanced wildly at Anthony, but no, he wouldn't have told anyone, not here. And not Cecil. When she looked back, she saw that Cecil had misinterpreted. He had gotten up too quickly, and his jovial expression had hardened into a practiced host face. There was no way for her to explain.

But she wasn't sorry to have him go. He had been trying hard, and failing, but of course the failure had been hers. Now she could be quiet again, she could try to disappear. It was tremendously hot and some of the adults indeed were starting to get into the pool. The younger parents were playing with their children, and the designated life of the party, Larry Stowell, his potbelly hanging over his trunks, did a cannonball off the diving board and made all the kids squeal. Anthony was still by the grill, and the bar too, she noticed, his shirt still on. Betsy sat at the edge of the pool with her legs dangling in, looking proper and lighthearted at the same time, her cotton dress pulled up above her knees.

In a burst of desire to be carefree, to belong, Marcella stood up, drew her black linen shift over her head, and sat down again on the chaise.

She was immediately sorry. But she did not want to put her dress back on again right away, so noticeably. She was conscious of her body as a foreign thing. She stretched one leg in front of her and examined it: the foot, the calf, the knee of a stranger, all part of a body that had betrayed her time and time again. She placed a hand on her belly. Empty. She was empty.

She looked for Toni in the pool and found her after a moment, or rather found her feet, pointed skyward in an underwater handstand. Then the feet disappeared and Toni's head surfaced, as slick as a mermaid's. She arched her neck and smoothed the water away from her eyes and forehead and down the length of her hair. She knew that people were watching her. She was that sort of girl—she would be watched, and she would know it. It was beginning.

Nearby Betsy was still at the side of the pool, and her daughter, Callie, came and sat next to her. Callie was in college, with bright blond hair and a trim, athletic figure like her mother's. She murmured something to Betsy and they laughed, like girls together, like friends. *Will Toni and I do that?* Marcella thought. *Why am I so sure I will lose her?*

Just then Toni herself flew through the air, squealing, and landed with a splash. She came up sputtering in mock anger, shaking her finger at Jed McClatchey, who stood laughing in the shallow end. In the way he laughed, turned away, Marcella saw that he was being nice, had perhaps been instructed by his parents to entertain the kiddies. As if to confirm this she saw him next pick up a much younger child, six-year-old Sam Daugherty, and toss him after Toni, as Sam howled with delight. Marcella watched Jed's arms, how easily he lifted the boy. She watched the muscles shifting along his back. He was eighteen or nineteen, she guessed. How perfect young men were, once they had come out the other end of the gawky phase, once their skin had cleared and their noses matched the rest of their faces. She remembered the boys she had known in high school, how uninterested she had been, waiting for a man. That was what she had thought about Anthony, immediately: he was a man. She had not thought any words like *strict* or *humorless* or *harsh*. She had seen only that he was sure of himself, he had been raised to have no doubts about who he was and what he would do in life, and when he seemed to expect her to be in love with him as he was with her it had made sense, she could think of no objections. She had been relieved, dazzled, even, to ride the wave of someone else's surety.

Jed McClatchey had a hint of the young Anthony about him—he was dark, unlike his sister, and his body was compact and chiseled. There was something a bit sharp about his handsome face. He did not seem to have Cecil's easefulness. Instead he was slightly cocky, also like Anthony—but underneath, she sensed, imagined, that this young man was an observer, that he harbored doubts about life, that he guarded a tender heart. Something like Marcella herself.

It would be like this to have a son. Odd and wonderful to look for one's own qualities in a child of the opposite sex, to see them transformed. There was a reason, wasn't there, that a son and a daughter comprised the perfect family? Another reason, too, to envy Betsy McClatchey. Except that she was tired of envy. It did no good, it accomplished nothing. Neither did longing; neither did hope.

Just then Jed looked up, straight at her. Their glances tangled and she knew she was staring, as if at a picture, and at the same time offering a picture of herself. *Here I am. Please see me.* She felt, for a moment, both naked and completely unselfconscious. Then Jed looked away and it was as though it had never happened; she could not say for sure that she hadn't imagined his dark eyes piercing her. She looked down at herself again, her striped bathing suit, her hands lying quiescent on either hip, and felt more real, more solid. She flexed her feet and thought, *That is me.* She sat up and swung her feet to the ground. *The me who is going home.*

ANTHONY SAW HIS WIFE plant her feet on the flagstones so purposefully. He was glad to see any sign of determination from her, after the past few days. He was not much of an observer—they both knew that; but just now he had seen her thoughtful hands on her stomach. Of course he had. Of course he had wanted the baby, just as he had told her. Long ago, however, even before this pregnancy, he had quit picturing him, his son. Pictures in one's head were not reality.

He took another sip of his mint julep. Silly drink but he had to admit that Cecil McClatchey hadn't skimped on the bourbon, even though he had gummed it up with sugar; and he hadn't used some crap brand either; he saw the bottle right there on the bar. With someone else Anthony might have thought he was showing off, but with Cecil he had the sense that he just knew how to do things right. The whole family had that effortless air about them.

By all rights, he and Cecil McClatchey should have been good pals, as much as Anthony was pals with anyone. He could tell that they had been raised the same way, with Southern and Northern variations—that they had both been expected to be smart, polite, and well groomed; conservative, but canny risk takers when it came to money; good at sports, particularly tennis, since it was practical and lifelong, but also team players; early risers, moderate drinkers, regular but not overly inspired churchgoers; and loyal, but realistic, friends, fathers, and husbands. Despite all this, he had never found much to say to Cecil. He sensed something soft in him. Rotten, even. Although surely that was too strong a word.

Betsy, though. He had always admired her and had the sense that she approved of him. She was sitting over there with her daughter, at the edge of the pool, her flowered dress hiked up around her knees. It could even be that she'd stuck her legs in the water to try to make Marcella feel better for being the only woman actually wearing a bathing suit. Not that Anthony hadn't noticed other men noticing his wife; not that she wasn't beautiful. And not of course that she was displaying herself on purpose, because he knew she never thought that way (odd because she so easily could have); still, it was an embarrassment. Marcella was his and he was sure other men envied him, but what if he had had a wife like Betsy McClatchey, who could always be counted on to do the right thing, a wife who maybe did not provoke covetousness or desire but neither looked at her husband—of this Anthony was sure—waiting for something unnamed that he couldn't give?

Did she? Did sturdy, matter-of-fact Betsy McClatchey have passions and yearnings? Of course she did, everyone did—and for a moment he imagined her alone, *not* in that dress she was wearing, and not asking him for something but rather giving—

God. What was wrong with him? He took a sickly-sweet gulp of his drink.

Marcella had gotten up from her chair, he saw, and put her dress back on. Good. Maybe she wanted to leave; that was fine with him. He would much rather be at the courts, as he was most Sundays, than at a party. Although no one else had left yet, and Toni would want to stay, he was sure.

"Hello, Anthony." He started. Betsy was right there beside him. He hadn't even seen her get up from the pool. He shuddered at the idea that his crazy thoughts would be visible on his face, but she didn't seem to have noticed anything. "I've been watching Toni. She's practically grown. Such a beautiful girl," she was saying, with the direct, slightly effusive admiration that he thought of as particularly Southern.

Nevertheless he felt a real smile come to his face. "That's kind of you to say." He cleared his throat. "Wonderful party, Betsy."

"Well, we're so glad you're here." She glanced across the patio, and then looked back at him frankly. "Is Marcella all right?"

"Yes, yes. She's fine. A little under the weather." He gazed out at the pool, as if he were looking for Toni. Took another sip of his drink. That was all he needed to say, all he should say, but Betsy let the pause hang, as if she knew he was deciding. "Had a bit of a disappointment recently," he said. "That is, we did."

It took her only a second. "I'm so sorry."

He wasn't sure how he had known she would understand. He looked down; she was looking straight back at him. Her eyes were a clear, forthright blue. "Of course please don't say anything—"

"Of course not." Her hand was on his arm. There was a pause, full of feeling. "I had wondered."

He stiffened with surprise. Normally he would have been offended at such an offhand confession of prying thoughts. It was not the sort of thing one admitted to. But he found he didn't care. "Wondered?"

"I have thought sometimes that it seemed like you were waiting for something. Both of you." Her eyes held his. Her hand was still on his arm. She patted it and let go. He wished she would not be maternal. That he knew her better. That she would keep talking.

He imagined how her life was with Cecil, well ordered, legible. How there would never be sentences left uncompleted, or unmet desires darkening the air, or baffling, impenetrable dead ends ruining straight, clear paths.

He thought of Marcella in the bed on Saturday afternoon. Of how he had not even touched her. Not even squeezed her shoulder or stroked her hair. He thought Betsy would understand if he told her that what he had really wanted to do was lie down, wrap himself around Marcella, consume her. To peel himself back and show her all the mess of his wrecked hope. He thought that, if he asked, Betsy might be able to tell him why he hadn't done this at all.

But she was looking beyond him now, her face changing, welcoming, and then Anthony felt a different touch on his arm, glancing as a bird's wing. "Betsy, I am so sorry," Marcella said, in her soft, musical voice. "I must go."

There was the briefest of pauses and then Betsy said, "You are a doll for coming. I was just telling Anthony how lovely Toni is. Lovely." There was a ringing tone in her words that was a message to Anthony: of course, she wouldn't reveal his confidence. She would reveal nothing. And neither would he.

He looked down at Marcella. There were circles under her eyes, and thoughts and regrets be damned, all at once he wanted to stroke them, like gray velvet, he wanted to smooth them away, his touch melting into her cheek, all of him sinking into her. But he kept his hand at his side. "Let's get you home," he said. He meant to sound kind, but it came out brusque. Marcella turned away. She looked sad and, worse, unsurprised. God, he was helpless to change himself; he did not know what to do with her sadness. He hadn't learned, in all this time, and she hadn't taught him. Of all the things he hated, he hated feeling helpless the most. He wanted to tell Betsy this too.

He turned to her but there were other people near her now and the expression she gave him was genial, set, her eyes glancing away. He raised his hand in farewell; he wasn't sure if she saw. It could be that he had imagined any connection. Perhaps that was better. Because otherwise he knew she was watching his failure with his wife, that she had seen it all along.

She had told him not to knock, ever. *Because I would always let you in,* she said. Instead she left the door unlocked. He would call from the road to tell her he was coming—he could never keep himself from doing this because his anticipation was so great, as he drove, that he always thought he might burst, and hearing her voice helped him. So she was always ready when he arrived, freshly showered, her hair loosely twisted up, wearing one of her long silky skirts. She was lovely, but he regretted what he had missed—the dirt from her garden, the sand and salt from the beach. It was how he loved to see her, and he would, the next day, sweaty and summer-dirty, as rough as Marcella Atkinson ever got. She would stand at the sink in her sun hat and old shorts, scrubbing her hands. "Don't wash," he would say. "Don't wash too much."

"I am a dirty woman," she would say.

"No. You're not. You're all I want."

It was easy, at the beginning, not to think. He swam, constantly, in desire. One weekend he left her house to go for a run, and as he ran, on the sand-edged roads near the beach, he felt he was more fully aware of his own body than he had ever been before. He could feel every strand of muscle flexing, every drop of blood rushing through his heart. This was what desire was like. He had had girl-friends before but never someone he had craved, like a drug.

He had intended to run longer but suddenly he couldn't stand being away—it was a ridiculous waste of time, not being with her—and he turned to go back. As he retraced his steps, panting, he was sure his father had not felt this way. He couldn't have. His father—carnal, lustful? Distracted, so distracted that he could think of nothing else, wanting only to go to her?

His father had felt differently, his father had not loved her in the same way. His father was not here. He, Jed, was.

He slowed a block away from her house and made himself walk but when he got there he did not stop to stretch. He burst into the house; she was not there. He went to the bedroom and there she was, lying on the bed, naked under the sheet, as he had left her, reading. She looked up at him with a slow smile that grew more somber as she saw him standing there, breathing hard, in the doorway. He took off his shirt and wiped his face. "What's wrong?" she said.

"Nothing," he said. "Nothing is wrong." He stood there with the blood still surging through him and felt enormous. *I will fill this room,* he thought. *I will be all she will ever think of, ever want.* He was at the bed in one stride, standing over her. "Listen to me," he said, "listen."

She was still smiling, like he was playing a role, but there was a question in her eyes. "I am listening," she said softly, and although he knew she had not meant it as a rebuke it felt that way. He took a deep breath, tried to make his heart slow down. Carefully, he lowered himself to the bed, beside her. He did not know what he was going to say.

It was an overcast Saturday afternoon, and in the flat light he could see each of the fine lines at the corners of her eyes, the single straight worry line across her forehead. He touched the groove gently and thought of all that had gone into it, all the years she had lived, without him. Something in him broke open. "Listen. I love you," he said. "Right now. I love you."

He didn't see or even feel her face moving; weren't his fingers touching her skin? And yet somehow sadness came and settled like a shadow. It was because of time, the impossibility of it, of them in it.

Or maybe the shadow on her face was the same shadow that never left them, the shade in the corner of the room, the shifting will-o'-the-wisp of his father.

He withdrew his hand, got up from the bed, and walked over to the open window. The overcast day made the colors outside more vivid and he looked out at Marcella's garden, at the green grass and the perennial border with its drifts and heights and valleys of bloom, and thought how much time she had spent there without him, and would again, after he was gone. He was breaking a rule he had, of never speaking or even thinking of time, of any sort of progression. He had barely broken it now but he felt that, still, she knew. He felt her knowing, behind him, on the bed: it was her garden, not his, not theirs. He did not know what sort of fragile structure they were making, but he did not want it to crumble. He had said he loved her. He turned away from the window, back to her.

She had thrown off the sheet and was lying uncovered, on her side, a leg drawn up and her arm over her breasts so she was almost modest, a nude in a painting. Her head lay on her other arm and she was looking straight ahead, far beyond him, not dreamily but intently, as if she had been instructed to train her eyes on the horizon. Then she drew her knees up halfway and Jed thought that maybe she was cold, or ashamed, or afraid, and that she would curl herself into the fetal position and they would be miserable and separate. But as he watched, she turned onto her back. Her arms fell to her sides, her palms up, open like shells. She looked at him with her sad green eyes and slowly he turned full to her, and she let her drawn-up knees fall open until she was completely exposed to him, her primitive secret folds of her opening to him, and then the glistening beneath. She lay there exposed and secretless and waiting.

I am old enough, her eyes said, *to have learned to ignore time.*

He knew she was wrong but he went to her anyway.

THREE
WISTERIA

When Jed pulled into the driveway Sunday night, the house was dark except for a blue glow in the living room. He went in through the kitchen door and could hear, faintly, the meaty voice of the Red Sox announcer.

When he was growing up there had been no TV in the Cape house, but the first time Billy visited, before he and Callie were married, he said, *What's the deal? No baseball, even?* And Jed and Callie, who were both eager for Billy's cheer and health, looked at each other and said, *Why not?* At the time Jed had felt inordinately grateful: hardly ever was his parents' absence a cause for celebration. He and Callie had begged for TV for years, and when they bought a set and installed it, on their own, they felt almost nothing but glee. But since then Jed never had been able to get used to it. It was mainly Billy who turned it on.

Jed opened the refrigerator. "Hey, man," he called, "you're still here!" From the living room, Billy waved at him but didn't answer, and Jed knew that Callie must be asleep. He held up his beer and Billy nodded, so he took out another one and closed the fridge.

Billy was slouched in the middle of the sagging old sofa. "Thanks," he said in a low voice. Jed plopped into the chair next to him. "Thought I'd go back tomorrow," Billy continued. "Hang out in the morning for a while. Callie's a little low." He gave a shrug.

"What's going on?"

"I don't know. Won't talk. Just low. She misses her baby brother. Who's busy off gettin' some poon—"

"Oh, shut up." Jed took a long drink.

"So how's the Jersey girl?"

"Fine. Good."

Billy straightened a little. "Is she fine and good?"

Jed matched Billy's new tone. "Yeah, man." For the first time in what seemed like weeks, he felt himself grinning. "Yeah."

"When you going to bring her home, meet the folks?"

"We're working on that. Patience." In the comfort of the familiar living room, the wholesome sounds of baseball in the air, Callie gone, Jed felt he had temporary immunity from his usual caution.

"Mmm. Well, we miss you around here," Billy said. "Not the same without you, brother. You know—this is nice." He gestured with his bottle to the couch, the TV, the two of them watching it. Jed nodded. It was what he had thought his summer would be; it wouldn't have been bad. He felt a pang of what seemed like nostalgia—except, of course, that wasn't possible. For a moment time felt utterly confusing—what had already happened, what was happening now, what had he expected or imagined? "Jamie misses you too," Billy continued. "I'm telling you, I'm chopped liver. It's Uncle Jed this, Uncle Jed that."

"I love that kid," Jed said, with a force he had not intended. "I love both of them."

"I know."

"So Callie's okay, right?"

Billy didn't seem to hear the edge of challenge. "Yeah. Just the blues. Thinks about your parents. I'm telling you, it's worse when she's here, but she wants to be here." Billy was quiet a moment, then continued, his tone elaborately offhand, "Hey, my mom sent me this article from the *AJC*. She's always sending me random stuff, you know? Well, it was this thing about unsolved murders." He stopped and shifted in his seat, and Jed saw he was already wishing he hadn't said anything. "Cold cases," Billy continued, reluctantly. "It just—I didn't like seeing it in print again." He glanced at Jed. "She's clueless. Mom."

"You didn't show it to Callie."

"No. It's just been on my mind." Billy paused. "Sorry. Shouldn't have brought it up."

"S'all right." Jed watched the Rays' fat but agile shortstop fire to third and the Boston runner get tagged. "So," he said, not looking away from the TV, "they solve it?"

"No."

"Damn." His head was light, he watched the little men in white running on the manicured green field; funny how there was hardly any movement at all and then the sudden soaring, the energy spilling out and rounding movements like a dance, and then all at once the ball shot across the diamond and now the runner was out at first. He thought of facing Anthony across the net, waiting for him to serve. "I might give that detective a call," Jed said.

"Really?"

"I mean, obviously the file's open. Did it mention my dad? The article?"

There was a pause. "Yeah."

"What a load of *horseshit*." Jed felt weightless, giddy. He really did feel angry at the detective but it was an anger as clean as cold water. "I wish they would do their fucking jobs and clear his name!"

"Shh." Billy took a pull from his beer and then said in a lower voice, "Damn straight."

Jed turned on him. "*You* don't think he did it, do you?"

"Of course not."

"Somebody's out there, some animal, and they haven't caught him yet because they're sitting around on their asses blaming my father."

Billy stood. "You want another one?"

"Sure."

While he waited Jed stared at the TV, at the expressionless concentration on the pitcher's face. That was it. Purity. Jed's mind was racing, his thoughts felt as unclouded and hard as the pitcher's eyes. The pitcher threw another strike.

He heard the refrigerator door close and then Billy's returning steps. "Here," Billy said, handing him a bottle and plopping back on the sofa. "Look. Are you really going to call the guy?"

"Don't see why not."

"They'll let you know if anything turns up." The pitch was high and outside.

"Yeah, but I could still light a fire under their asses." *I could tell them something,* he thought, and it was not until that moment that he realized he could.

Billy sat up all the way, held his own bottle in front of him with both hands, like an earnest offering. "I don't know if you need to stir it up. It's been seven years, man—"

"Almost eight." *I could tell them something. He wasn't there, he really wasn't, I know it for a fact.*

They would say, *How do you know that, son?*

And then? he thought. *Then what?*

"Callie's come to terms with it," Billy was saying. "She knows they'll never find the guy. She knows he'll rot in hell, whoever he is. She's not sitting up nights."

"Neither am I." *And then what?* His father guilty in a whole new way. If Callie had answered her questions, there was no point in forcing her to ask new ones, making her wonder if their father had even loved their mother—right?

"I'm just saying." Billy sighed.

"Callie talks about it?" *Whoever he is.*

"Not really. Not anymore. She's tough." Billy drained his bottle and set it down on the coffee table, finally sat back. "All right. Full count. And—damn. Look at that."

The ball was sailing, out and away, above the expanse of green. As the crowd at Fenway roared, the TV camera closed in on the pitcher, his eyes following the course of the home run, his face still expressionless, and yet somehow the intensity turned to resignation.

"That's the way you play it," Billy said, slapping his leg. "That's the way you play *that* game. See? You never know what's gonna happen."

"No," Jed said. "I guess you never do."

WHEN BILLY D'AMBROSIO HAD MET JED MCCLATCHEY, and then his sister, during his and Jed's first year of law school, he'd been dazzled. He hadn't wanted to admit it, but it was true. They had been in the papers constantly, and yet here they were, leading their lives, getting A's. Callie was beautiful, she looked him straight in the eye, she didn't seem grief stricken at all except in the most understandable of ways. When she talked about her father she would often cry, pretty tears that didn't frighten him.

They quickly formed a tight threesome, they were all practically roommates except that Billy and Callie, in those days, had lots of rollicking sex. He and Callie got married and then they had Jamie and everything was proceeding nicely and Jed came over all the time, and Billy couldn't quite say what it was that made him start to quietly job-hunt up north, except that when he held his baby son, James Duncan D'Ambrosio—named after Jed, not him—he wanted him to never know grief. Even then he was starting to feel adjunct to Jed and Callie, that their history with the parents he had never met was like another person in the room, filling all the space and draining it of air and life. He was afraid of them, these dead parents. If it had been only one—but it was both, Callie and Jed were too unmoored, what had been impressive now seemed unnatural.

Billy had his little family and he loved them and he had not wanted Callie to leave this summer. He had managed to convince himself, though, that it was simply old-fashioned, an argument Callie had used herself—that women used to do this all the time, the men out, away, hunting and gathering in their city offices, the women and children safe in their summer idyll. That Callie had never before argued for old-fashionedness, or idylls, or madonnas tending hearth, he ignored. He had long ago become used to Callie being right, he wouldn't argue now; besides, he could come home late and get up early and impress his firm, and become more and more convinced that he had done the right thing, moving them here, and that this summer's separation was temporary.

He was glad his brother-in-law was off doing something normal, getting laid or falling in love or both. He was glad he had something to rag him about and felt old crude humor rising to his lips, things he hadn't said since college. It was a little weird, this whole scenario with the girl—he couldn't say why exactly, he just felt it—but he didn't blame Jed if he wanted to escape every now and then. That was something he could understand.

JED HATED TO ADMIT IT, but when Billy left Monday morning he felt himself relax. He'd gotten used to being the man of the house, and to not being watched. It was not that Billy was looking for signs of trouble—rather, Jed felt that Billy was always trying to figure out where he himself fit, where he could insinuate himself. This was new. He might ask Callie about it, one of these days.

After waving good-bye in the driveway, everyone else went back into the house and Jed got out a ladder and shears to clip the wisteria arbor by the patio. It was in full sun and Jed was up on the ladder sweating already when he heard the sounds of agonized protest coming from the house. He could make out Jamie hollering *Mommy* and *no,* and as this was not so unusual he kept clipping. Besides, Toni was there too; wasn't she supposed to be useful? After a few minutes the yelling escalated, then stopped, and soon after he saw Callie sprinting down the driveway, pushing the double stroller. He watched her until the overarching oaks on Whig Street blocked his view.

He balanced the clippers on top of the greenery, took off his shirt and wiped his forehead with it. Callie often went for a run in the morning, but alone, or only with Grace. Now she was pushing that stroller in this heat. He threw his shirt down to the ground and picked up the shears. It felt like 90 degrees already. And humid. He thought of Marcella in the heat, sweat at her hairline. Thought of them moving together slowly through the thick air as though they were swimming—

He was standing immobile on the ladder, the long blades poised in the air. Stop. Ridiculous that he was pruning the wisteria now in the heat. But good. Good to punish himself, sweat to death in straight sun.

"What are you doing?"

He looked down, startled. Toni was at the foot of the ladder. He resisted the impulse to give a snippy sixth-grader sort of reply—*Playing football, what does it look like I'm doing?*—and took a deep breath. "Did Callie take both the kids?" he said, trying to keep accusation out of his voice.

"I was going to keep Jamie," Toni said. She sounded defensive anyway. "He totally pitched a fit, though. He hates me."

"No, he doesn't." She was looking up at him with her eyes shaded against the sun, her weight on one leg, chest thrown out. It really seemed to be unconscious. He tried to will himself into a fond sort of amusement. "Really," he said, and started snipping again.

Toni said, "Is Callie okay?"

"She's fine. Just tired."

"I can't imagine having to wake up in the middle of the night like that all the time. If it were me, I'd look like shit."

The answer was obvious: *No, you wouldn't.* So he didn't answer. Chunks of tangled vine fell to the ground around him. He finished everywhere he could reach and climbed down. "Excuse me," he said, and when Toni had backed away he moved the ladder to a different vantage point and climbed back up.

"Aren't you cutting kind of a lot?" Toni said.

"You can't kill this stuff," Jed said. "In Atlanta, this is a weed. Pulls down trees. If I didn't prune it, it would take over the whole patio."

"So why do you have it here?"

"We didn't plant it. It's always been here." He reached through the vines and shook the peeling white wood of the arbor. "This thing is going to fall apart before too long."

"Does it bloom?"

"In the spring sometime."

"So you never see it?"

"No. My parents saw it once, I think. My mother always said someday she'd be here in time to see it bloom again."

Toni said hesitantly, "But she never was?"

Inwardly, he cursed. "Nope."

He didn't look down at Toni. He couldn't believe he'd let himself get into the maudlin zone. He knew what the expression on her face would be—he had seen it before, in all the girls who thought a grieving man was romantic, that he was in need of tender care, like a puppy. Marcella wasn't like that. She seemed more wounded than he. He had never considered this before. He lopped off a long trailing twist of vine and a hole opened up in the thick tangle of green. "If you want to be useful," he said, and tried to grin cheerfully without meeting her gaze, "you can go get that wheelbarrow over there." Out of the corner of his eye he saw Toni scurry away.

When she came back he glanced down and saw her bent double, moving fast, gathering the clippings from the ground. He was more used to her languid. "You don't have to do that," he said.

"No, it's all right."

"Well, I'm done, anyway." He climbed down and began to help her. "I'll just go dump it in the woods."

"I'll go," Toni said.

"There's a lot of poison ivy back there."

"I know what poison *ivy* looks like." She trundled away, wobbling, with the barrow. *Poor kid,* he thought. He made himself think of her that way. It felt good to feel sorry for someone else.

The sweat was in his eyes and he wiped it away again, and then walked over and dove into the pool. The sudden cool was bliss, it was rebirth; he wanted to stay under water forever. He did a long slow lap but then saw Toni was back, and got out of the pool. He didn't want her watching him swim. He didn't want her there at all. But she lay down on a lounge chair and it seemed to Jed that though she flopped down on it casually enough, she then arranged herself with some care. Finally she was still, her legs crossed, her eyes closed to the sun. Even with her self-consciousness, her body had a freedom to it that Marcella's didn't. She exuded energy, expectation. He said, "Isn't there some laundry to fold or something?"

"I did it all," she said, not opening her eyes. "And I did the dishes. But I'll leave if you want me to."

He let silence fall. "No, that's all right." He lay facedown on a chaise and closed his eyes, guiltily aware that both kids were gone and he was glad for the break.

"So," she said, "how's Marcie?"

"People are awfully interested in Marcie," he said. Toni did not respond to this. "She's fine." He made his mind blank, a cube of air, the pictures of Marcella invisible.

"Do you know what Callie told me?" Toni said. "She told me you were a bad bet. She said you haven't ever had a girlfriend for longer than two months."

"That may or may not be true."

Toni considered this for a moment and then said, "It's, like, one or the other."

"Callie likes to keep track of these things," he said lightly. Like some callow Casanova. *Danger! Stay away!* "But I don't." He did not ask why the hell Callie had been discussing him with Toni to begin with.

"You better not wait too long," Toni said. "For the right one, or whatever. You'll get all shriveled up."

He laughed and turned his head to look at her. "How old do you think I am?"

"I know how old you are." She looked back at him frankly, not even flirting. She was simply laying herself out for him. Offering. "I mean"—and he could swear she blushed—"not your body shriveling. Your—your happiness."

Jed thought how little Toni knew him.

"Like my parents," she continued. "I don't think they've dated a single person since they split up. Either one of them."

"So why did they split up?" His breath was coming too fast.

" 'We've grown apart. Blah blah blah.' *I* don't know," she said, with sudden vehemence. "Just 'That's it, it's over, you're going to boarding school.' "

He swallowed. "That's tough." *But why? What happened? Any hunches?*

She sighed. "Whatever. My dad is sort of tough. I guess. I mean, I love him. My mom is beautiful, though," she said abruptly. "Do you remember her?"

He turned his head away again. "No. Not really."

"Well, she is. But I guess it turns out beautiful people get divorced too."

He wondered if he made Marcella happy. He was suddenly ashamed: he hadn't even wondered that before now. "Do you see her much?" he said. "Your mom?"

"Some."

"You don't get along."

"We get along fine," Toni said. "She's not that fun to be around. She's always so depressed and moony and out in her fucking garden."

He lay there, his eyes closed, barely breathing, waiting for something—for the picture of Marcella to coalesce. She was walking across her own lawn. Far away. The grace of her stride was almost palpable, if he just reached out a hand—

Toni said, "Did your parents ever have any trouble?"

Jed was so surprised he didn't answer for a moment. The picture of Marcella flickered and vanished. The subject of his parents was taboo with so many people. But Toni didn't know that. How could she? He shifted his head on the pillow of his arms. "No," he said. "Not that I ever saw."

"That's nice," Toni said, and her tone touched him unexpectedly, how wistful it was. "Nothing? No fighting? Nothing?" She paused. "They really loved each other?"

Jed's eyes were open now, staring away from her, into the denuded arbor. It seemed the strangest kind of betrayal, to lie like that, except that it wasn't a lie; he hadn't seen any trouble. The things he could have told her—that his parents had been college sweethearts. That in the photos that had hung in their hallway in Atlanta, the Kodachrome had faded to a candy-colored flatness that made the bubble hair, the skinny ties, the orchids around his mother's wrist, all the more perfect. That his parents had always looked perfect. That he had never even heard them raise their voices.

Why had his father done it? *It*. A different *it*. Had cared nothing for those pretty pictures. His head swam, his father was before him, hazy, less guilty than before, now merely an ordinary, unremarkable asshole. Jed clenched his hands, dangling off the end of the chaise, into fists. He didn't want his father. He wanted only Marcella, alone.

"Jed?"

He started. Toni was crouched beside his chair. She put her hand on his bare shoulder. "I'm sorry," she said.

If he just turned over, right now, Toni would be there, her mouth close, her full breasts inches from his touch. Things would take another path entirely, the normal, red-blooded path they were supposed to take, and he would never have to think of Marcella, of his father, again—

He felt a sudden rush of sorrow. He wanted to think of Marcella. God, God, he missed her. And he had no right.

He said, "Please don't," and the hand went away.

"I'm sorry," Toni said again, and then he heard the whisper of her feet moving away across the dry grass. He did not watch her walking, did not watch the sway of her hips or the light on her hair, did not breathe until he heard the slap of the screen door.

Then he turned over and sat up.

He looked at the pool and tried to see his father in it, standing at the side, his bare chest above the water. Sliding in, doing one of his slow, long-limbed laps. And his mother beside him, her head turning mechanically, her compact athlete's body slicing through the water—

But he could not make the picture come. His parents side by side. That picture was gone.

He saw other pictures instead, different altogether. He did not want to remember, but he couldn't stop. He had been wrong about so many things.

JED WAS IN THE KITCHEN, in Atlanta, a few weeks after his mother had died. He and his father and Callie were sitting around the kitchen table. It was during the time when it seemed like they were always sitting around the kitchen table, about to decide something terribly important, only no one knew what it was. It seemed like it was always night. The alcove where the kitchen table stood had been designed for breakfast, for sun, and the bay of naked windows around them shone cold with the darkness outside, superimposed with the glare of the kitchen lights and their own distorted reflections. It was the end of December. Spring semester would start in a week. "I think you should go back to school, Callie," his father was saying.

"No," she said.

His mother's body had been in here, in the kitchen. Jed didn't know where. It felt unnatural to think of the physicality of his own mother, her body, the thing he had touched. Her humanity, her helplessness. He scanned the floor now as he always did: there? there? As usual he could find no trace, but it seemed that if he kept looking he would detect something. A scrubbed dullness, indicating the removal of blood. A malevolent glow. Someone had decided that he and Callie shouldn't see the crime scene—that is, their house—until the police were finished and the place was washed clean. About this he felt both gratitude and fury.

"Dad," Callie said, more gently, "I'm sorry. But we can't go back. We're going to transfer to Georgia State. We'll stay here in the house with you. We've already decided."

"Jed?"

"I'm staying, Dad." His voice came out in a croak.

"It's not what your mother would want. It's your senior year, sweetie—"

"Dad, come on," Callie snapped.

Jed flinched at the impatience in her voice, but kept his eyes on his plate. It wasn't really contempt, only ferocity, the Callie-ness magnified to an almost unbearable level. How could his father think they cared about school? About Callie's senior fun? He seemed to need them to be, alternately, either much younger or much older than they were.

"I've already paid for this semester, you know." Jed glanced up. His father was smiling weakly, defeat already on his face.

"Then you can just call them and tell them you want the damn money back," Callie said. "Or I will. And if they won't give it back then I'll just say, fine, that is my first and last alumni donation, and if you ever ask me for money again I'll sue you faster—"

"Callie, honey—"

"Daddy, I'm sorry. But I'm not going."

His father looked down at his own folded hands, like foreign objects, on the table. "Well. It seems you two know what you want."

Jed heard his own voice. "It isn't what we fucking *want*."

"Jed," Callie said. "Jesus." Their father just looked at him, stricken.

Jed didn't say any more. Dinner lay half-eaten on the plates in front of them. He didn't know who had made it; the fridge was stuffed full of the food people had cooked for them. Shirley Barnes, who had been with Betsy the night she died, who had dropped her off at the house—empty, they had thought—after a movie, brought something several times a week, like she was trying to cook away her guilt. But at least now they were alone more. Not always—not even half the time; people still seemed to think they could fix everything with the balm of their presence—but every now and then, like tonight, they had an evening to themselves. Jed knew his father hated it, wanted people with him all the time. It didn't even matter who they were. But Jed welcomed the quiet. It was stark and bleak but it was the truth. His only wish was to grab truth by the shoulders and look it straight in the eye, but he could not seem to get hold of it. He knew his father did not have the same wish.

The phone rang and Callie gave a harsh sigh.

It rang again and she made a halfhearted rising motion, but their father put out his hand and went to answer it himself. He walked so slowly that Jed thought he wouldn't make it before the answering machine picked up, but his father reached the phone on the last possible ring. "Hello?" he said, his back to them. "Yes. Hello, Detective. Fine. Thank you."

They no longer snapped to full attention when the police called, but Jed saw Callie's back stiffen. For himself, his ghost of a hope— *They have news, they caught someone*—had been replaced by sickening dread. *They have what they need now. They are coming here to get him. To get Dad.* Although, of course, they wouldn't have called first.

"No, no problem. We're just finishing. Hm-mm. Yes, well"—their father turned away, walked toward the door, the old-fashioned phone cord stretching, but his voice was still audible—"I'd rather come to you, if you don't mind."

Callie got up and began clearing the dishes, loudly, but Jed still heard *Yes, nine-thirty, thank you.* When Cecil hung up he walked out of the kitchen without looking back at them.

"All they do is keep asking him the same questions," Callie said at the sink. "He told me. Sometimes that red-haired one, sometimes other people." She thrust the faucet handle open, and the water shot out full force. "Over and over. Like they think something's going to change. They *know* there have been other break-ins. They haven't caught *anyone*. Why don't they leave him alone?" She looked at Jed, waiting for him to agree, for him to declare allegiance. Fidelity.

He brought his dirty plate to the sink, dropped it in the soapy water, and walked away without speaking.

There were times when Toni and Jed had everything under control and Callie found herself with nothing to do. She knew that this had not been her plan, that Toni and Jed were supposed to be merely her lieutenants, but she felt powerless to insert herself. In the past she would have constructed an elaborate schedule so that she would not have to make continuous decisions about how to spend her time; but this summer she had listened to the notion that she would want "relaxation," "downtime," "freedom." Freedom from what? She felt anything but free. At any rate, one day, feeling superfluous, she managed to rouse herself enough to make a plan, or at least a move. She took Grace, put her in the car, and began to drive.

It was a hot day and being in the air-conditioning was a relief. That was a good thing, she thought, trying to make a mental list of good things. She was vaguely aware that once optimism had been habit, even a reflex, but now the mechanism eluded her. She drove down Route 134 and got onto the Mid-Cape, driving east toward Provincetown, and then glanced in the mirror: Grace had already fallen asleep. Billy had attached a mirror to the back window, pointing toward the baby, who faced backward, so that when Callie looked in the rearview she could see her. The wonderful car. The sleep machine. That was what she and Billy had called it when Jamie was a baby. That was when Billy had rigged up the mirror. They had thought they were so clever. Thinking of those times, Callie felt she was on a high mountain, the air too thin, looking down toward a lovely promised land she had been forced to leave.

She looked in the mirror again and observed that Grace was adorable, exquisite. She waited to feel a bloom of appreciation or joy. There was nothing.

Instead she concentrated again on the road, on the heat waves rising from the asphalt. She could drive forever through this wavering light, if Grace would keep sleeping. She would drive and drive, and eventually she would be in Provincetown, bouncing down the planks of some pier, then the car would be angling, falling, sinking fast till they were at the icy-cold bottom.

Well.

Just go. A destination would arise. And Jed could manage at home anyway. Jed, her self, her surrogate. Jed was the only one she didn't worry about, who made her own worry ease. She had convinced him to come here. She hadn't realized she was doing it—she remembered asking, but when he appeared and said he had left his job for a while, she'd been baffled—had she asked for that? Surely not. She should be angry at him; it was a ridiculous, irresponsible thing to do. But she couldn't summon up any outrage. She needed him. It was one more thing to think about later.

And then, when they were almost to Orleans, Grace began to fuss. Callie felt a prickle of panic but tried, automatically, to soothe herself: look at the clock, almost three hours since the last feeding. And she needed a task. If she could not tell herself what to do, her baby could. "Good girl," she said, but Grace's cries grew louder. She was at the rotary, and pulled into the first parking lot she saw.

As she nursed Grace in the backseat, she realized she was at the old Army Navy store. It had been here forever. Maybe she would go in when Grace was done. A purpose. That was the way things worked—

you drove your car toward a goal. She would buy something for Jamie, she decided. Maybe even a tent. There was an idea: see, she could have them. He and Jed could camp out in the yard. She could picture them there, how much Jamie would love it—would Jed? Well, he would do it, probably, if she asked. She could buy them flashlights and mess kits. The kind with the collapsible cup and the plate that turned into a frying pan. Happy, happy childhood. She had had one of those kits, aluminum, in an olive-drab case. Her mother had bought it for her—bought it here. Callie had been going to Girl Scout camp. A long time ago.

At her breast, Grace was falling asleep again. Callie looked down at her closed eyes and drowsily sucking little mouth and felt abandoned—*Don't leave me, stay awake. I need company.* As if a baby could be company. But even after Callie detached her, strapped her into the baby carrier and put it on, Grace's eyes didn't open.

Inside, the store was barnlike and gloomy, with a corrugated tin roof high overhead. It seemed bigger than she remembered; wasn't it supposed to work the opposite way? Weren't places supposed to get smaller, less bewildering? As she made her way deeper into the store between towering stacks of military surplus, she was almost overcome by the smell of rubber, of metal. A foreign, heartless smell. Callie cradled Grace, attached to her front. All this testosterone, this love of war, this *maleness*—why had she brought her baby here? But she hadn't felt this way before, years before, as a skinny nine-year-old, legs covered with mosquito bites, begging her mother for an aluminum mess kit.

Her mother had looked down at her with cool eyes. "It's not on the list, Callie. You don't need it."

And Callie had felt a familiar indignation. She remembered looking at the picture on the box, at the way the aluminum pieces fit together snugly in their pouch, how they could come out and be plate and bowl and *everything* you could possibly need. She had imagined the kit bouncing hollowly against her hip as she hiked through the woods, how it would bang against the canteen they had already bought. She would be like a soldier on the march. "I *do*," she had said. "I *do* need it." But her mother's face had not changed. That implacability. That efficiency that did not allow for poetry—the poetry of a girl tramping through the woods: indomitable! invincible!

She hated to think of moments of disagreement. That had been a small clash, but in her mind it was one seed of the separation she had felt when she was nineteen, twenty, twenty-one, so full of her own possibility, convinced she needed no one, least of all her mother. For a time she had been sure her mother had nothing to offer her. No examples, no wisdom. Had she really thought that? Her memories had grown hazy and confused along with the rest of her thoughts. All she knew was that when her mother died there had been a long, long moment when every cell of her had seized up and cried, *I didn't mean it! Please come back!*

And then she was back in the echoing olive-green aisle. The mess kit. Had she begged for it? Had her mother caved (no, surely not), had her mother surprised her with it later? Because she had ended up with that mess kit. She remembered it so clearly, could feel the flimsy aluminum in her hands, could taste the metallic tang of the cup's rim. Couldn't she? Now she wasn't sure of that either. She stood in the empty aisle, poised, absolutely still, waiting to know if her memory was true or not, patient, patient, but then Grace stirred in her sleep and Callie's concentration dissolved. Her back was aching from Grace's weight.

She began to walk again, more quickly now. A faint, menacing hum seemed to emanate from the shelves. She cut her eyes one way, the other: she needed to escape. She was different now, her mother gone, that valiant girl gone. She could see herself, scuttling through the aisles, hunched around Grace, surrounded by tools of violence, of survival against too-high odds. *Calm. Calm.* She felt her mind straining like a wild horse. She held it under tight rein. It wasn't like she had seen any actual weapons. *Grenades! Rocket launchers, aisle 6! Ha!* She found the tent section, grabbed a cheap two-person model, and hurried back to the checkout.

Her fingers were trembling, and she put her credit card down on the counter with a loud *snap.* The salesman looked at her strangely as he picked it up. He was a tall guy with a buzz cut and a camo jacket, fresh from the recruiting center, Callie thought, except he had a fuzzy beard and his fatigues were less than crisp. A wacko. Some crazy Unabomber. She couldn't meet his eyes, couldn't see if they were kind or not, and how would she know? It didn't matter, didn't matter. She was almost done.

He said, "Would you like some help getting that to your car?" He cleared his throat. His voice was thick with a Massachusetts accent, but deep and almost courtly. "Seeing as you've got the baby?"

"No," she said, horrified at the thought of him following her outside, preventing her escape. "No, thank you—" Then she stopped.

The man turned to look behind him, following her gaze to a flat glass case, locked, with a pegboard inside. Attached to the board was a long row of knives. "You need something? You—ah—want to see one of those?" He glanced back at her. "I don't have the key. I'll have to get the manager."

Her mind was about to go galloping away, down the dark path she hated, and she would not be able to stop it. She shook her head. The register flurried with beeps and tickings and the man ripped off her receipt and pushed it and the pen across the counter. "Miss?"

The knives were arranged by size, the shortest ones starting on the left. You could read the row like a sentence, a long sentence ending in a scream. Her eyes slid along against her will. They inched past the ones you might use to cut a steak or whittle a boat or maybe clean a fish, *clean,* Girl Scout things, safe things, happy camping trips with your new mess kit, yes—but then there were bigger ones, for animals, probably, yes, just for crazy cruel hunters. And there was a machete, God, where was she supposed to be, anyway? A field of sugarcane, a rice paddy? God, how could someone hold a blade that long, that sharp, far too dangerous, the things it could do, flashing in the light—

She saw Grace cut in two like Solomon's baby, too late, too late. She saw her own blood, pumping out of opened veins with the beat of her own heart. She saw her mother's kitchen, how the floor was freshly washed, how her mother was not in it.

"Miss?"

She felt a mask come down, a hard, shiny smile. "Why, I'm not a miss! I'm a ma'am. I've got a *baby.* I can tell I'm not in the South! Why, thank you so much!" Her hands grasped the box and she fled. Outside in the parking lot someone, her shadow self, took the sleeping Grace and buckled her in, this other lying self found the keys in her purse and steered the car back onto the road and around the rotary and toward home, while her real self huddled in the corner of her mind, rocking rocking, knowing she had seen both the past and the future and that she could not fend them off for much longer.

It was noon on Friday, and Marcella was making a marinade for their dinner steaks. She chopped garlic, poured in wine and olive oil and vinegar. She crushed rosemary from the garden with her hands. She was humming. She had taken a shower a little while before and her damp hair, twisted at the back of her head, was pleasantly cool, as was the kitchen floor under her bare feet. Although she was alone in the house, she could already feel Jed's presence. She looked through the door into the living room, imagining him lying on the sofa reading, as he often did; from where she stood she just would be able to see the top of his head. She turned back to the counter and breathed in herbs. He would arrive before sunset.

At her house, Jed read only books he found on her shelves; he never brought his own. Sometimes he would pick up a book in Italian, and puzzle through some of it with a dictionary. He got her to read bits out loud to him, and asked about the translating work she did. She said it was only something to make her feel useful. "But you want to think of me as a literary woman," she said, laughing—"so be it!" He read books in English too, serious and light indiscriminately, with, it seemed to Marcella, a kind of abandon. "Don't you read at home?" she had asked him.

"I concentrate better here," he had said, but she knew this wasn't true. She had never seen him finish a book; he rarely even picked up the same one twice. This was disturbing to her but she could not say what it might mean—

The phone rang.

Her first thought was that it was Jed, something was wrong, he wasn't coming. There was bad news, she felt it; when she answered and found it was Toni, her heart lurched, still believing her premonition. "Mom," Toni said, "I'm on the road. I'm about an hour away—"

"What happened?"

"Dad and I— Can I come stay with you?" For a moment Marcella felt nothing—the blankness between fear and joy. She could hear the sound of traffic in the background. She saw Toni, one hand on the wheel, the phone clutched to her ear. Needing her. "Mom?"

And then it came, happiness in a great swell: Toni was coming. "Of course, darling," Marcella said. "But what is wrong?"

"I had a fight with Dad. I *hate* him."

"Toni," Marcella clucked, trying to sound relaxed, because it really was nothing. Trying not to sound surprised: when had Toni last turned to her? Seemed to need her?

"Don't *you* . . . I had to get out of there." She launched into a long story of how she had been at the Woodshed in Brewster and her fucking ride had left and she'd been late getting home, but she was in college, *Jesus* . . . Marcella was quite sure that Toni was leaving in her profanities on purpose, but she didn't know to what end, and anyway all she heard was her little girl saying *Listen to me, listen to me.* She looked down at the steaks, feeling unsteady.

"So I'm almost there," Toni said. "It'll just be tonight I guess. Well, tomorrow night too. I have to be at work on Monday," she said, and Marcella heard a little pride in her voice, and again saw her daughter holding Cecil's grandchild, this mystery child who, perhaps, looked like Jed. "Mom?" Toni said. "Are you *doing* something? You're *distracted.*"

Toni's main criticism was that her mother had no life. But at the first sign of one, her resentment sprang up. Marcella wiped her hands on a towel, picked up the pan of steaks to put in the refrigerator. Toni liked steak. "No, sweetie," Marcella said. "I'm not doing a thing. Not a thing except waiting for you."

When she got off the phone she took a moment to compose herself. Jed usually called, too, from the road. What if he didn't? What if his phone wasn't turned on? Of course it would be but she sat down anyway, her confusion overtaking her. What if he was here when Toni got here? Could she call the house in Mashantum, ask when he had left? How laughable. A cheery conversation with Callie, chatting, *How are you,* nothing to hide, *yes, I am Jed's girlfriend . . . girl . . .* For a moment she saw how life could be, someone else's life; felt a moment of sharp, bitter yearning; and then let herself plunge back into the strange richness that was reality. He would be angry. She had never thought of Jed angry, at her. She would call in a minute but for now she stood and began moving quickly, her eyes darting. Because she also had to purge her house of any signs of him.

She tried to smile as she searched, to feel devilish, but no, she did not enjoy playing such games; it was one of the reasons this could happen between her and Jed, because here in Connecticut she had no one to hide it from. Until now. She did not want to think of Cecil, of how years before in Mashantum they had had to plot and sneak. She had tried to avoid subterfuge then, as much as possible; she had tried not to lie. Instead she simply hadn't said. And Anthony hadn't asked, had not, she believed, even cared, and there was no one to care now—but she must not think of Jed and Cecil together at the same time, she must not.

She kept going, kept looking, but there was nothing to find, not so much as a razor or toothbrush, things Toni would not even notice. She was almost disappointed she couldn't put her frantic energy to

use, but she wasn't surprised. She suspected Jed had made a tacit
pact with himself not to leave a trace. Every Sunday night, she
noticed that he had even filed the books he had been reading back
onto her shelf without marking his place, and she thought she knew
why. If they accumulated too many routines, too much familiarity, it
placed them in time, and he wanted more than anything to believe
that they existed on an island of eternal present. In the pure present
there was no threat of past or future, of memory or loss. She wanted
to tell him that she knew of this belief, but then she might also tell
him that it was no good. She might tell him that on every Sunday
night, she laid her face in his pillow and breathed the absence of him
in. He might have left no physical traces of himself, but it did not
matter.

She stood still for a moment and thought how, this weekend, she
would not have him. She realized she was hoping he was almost here.
That she would have time to see him at her door, to touch him, before
she turned him away.

But she made herself keep combing the house. Toni was coming.
Finally she stopped at the doorway of Toni's bedroom. Where Jed had
slept that first night. She had put this room together so carefully after
the divorce, in those days when everything she did or said felt like
apology. She felt a sudden jolt of longing for her daughter, not just her
presence, which she would soon have, but to hold her close, to gather
her to herself completely in a way that was no longer possible, physically or otherwise—Toni who was still so angry, Toni who, Marcella
believed, quite simply loved Anthony more. She was hungry for Toni,
hungry for Jed, and she couldn't believe she could feel both at once;
that was why her legs shook, why she was holding on to the frame of
the door. It was standing here, it was thinking of Jed in that bed.
Almost reluctantly, she walked into the room and slowly sat down on
the pink comforter, as if something might break in the room, or in

herself. This was what Toni would see when she lay here. This was the view her girl saw out the window.

Marcella's own bedroom was last. Nothing. But her glance fell on her made bed, and irresistibly she thought of Jed in it. She walked over and buried her nose in the pillow he used, but it was fresh and bare and smelled only of the laundry.

An odd calm was creeping over her. When she called Jed, and told him to turn around, she would feel the heat of his desire, and her own desire too, in every cell, like sickness. Her spirit quailed but then she steadied herself again. She would try to tell him how clean it was, this automatic love for one's child. How unhesitating the *yes*. How there were no questions, how she had gone too long without taking all of her daughter she could get, in greedy handfuls.

She picked up the phone.

FOR HOURS CALLIE HAD BEEN FLOATING in dread, as happened now every Friday, starting in the morning, sometimes spilling back even to Thursday night, when she would lie awake exhausted, her open eyes glued to the blackness that was the ceiling, knowing what was coming . . . and now it had happened, Jed had left, Billy had arrived, the changing of the guard, the men here to watch over her. To inspect. She didn't know if she dreaded Billy because he saw too much or too little. He reminded her that this summer was temporary. His presence, meant to fulfill her, reminded her of the yawning chasm at her back where her mother and father should be. He reminded her that they had a life in foreign Connecticut and when fall came it would be her duty to build it up, in the strange place with the house and roads and people that would never, she was sure, feel familiar. When Jed was there she still fought every day to shuffle through in a straight line, to force herself from one hour to the next.

Jed noticed, a little, but his noticing did not make her feel exposed. But when Billy came with his laughter and his tossing Jamie up in the air and his awkwardness with his own baby daughter, it reminded her of the person she had managed to be before Grace came and how since then she had failed. During the week, she was alone in a cell with Jed and her struggle was contained, but then Jed left and Billy came and the door opened and it became a public matter—

She was standing at the sink washing dishes. The children were finally in bed and even though it was already dark Billy was outside at the grill, cooking their dinner. That was what happened up here—the days grew shorter even in the heat, even in the thick of July. Time hurtled. The window above the sink was open. Above the slosh of the dishwater she could also hear the hiss and sizzle of the meat, and then a car pulled up. The jerk of the hand brake and the slam of the door, the crunch of steps on gravel. Her brother's dark form walked over and stood with her husband's.

"Her fucking parents," she heard. "Fucking *surprise* visit."

"You don't want to meet them?" Billy laughed. "Jesus, *did* you?"

"She— I called before I got there." Jed cleared his throat and Callie thought he sounded odd, shaky. "Thank God," he said.

"Not quite up for that, bro?" Billy clapped Jed on the shoulder. "Glad to have you back. Just like old times."

She was washing Jamie's plastic cup, the one with the red cartoon fire engines circling it in endless emergency. She could not even move her hand away from the faucet, she could only watch the water filling the cup and then overflowing, spilling to the white porcelain floor of the sink and down the drain, wasted, as she shook with her reprieve.

IN HER BED THAT NIGHT, Marcella lay wide awake. Toni was in the next room, but Marcella didn't even realize she was listening and waiting until she heard Toni click off her lamp; then the crack of light coming under Marcella's door disappeared and she let out a breath. In a few minutes, the silence deepened and settled and she knew that Toni was asleep.

There was nothing, nothing, there was nothing like knowing your child was safe asleep in the next room.

Unexpectedly, she thought of Jed. She wanted to say to him, *Someday you will have that,* but then loss washed over her in a gentle wave and she did not let herself think about that anymore.

It was a minor crisis that had brought Toni to her, but she would take it. She wondered if maybe, just maybe, Toni was starting to feel an iota of obligation toward her, and wondered if she wanted that or not. Obligation had not served her well with her own mother, who had felt so beleaguered by life that she believed she had no power beyond inducing guilt. *But I am a mother,* she thought, *and I want my child however I can get her.* Maybe Toni just wanted to annoy Anthony by leaving, maybe she wanted Marcella to slip her some cash too, but Marcella would not be convinced that she didn't also want some elemental safety, something only she, Toni's mother, could give. Marcella had cooked her the steaks meant for Jed, she had put the extra pillows on her bed, she had cut phlox and black-eyed Susans and the last precious delphiniums for her room. And it might have been Marcella's imagination but Toni seemed just a little bit softer, hugged her a little more convincingly, even though as usual she said nothing about the flowers or the food. She was comfortable, that was the thing Marcella could give her. Marcella hadn't given her enough. She had let Anthony take over, long ago; she had deferred to him, and somehow, by the end, it felt like she had abandoned Toni, the exact opposite of everything she had ever wanted.

So she wasn't sorry she had sent Jed away. Nevertheless, she lay in the dark and missed him, and wondered where he was. He would have gone back to Mashantum, of course. But it occurred to her he could go anywhere. He could have kept driving west, to New York. She did not like to think of him there. He would be so alone, lost on sidewalks thronged with people for whom it would be easy to imagine intricate lives.

She was beginning to get sleepy. She felt herself relaxing, her limbs growing heavy.

Across the hall, Toni made a noise in her sleep, a cooing and sighing. A comfortable sound. She thought again of Jed. She realized she was afraid not that he would be lonely in the city, but that he would look around at all the purposeful souls and begin to walk with them. He would see that was where he belonged, with other people, moving, moving away from her.

But Toni was *here*. In bed in the dark, alone, Marcella thought that she should have gotten Toni another pillow, or two. Maybe Toni had gotten them herself from the closet. She liked a lot of pillows, to go to sleep propped up like a princess—although she then slept like a wild thing, tossing and turning, and in the morning the pillows would be scattered on the floor. Marcella smiled to herself. See, she had that bit of knowledge. That, and much more. Toni would never believe it, but Marcella knew her better than anyone in the world; she knew her in her bones, the way mothers were supposed to. Yet she, Marcella, did not believe that her own mother had known her that way. And so that was what daughters did—disbelieved. Was that where it started? The yearning to be known? She would do anything to spare Toni that search. It was the desire that led to all trouble.

As Marcella's body healed from her fourth and final miscarriage, August stretched itself out and melded into September. The light deepened and the nights turned cooler, the Atkinsons went back to Wellesley, but still she could not shake her sadness. She had girlfriends but she knew they would suggest exercise or antidepressants or a spa, or the fertility doctors Anthony didn't want. She was getting too old for that anyway, she was worn out. She did not want that exhausting hope to swell in her again.

She found herself, strangely, longing to go back to the Cape. Usually she felt it was Anthony's place, not hers. Their house was full of his family's spartan artifacts, ladder-back chairs and Latin dictionaries and old tennis trophies, strange things that had once charmed her but which she now found difficult to love. The appeal of the Cape had never really sunk into her—she thought the scrubby trees and the small-windowed houses were pinched and meager. But now she thought of the few times they had gone in the off-season, when it was still warm enough to sleep in the unwinterized house, and remembered that it was different then, still and quiet, the wildness of the place closer to the surface.

That evening after dinner, when Toni had left the table to go do her homework, she said to Anthony, "I was thinking of going to Mashantum this weekend. If I could arrange it—if it would be all right with you." She found she could not meet his gaze, and got up to begin clearing the dishes.

Anthony raised his eyebrows for a moment in mild surprise but then he nodded. "Of course, Chella," he said, and nodded again, definitively. "You need some time away."

He said it almost as though he had proposed the idea himself and she had just agreed. When had he begun to use that tone? Condescending, but more than that—retreating? He wasn't asking why she wanted to go, what she thought she was going to do with herself. Why being alone there would be different from all the solitude she had here, all day long. "Darling," she said, surprised even as she said it, "perhaps—you could come too?"

"That would be fun. But, then, where would Toni go?" Anthony said jovially. He picked up his own plate and went into the kitchen, and almost reluctantly she followed. She set a serving bowl and glass on the counter and realized Anthony was moving toward her, and for a split second she had the urge to cringe, not from him but from a shadowy something else, waiting to swoop down on her. She held herself still, however, and Anthony took her in his arms, seeming not to notice her stiffness. "It would be a relief, to have a rest, wouldn't it," he said. He was patting her back, like she was a child.

"I don't really need to rest," she said in a small voice.

"Oh, you seem a bit tired. You need to get away from it all."

She didn't answer. She didn't say, *I don't want to get away* from, *I want to go to.* Right now he was being solicitous, even sweet; she didn't want to ruin it. But he was the one who was relieved—she felt it relaxing him, this fresh conviction that she had some benign problem that a ladies'-magazine solution, a little getaway, would solve. Reflexively she tried to think of their vanished babies but their images were hazy, diffuse, and she knew for Anthony they were barely dots on some disappearing horizon; he was not even looking in that direction anymore, he had turned somewhere else, and though she knew it was her job to pick up and follow him, in her mind she squatted down and held herself stubborn and immobile while he kept moving, grew smaller and smaller. His arms were still around her but she could barely feel them. She stepped away and smiled, not meeting his eyes. "Thank you, darling," she said. "It will be nice."

"Sleep in. Do some shopping." He was already turning away, just as she had seen in her mind.

"Yes. It will be lovely." Terrified—because she knew she was causing it, her spirit suddenly dogged, inflexible—she felt something in her, the line from her to Anthony, stretch thinner and thinner, hairsbreadth fine, and then give way.

She arranged for Toni to sleep over at a friend's and drove to Mashantum on a Friday midday toward the end of September. She went to the house, feeling like a trespasser, dropped off her things, and then went straight to the beach. It was high Indian summer, the sun warm and the colors rich. The parking lot, which required a permit during the summer and usually had a line of cars waiting, was unattended and nearly empty. The boardwalk had been taken away and she walked the uphill path barefoot in the warm sand. At the crest of the dunes, the beach and blue water and wide horizon were spread suddenly before her like a new world.

The beach was deserted, save for a few walkers with their dogs, rollicking faraway dots, and a lone man in a beach chair, his back to her. Marcella felt a lift of quiet elation. Alone, alone, no one expecting anything of her. Then the man in front of her shifted in his chair and she glimpsed his face, and realized that it was Cecil McClatchey.

She stopped dead in the sand, holding her own chair and towel and book. Her elation evaporated. She realized she could leave. She had only come to this beach, their usual one, where she was most likely to see someone she knew, by force of habit. Mashantum had dozens of beaches. She had forgotten that she could choose.

But she stood in the sand, unmoving. As she realized she had been undetected, she relaxed. Choice, indeed. She could choose to stay or go, to speak to Cecil McClatchey or walk away; she could be rude, but if no one knew, was it rude? And what, oh what, did it matter? She felt the sun, straight above her, warming the top of her head, her bare arms, and she could feel the fear—for that was what it had been—running off her like water after a swim. And then, as though it had been her plan all along, she found herself marching straight down to Cecil's chair.

She stood next to him, as bold as a teenager, and he sprang up, grabbed her hand, and pumped it like she was a long-lost friend. "I thought I was the only soul left on the Cape, indeed I did!" he cried. Then he was unfolding her chair for her and settling it in the sand next to his.

"I don't want to invade your privacy," Marcella said. "One so seldom gets the chance to be alone."

"Not at all! Not at all!" A look of distress came to his face. "But you probably don't want to be stuck talking to me."

"I don't feel stuck," Marcella said, and laughed, hardly believing it was her own voice.

And how was Anthony? How was her daughter? They were fine. She needed a little retreat, just a little quiet. "I admire a woman who doesn't need to talk all day long," he said. "Going to do some shopping?" She shook her head. "No? Even better."

He was courtly in an old-fashioned way; she saw he would give no hint of having a life of his own, would contentedly discuss her all day unless she gave him leave to do otherwise.

"Betsy's not a shopper, I'll bet," she said.

"No, no. She's a sensible woman," he said, as though she were a character in a book.

Eventually he allowed that he had been in Boston for business and had decided to take the weekend. He'd wanted Betsy to come join him, but she'd already had some plans with her lady friends. "I guess you know how that is," Cecil said. "But I'll tell you. This empty-nester business is something. Both the kids off at school, and we could just take off whenever we want. We're not used to it."

"Have you traveled much?" Marcella asked politely.

"No. Not yet. I guess Betsy's a homebody. I'm the one with itchy feet."

Marcella pictured Cecil and Betsy in a sunny breakfast room, the morning paper strewn in front of them on the table, half-drunk cups of coffee—and a note of discord. This was something new. She imagined Betsy would be as calm as always, unmoved by her husband's innocent, mysterious longings. *Oh, men,* Marcella would have said, if Betsy had been sitting there talking to her instead of Cecil. Agreeing with her. *Men—aren't they silly?*

But it was not Betsy sitting there, it was Cecil, and she found herself being charming. The ease that always eluded her appeared from some unknown place—out of the warm sun, perhaps. "Do you ever go back to Italy?" Cecil said.

"It's been years," she said. "I have very little family there anymore. It is so hard to get away."

"Brothers and sisters?"

She shrugged. "I come from a long line of only children."

"Oh," Cecil said. She saw that he thought this sad.

"Not by choice," she said. "I mean—of course one doesn't choose one's family—I mean, no one meant to have one child. My grandfather died in the war, when my father was a baby. And then my father died in an accident, before I was born. And Anthony and I—" She raised her hands and opened them, releasing old hopes to the sky. "It didn't happen." She looked at Cecil and saw he was looking straight back at her, and she had the oddest sensation that she someday would tell him more, all of it, that maybe he could see the outline of it all in her eyes right now. That he *saw.*

And as they talked she also realized, in some part of herself that had been asleep for a long, long time, that she was being watched. It was surprising how quickly the girl's tricks came back to her: smoothing back her hair, closing her eyes and turning her face to the sun, presenting Cecil with her profile. It was a part she was playing: she was gliding across a stage. He seemed to believe her life had an elegant, exotic shape, and she did not tell him otherwise.

As the afternoon wore on, the effort of pretending not to notice each other in anything other than an old-neighbor sort of way became delicious. They were beside each other in their chairs, not face-to-face, the convenient horizon in front of them. They could deflect desire, turn their longing out to the open sea, if this innocent pretending was desire.

Marcella looked sidelong at him when she could. She had always thought of him as generically handsome, but now his straight, prominent nose and strong chin seemed to her uncommonly distinguished. His thinning hair, once blond, was now almost completely gray, but still wavy, a little long at the back. How handsome he must have been when Betsy first met him, with his blue eyes and blond curls. She could see him somehow, years ago, when she herself had been a girl as well. They had all once been tender and inexperienced and unlined. She felt an odd, intense mourning that she had not known him then, that there was so much she would never know. "Did you and Betsy meet when you were young?" she said.

"Sophomore year of college," he said. "In English class. Betsy was the smart one."

And you the good-looking one, she almost said aloud—but that wasn't fair, Betsy must have been striking in her own way. Confident and athletic, slimmer then (she wasn't heavy now, Marcella reminded herself, only had a middle-aged thickness), with dark hair in a shining, perfect pageboy. "And you were smitten," she said.

"Yes, I suppose I was."

"So you have grown up together. In a way."

"That's about right. Not what they do now as much. Seems like people wait longer to settle down."

"It was the same with Anthony and me," Marcella said. "We met in university. I was terribly homesick. It seemed—"

She stopped. She had been going to say, *It seemed like Anthony was the person I had been sent here to find.* Instead she said, "He was so American, you know—so sure of himself." She glanced at Cecil and saw one corner of his mouth twisted in a dry smile. His eyes met hers, then moved quickly away.

"It is best, don't you think? To meet when you are young?" She heard the forced gaiety in her own voice. "Because you know each other so well. Inside and out."

"Go through a lot of changes together," Cecil said.

"Yes."

Marcella gazed out at the water and dug her feet into the sand. She was aware of his eyes on her, aware that she was stretching out her leg in a way she ordinarily wouldn't. She felt ashamed of herself but also defiant. "I am sorry I was so strange at your party," she said. "I wasn't myself."

"I don't remember you being strange."

"Oh, of course you do." She looked at him frankly. "I was sitting all alone."

"Well, I just remember you looking lovely."

"You are being chivalrous," she said, but he didn't answer, and she was sorry she had said it. She wanted to stay on the stage but it seemed to her that now he was standing in the audience staring at her, daring her to come down. Although of course she was imagining that too—all of it, all of it, in her head.

I don't dream like you, Anthony had said.

"You're shivering," Cecil said.

"Am I?" She gazed appraisingly at the sun, as though she had not been tracing its path for the last hour. "It has gotten so late!" She glanced beside her at the long shadow she cast, and reached down and felt the shaded sand, sifted it through her fingers. It was cold. She said, "I suppose I should go."

Cecil leaped up, just as he had first leaped up to greet her, and she thought, *I have misjudged. He is tired of this, he wants me to go, he has been too polite to say. He is like this with everyone, anyone.* "Let me carry your chair," he said, and mutely she stepped back, let him fold it and pick it up. They made their way back toward the dunes.

The beach had been bathed in the late light, but on the other side of the dunes the parking lot, empty but for their two cars, was in shadow, and the road winding away from it was almost fully dark at the curve. "The sun goes down early up north," Cecil said.

"Yes," she said, and forced a smile back. "I suppose it does." She couldn't say why she both longed for the winter dark and dreaded it.

"Strange, isn't it?" Cecil said. "The parking-fee girl usually sits over there. There's a line of cars up thataway. There are people on those porches. I guess I'm not used to it in the off-season."

"Do you think it's lonely?"

He considered, and then said, sounding surprised at himself, "No. I like it."

She looked up past the dunes to a row of three cottages, all with identical flagpoles out front, now empty, and with the same weathered shingle siding. Each house had different color shutters—green, then blue, then red, down the line. She wondered if they were rentals, or if they were all owned by the same harmonious family. The shutters were closed over the doors and windows. She had never noticed people in the cottages before, but they were now obviously, utterly empty.

She stood fighting the sadness but suddenly it overcame her— not self-pity that she was going home to an empty house, but a sorrow she had felt before, she realized, one now fanned by the sight of the vacant cottages, by the thought of winter. It was the time of night when the lights should glow yellow in the windows, a time when she should be opening the door to a kitchen warm and full of people—a kitchen in her mind that she had never seen anywhere else, with a wooden table and baskets of bread and the cheerful bustle of adults and children together. In it, she was never sure if she was mother or child. "Why, Marcella," Cecil said, "what's wrong?"

"It's—it's just the hour when people go home." She was sure he would not understand and she cringed when he opened his mouth to speak. She was not even curious what he would say, what he would make of her strange tears, she was just sure it would be wrong. She felt she had never been able to explain herself to anyone, and she cut him off. "Never mind," she said, "oh, never mind."

"You shouldn't be so sad." His face was no longer jovial, but gentle. His eyes took in her sadness and reflected it back to her, made it a softer thing, less frightening. When he moved toward her she thought, *This is innocent, a hug from an acquaintance.* Then, *This is a mistake.* And she thought, too many thoughts, but now not a cacophony, instead a song—*I am safe now.*

NEITHER OF THEM WAS THE TYPE: that was what they kept saying to each other. Their mutual bemusement became part of their bond. Cecil traveled often to Boston for business, Marcella had her days free, and at first it was amazingly simple to arrange. For a time, she was able to hold her guilt at bay.

It was at a hotel in the suburbs that Cecil spotted the bathing suit in her suitcase. He pulled it out. "What's this for?"

She shrugged, blushing. "I thought if there was a pool. Or a hot tub."

"You thought you'd have some time to kill?"

She looked up at him through her lashes. "No." Then she looked at him more carefully. "What do you want?" He didn't answer and she studied his face some more. "You want me to put it on," she said finally. She furrowed her brow. "And—?"

He began to smile. "And I want you to wear it for a while. For a little while. So it smells like you. And then I want you to take it off," he said. "And give it to me. To keep."

It was when she thought of such moments, always at the most mundane times—standing in line at the grocery store or driving down their street to begin the carpool or picking up Anthony's shirts—that Marcella felt how loosely she was bound to her life. One day Anthony suggested they plan a trip to Europe and she burst into tears; it seemed she would miss Cecil even more if she was not in her familiar surroundings, where she had learned to negotiate her longing, fit it into the cracks and crannies of her days. She was able to convince Anthony that she was just her usual overemotional self, although at the height of her tears she thought, *I should just tell him*. For a moment she even fancied it would be a relief. But then she remembered it was Cecil who was real, almost painfully so, not this other life, it was Cecil with whom she felt alive.

What she couldn't believe was the energy she got from her love for him. He needed to be present only in her mind and she felt radiant, focused; and he was almost always in her mind. The only way to scare herself away from him was to think of Toni, of being separated from her beautiful little face and young body, that body she had held and nursed in its earlier, smaller incarnation. But even then she was not frightened completely. She did not want to think of logistics but she was sure it could all be worked out, if such a time ever came. She tried not to imagine an alternate life too fully. When her thoughts became concrete, she heard the voices of her mother and grandmother scolding the loudest. But in spite of herself she was rapt whenever

Cecil let slip a comment about Betsy, his boredom, their lack of passion, and let the vague and general notion of a life with Cecil and the completion she would feel grow brighter and brighter. At her most feverish moments, moments she secreted in a corner of her mind, she even let herself imagine having a baby with him. It was easy to dream that her body's recalcitrance would dissipate along with her old wooden life, that rebirth would be complete in every sense.

So all winter and spring her thoughts and their time together were private, hidden from the world. They saw each other once or twice a month. They spoke of how it would be that summer in Mashantum, when they would see each other more often. Anthony would be in Boston much of the week and Toni would be in camp. Cecil did not say exactly how he would arrange things—she appreciated that in him, he would not gloat, would not plot and plan out loud, he was a man of honor, as strange as it might sound; she knew that. But if she stopped to consider, she knew he could say he was playing golf, and be safely gone for hours. The thought of being in the same state, the same little town, of having Cecil sleeping only a few streets away, made her nearly delirious.

They had planned their first meeting that summer carefully. He was going to come to her house, and probably ride his bike; if anyone saw him he would just smile and wave, keep going. The bike would be easier to hide, of course, although neither of them said that. For the occasion Marcella had cleaned the guest room, a room that she had never slept in, let alone she and Anthony together. She had stood in the low-ceilinged room with a rag in her hand and the dust motes sparkling in a beam of light, and in a shiver of anticipation that bordered on revulsion thought of herself and Cecil together in the unfamiliar bed. She was intoxicated at the thought of her and Cecil's life together becoming more daily, but as his arrival in Massachusetts crept closer she also felt panic that the fairy-tale hotel-room affair was ending, that something more real, less deniable, would take its place. It was not that she did not want it. It was that she wanted it so badly. She had gone over it and over it in her mind: the sound of the bike on the driveway, Cecil standing there in the flesh, in life, her life. He would have that open, honest look of delight on his face, as if he had just discovered her. And the whole summer, an ocean of time, would stretch before them.

But then she saw him before she was prepared. That very afternoon, she was dropping Toni off at Nobscusset for her first tennis lesson and there he was, two courts away, in his whites, playing Fred Sprague. She knew she shouldn't stare but she sat down on the nearest bench anyway. Her heart was racing. There was something wrong, so many people around, she was not so naturally daring, she would give it all away. For a dismayed moment she thought, *I am not meant for this after all*.

He and Fred finished their set and Cecil walked to the fence, drank from a water bottle. His back was to her but she knew, from some stiffness there, that he had been aware of her all along. When he finally turned and looked at her it was with a hunger that slammed into her with bodily force, and she knew, all at once, that what they had was not going to fit into their life here at all. Even if they were not discovered, she knew this thing would somehow burst the bounds they had carefully made for it. In spite of all her daydreams, this was not something she had considered, that her life might be completely transformed.

V

On Saturday morning, at Marcella's house, Toni acknowledged that going to the beach was nothing new. "But at least I won't be there with little kids," she said.

"Believe me, there will be plenty of little kids."

"But if they cry or take a shit, it won't be my problem."

"*Basta*. You love those babies. I can hear it in your voice, *cara*." Toni bit her lip and Marcella had to restrain herself from going on: *What do they look like, what do they feel like, what is Jed's face like when he holds them?*

They arranged their towels on one of the few empty patches of beach, down near the water. The day was clear and dry, and every now and then the breeze was shot through with coolness. Marcella noticed boys, and men, noticing them, many more than would have noticed if she had been alone, and she smiled to herself, feeling proud of her daughter's ability to attract even though she knew it was not the proper feminist thing to do. Toni was abundant, she was overflowing that bikini of hers. Marcella herself had never looked like that but she imagined that Toni would slim down one of these days, lose her college-girl puppy fat—she knew perfectly well it came from beer, she was not stupid. She also noticed, though, as usual, that even if she were thinner Toni would not have had exactly her build but instead a figure Marcella recognized from her own mother. Broader shoulders, a thicker waist. A powerful girl.

Marcella supposed she should feel old, but she didn't. She had had friends back in Wellesley, slightly older, whose daughters had been full and lush like Toni was now, and she had seen how quietly frantic they were to regain something they thought they had lost, how they truly thought their daughters were at the peak and they themselves dwindling. But Marcella had never felt young like that—felt that the world was open before her, that she was invincible. She stretched and thought of Jed's hands on her with an unfamiliar smugness. No, she did not feel old.

Toni had been propped on her elbows pretending not to eye the boys eyeing her but then she sat up, all pretense at subtlety gone. She stared for a minute from behind her sunglasses. Then she took them off, squinting. Marcella knew she was not supposed to ask. She waited. Toni put them back on. "That guy over there," Toni finally said, reluctantly. "He looks like Jed McClatchey." Marcella felt her chest go icecold. "I mean, not exactly. But there's this thing about him. I don't know."

Marcella swallowed hard and tried to keep her breathing very even. She followed Toni's gaze and saw a man she immediately knew was not Jed. His hair was lighter, he was a little taller. And yet. Toni was right, there was something. His body was slight but muscled, with a tautness around his shoulders. There was something watchful about his face; he had the same straight nose. She looked again at Toni. As her daughter watched the man, Marcella saw wistfulness break through her disdain.

She reminded herself that Toni worked at Jed's house, that of course she knew what he looked like, had, in fact, probably spent more hours with him than Marcella herself had. And also that she was with Callie and with Jed's nephew and niece, and it would be like Toni to notice the resemblances, to see the shared genes manifesting themselves. That she had happened to notice a person who looked nothing like Jed and yet did—that she had caught Jed's essence, something that one might say could be detected only after concentrated, deliberate observation—it meant nothing. Nothing.

"I don't remember Jed very well," Marcella said, and prayed she would be better than usual at pretending.

"He's definitely not my type," Toni said, too quickly. "He's too short. Way too intense. It would give me a headache to be with him."

Marcella felt like a butterfly skittering along the surface of a vast sea, with nowhere to land. Stay aloft, aloft. "Well," she said, "he's had tragedy in his life."

Toni shrugged dismissively. "Yeah," she said, and her face softened, and Marcella saw that she found Jed romantic, for the very reason of his losses. She wanted to shake her and shout, *Silly girl!* But of course she wouldn't. Toni was confiding in her.

"He's cute, though," Toni was saying. "Right now he's going out with some girl he met in a bar."

"That doesn't sound good."

"I don't think it will last. Callie said with him nothing ever lasts."

"Well, then." Marcella lay back down and closed her eyes. Her thumping heart seemed to slide into her stomach, and she thought she might be sick. Trying not to clench her teeth she said, "I would listen to his sister, Antonia. He is too old for you anyway."

"Not really. Eight years."

"Eight years! And not your type. You say."

"No." Marcella heard Toni's voice moving, heard her turning over, arranging herself. "Definitely not. Can you untie this for me?" Marcella opened her eyes and saw Toni's arm crooked around to her back, holding the straps of her bikini.

"Darling, it's indecent."

"You're just saying that because you're my mother."

"Exactly," Marcella said, marveling at how easy this conversation was. She hesitated for good measure, and then leaned over and untied the strings, and sneaked in a quick stroke down the smooth skin between Toni's shoulder blades.

"Mom."

"There was sand."

"Mo-om."

Her heart was still beating too fast, her stomach swirling, but Toni was so unquestionably real, flesh of her flesh so beautiful, so bright, that Marcella could almost pretend this absent Jed was someone she—they both—had imagined. If there were any real threat, she could will it gone. Toni's head was turned away, her eyes closed again, and so Marcella could stare to her heart's content. At Toni's age, Marcella had been about to lose her mother, about to meet her husband . . . but clearly, obviously, Toni was far too young for such things. Marcella felt as though she were sprouting roots of iron into the sand, anchoring her forever to the earth, next to her daughter. *I will always be here,* she thought, *always with you, if you want me.*

She had never imagined she would have to remind herself of this truth.

It was hard to know when it had started, the retreat from her own child. But she did remember one day, in particular: Howes Beach, the sun high, the tide going out. Toni had been three, and there had been something mildly celebratory about the day—perhaps it was a weekday that Anthony had taken off? Back then they had gone to Mashantum for only a few weeks each summer. It had felt like a vacation, not an exile.

She had been sitting in a chair under a beach umbrella, her finger holding her place in the book on her lap—a lady of leisure. Her other hand lay across her stomach, which was still flat. But she was newly pregnant, again.

Her doctor had already told her there was nothing to worry about, that there must have been something the matter with the first one she'd lost and she should be grateful. There was no reason not to believe him; Anthony did. "Of course there's nothing wrong with you, Chella," he'd said. "It's just a little bad luck, that's all." At the time she had wondered if he was so entranced with Toni that he really didn't care, but when she had told him she was expecting, a few days before, the exultation that had blazed across his face told her she had been wrong. He had picked her up and begun to swing her around but then thought better of it, and as he set her down, very gently, she thought, *Of course we are the same. Of course we both want more children, a houseful.* He stroked her cheek. "I've made you happy," she had said.

"Of course you have," he said. "Don't cry. Don't cry, Chella."

She thought of that now and wished he would look up at her. But he and Toni had just moved a few yards farther away, looking for water for the moat of their sand castle. She could still see them clearly, though. Toni was wearing a pink ruffled bathing suit and her blond hair was in two high ponytails—she had approached Anthony that morning with her brush and elastics and said, "Ponies, Daddy?" with that exquisite pout on her face, and it had amazed Marcella yet again to see Anthony put down the newspaper and, of all things, carefully do Toni's hair, while their daughter held so still, as though she knew she had performed magic.

Now Marcella watched as Toni pointed to the moat, and Anthony began enlarging it. Anthony gestured to a tower, and Toni began a matching one beside it. They worked so earnestly, with an unconscious, easy rhythm that Marcella thought she and Toni rarely had. Toni looked so serious, her little pink bottom in the air, digging for the wet sand; she reached deeper with her shovel, then straightened suddenly, reached for a different shovel, and backed up right through one of the castle walls.

She whipped her head around to survey the damage. Marcella, in her chair, held her breath, mildly worried: did this mean a tantrum? But instead Toni turned back to Anthony, her eyes wide, and clapped her hands to her mouth in an enormous *oops*. He looked at her in surprise and then started to laugh, just as Toni realized her hands were full of sand. Abruptly she ended her performance and began to make faces, trying to spit it out.

Anthony wiped her face with the edge of his shirt, still laughing, and then took it off so he could really scrub. Toni's eyes were screwed shut, her lips pursed enormously so he could wipe there too. Marcella watched the muscles shifting in Anthony's arm, his chest, and thought, *Look at what I have given her. Look at my child's father—he is so handsome, he adores her!* Marcella thought that if she had had a father she never would have known how to play the coquette as Toni did, in all her three-year-old glory. Surely now Anthony would catch her eye. The smile of camaraderie was waiting on her face: *Look at our star of stage and screen!* But he didn't. When he had finished cleaning Toni's face, she pointed imperiously at the moat and he went back to digging, but as soon as Toni was absorbed in her next task Marcella saw him sit back on his heels and watch her, as though she were the most fascinating creature he had ever known.

It didn't matter. It was what she had dreamed of as a child, a father not only to treasure her but somehow also to blot out her mother and grandmother—to send them firmly upstage out of the lights, to beckon Marcella herself down. Not that Marcella had dreamed of being any kind of star. She had wanted only to have the lights bright enough around her to make life clear, to make her clear to herself. In the gleam of Anthony's love, Toni would never doubt herself.

Yes, Toni was a genius for wanting Anthony. It was clear she wanted him more, waited for him, craved his attention. Marcella knew that in the many hours she was alone with Toni, she could have asserted her-self, staked her claim, erased the look of waiting from Toni's face. But she was not sure exactly how; she refused to scold and shame as her mother had done, or wheedle and scheme and dominate like her *nonna*. Besides, there was so much of Marcella's love. Toni was wise to take it for granted.

Yes, never mind. Never mind. Marcella had laid her book in the sand and let her other hand steal over her belly. Maybe this new child would stick to her side, as wide-eyed at the world as she sometimes felt herself to be. Carefully, she would ease him down into the lights, so he could be seen, so he could see. She had thought, that day at the beach, *We will watch your father and sister conquer, my darling, and then we will welcome them home.*

And now, years later, she looked at Toni beside her, asleep in the sun. She had thought for so long about invisible children. Mirages in her desert. But how ridiculous not to see what she had. Toni, only Toni, was right here.

On Friday, just after talking to Marcella, just after turning around and pointing himself back toward the Cape, Jed pulled off the highway for gas. He was in some cute Connecticut hamlet and the service station was next to a stone bridge, and as he stood there pumping the gas into his tank he realized how foreign it all was, how he was really so goddamn provincial. The air was different: in Atlanta it was soft and lazy, at the Cape it was salty and sharp, but here it seemed clear and uncomplicated. The trees were different too: they were not the Cape's scrubby pines or Southern loblollies or poplars but instead oaks and maples, sturdy, balanced trees out of a picture book. The pretty little prewar bridge spoke of an older, more steadfast civilization than the interstates of the New South. He could practically feel the self-satisfaction oozing from the ground. And there, hanging above the bridge, among the green foliage of a sugar maple, was one rogue spray of autumn-red leaves. Time was rushing, like the traffic out on the highway, always faster and faster. Everyone was hurtling along, he could not stop them. But, goddamnit, he just wanted to stay still, stay the same, with Marcella. Who had turned him away.

He felt a presence behind him, like his own conscience. He turned around. It was, instead, a dark-skinned man in green coveralls. The man's patient yet slightly superior expression immediately annoyed him. "Yes?" Jed said.

"It's full-serve," the man said, with an accent Jed couldn't place. He held out his hand for the pump.

"Oh," Jed said. "Sorry." He did not move.

"I'll do it, sir."

The name patch above the man's pocket said *Bob*. Jed resisted the impulse to ask if that was really his name. "I'm almost done," he said. "Thanks."

"I will do it, sir," the man repeated, unsmiling.

"Almost finished here, don't worry about it—"

The man didn't answer, didn't withdraw his hand.

Jed looked at the man's empty hand, the white script *Bob* on his chest, then around him at the lovely little village where things were done a certain way and no other, and though his mother had taught him manners, yes, she had, he suddenly didn't care. "Jesus fucking *Christ*," he said, and yanked the nozzle out of the tank and jammed it back into its holder, reattached the gas cap with a violent twist.

"Uh, sir—"

"*What?* What *now?*" The man had backed up a step and looked intensely disapproving. He cut his eyes to the pump. Clenching his teeth, Jed took out his wallet and thrust a couple of twenties at the man, whose eyes had somehow become his mother's. *Jed, really.* When had he ever been angry at his mother? When had he not listened to her? She had kept him in line, he had let her. He had always, deep down, agreed with her. *That is no way to act. Jed, really.* The man was no longer holding out his hand. "Take the money," Jed snarled, and finally the man took it.

He got in the car and slammed the door. Through the closed window he heard the man saying "Sir, sir," but he could not look at him. He started the engine. Possibly the man wanted to give him change but more possibly he was going to scold him or pity him, and Jed could not bear either; most probably the man just thought he was another garden-variety preppy prick, and that thought was the most bearable, but Jed was not going to wait to find out. He screeched out of the driveway and toward the eastbound ramp, over the little Yankee stone bridge, and all he could think was, *It's Marcella's fault, all her fault, goddamn her, all her fault.*

Someday I am going to lose her too.

He could not stand it. For a second rage encased him so that he was paralyzed, he couldn't see, but he pushed it away, he knew how to do that, God he was good at that—push it away and go back to *Goddamn her* or, even better, *Goddamn Toni,* and even though he knew it was childish, he let himself seethe this way for the rest of the drive back to Mashantum.

JED WAS FURIOUS all weekend. It was frustrated desire, was all it was. It came up, mutated, at odd times. He figured out a way to show a little of it: he said they had had a fight. He and Marcie. On the phone, on the way. Yes, about her parents, but that wasn't all—and *no,* he couldn't fucking explain. Billy and Callie began to tease him about another one biting the dust, but when he barked back at them they didn't say any more. Callie actually looked afraid, which made Jed even angrier.

Early Sunday evening, when he could stand it no longer, he called. He had become a creature of habit. Marcella was his habit, and Toni had deprived him. She had interrupted their precarious rhythm of weekends. As the phone rang he thought, *What if Toni is still there?* Simple—he'd hang up—or maybe, damnit, he'd just say *Hello, guess who*—

But Marcella answered. "Jed," she breathed, her voice warm and glad.

"Is Toni—"

"She just left."

He waited a beat. Finally he said, "Do you want me to come?"

"Yes, darling. Please."

He hung up the phone. His hand was shaking but it was the tremor of fatigue, of tense muscles finally relaxed. He could go. He could go. He felt like he had been straining at a starting line and the barrier had been removed so suddenly that he might simply fall over.

Collect yourself, man. Fool.

He had begun speaking to himself this way.

He might have gone straight for his car keys and headed out the door if he had not heard voices just then in the next room. Of course, he would have to tell Callie now, and Billy. As it turned out Callie was already in bed—she'd taken to napping at odd hours, disappearing at a moment's notice. Billy was watching a Red Sox game in the living room. "Hey, look," Jed said. "I, um, just talked to Marcie."

Billy, slouched on the sofa, his legs wide and slack, looked at him with a grin spreading over his face. "Her parents gone?"

"Yeah. I'm going to go see her. Uh, now. Just overnight." Jed did not sit down.

"Make-up sex. Hard to pass that up." Billy stretched his arms over his head, yawned. "But, you know, I've got to leave tonight myself. I'm just checking the score here." He lowered his voice. "Callie might freak."

Jed looked at Billy. He knew Billy wanted an ally and there was a time when Jed would have been glad to do it, but now there was something he wanted more, much more. He said, "Yeah, she might. Why don't you drive up tomorrow morning?"

Billy's voice hardened almost imperceptibly. "I've got an early meeting, bro."

"Yeah. You've got a wife too." He was swimming in rage again, floodwater from another storm, he knew that, he didn't care. Gritting his teeth so he didn't shout, he said, "This whole setup is fucking crazy."

"Tell Callie," Billy shot back, as if he had been waiting for a chance to say it. "I didn't want her to move to the fucking Cape." They glared at each other and then Billy slumped a little and turned away and said, "I'll call Toni Atkinson. Maybe she can stay over."

"Don't," Jed said instantly. His fist was clutched at his side. He was furious but also now cunning: all he had to do was drive back to Marcella, and he would not, not, not give that up. "Callie needs family," he said. "She needs *you*." As he said it, Jed knew that there was something looming in front of him, some reason to worry about Callie. He should sit down with Billy, figure out what was going on—but not now, not now! "And what about Jamie?" Jed said, shameless. "Sleep outside in that tent again with him. He would love it. My God."

Billy looked at Jed strangely. "He's in bed already," he said. "He's asleep."

"Oh. Right."

"Besides," Billy said, sitting back into the couch, something about his posture determinedly cheerful, "I'm still recovering from *last* night. My back'll never be the same."

Billy was a good man, a decent man, Jed knew this very clearly— a man who had once been one of his best friends. And this had changed. Jed did not know when it had. But he was still family; that didn't change; he didn't want to see this wide stripe of weakness running through Billy, part of the larger thing Jed was refusing to see. He knew that Billy didn't want to talk about Callie either, not really, and that he should make him, but he wasn't going to. All he wanted was to get back to Marcella's house and bed and arms, for just a little while. He felt quite clear about that. He would not think beyond that. Jed stood there, not backing down, and finally heard Billy sigh and agree. "I want to meet her, though," Billy warned, and although his tone was light his eyes were not teasing anymore. "I want to see what all the fuss is about," he said. "Because this seems like something different. It seems like there is something serious going on." He was no longer smiling. "Am I right?"

"You're right."

Billy looked at him, unsmiling, as though he wanted to say more, a lot more, maybe he wanted to talk after all, but Jed took a step backward. "I owe you, bro," he said. "Tell Callie I'll be back tomorrow night. Late." He was out, he was gone, he was already flying down the highway; his anger with Billy had not faded but instead migrated to a place where he stored pieces of puzzles, puzzles he fully intended to solve, later.

TONI WAS DRIVING DOWN THE DARK INTERSTATE and singing to the radio. It felt good to be alone in the car. The darkness outside seemed comfortable. Normally she didn't spend a lot of time sitting around analyzing; she'd rather move, rather act. But what else could you do on a car trip besides sit there and think? And she let her mind wander and finally settle on this odd new warmth she felt toward her mother.

Toni had always thought her mother was beautiful, but like someone from another world almost, sort of untouchable even though Marcella was always literally touching *her,* smoothing her hair or stroking her cheek. Toni had felt her to be far away, had always wanted more more *more* of her, not the love Marcella lavished on her but something else she couldn't name. The house when she was growing up did not have the relaxed feeling of her friends' houses and it was easier for her to blame Marcella than Anthony. Wasn't it her mother's house, anyway? Wasn't it her mother who was always there?

But she had had a good time this weekend and had not felt homesick in her own bedroom as she often had before. Her mother seemed happier for some reason—was that why? That didn't really make sense. Her mind wandered and settled on something different: it was Callie, Toni decided. Callie had opened her eyes, although Toni did not know how to tell her this. When she watched Callie with Grace, Toni felt an unfamiliar jealousy, wanted the feel of that tiny body, the charge of that utter neediness. And it was weird, but she also was afraid of Callie, and admired her, and had a very strange contempt for her, and one day she realized she was just afraid of what Callie had been through. She thought, *Well, at least I have a mother.*

It had been a revelation. She was not the kind of person who sat around and thought about what she already had. But then when she fought with her father over the Woodshed and her curfew and his ridiculous fear about her growing up—what was she supposed to do, never change?—calling Marcella seemed attractive. Before, she would have been mad at her mother even as her fingers dialed her number.

So she had that warmth behind her. She would rather have stayed with her mother, lounged around and gone to the beach with her, had a real vacation. She would rather not have had a job to go back to, and *babysitting* on top of it. But there was little Grace. And there was Jed. It was exciting and disturbing to think of him. Just as she was not used to appreciating her mother, she was not used to pursuing some guy and not having him like her back. She wasn't used to *pursuing* at all. The prickle of her thoughts became uncomfortable, and when one of her favorite songs came on the radio she turned it up as loud as it would go.

WHEN JED AWOKE AT MARCELLA'S on Monday morning, the bed beside him was empty. He slipped on his boxers and walked barefoot down the hall. The house was silent except for the first birds singing outside. The kitchen and living room were deserted.

He found her on the porch, sitting in one of the wicker armchairs, looking out into the trees and the growing light. At the sound of his footsteps in the doorway she turned to him, unsurprised. He said, "I thought you had disappeared in the night. I thought I would never see you again."

She only smiled, a soft smile that he knew should be all comfort.

He sat down in the other chair. For a minute or so he did not let himself look at her. Instead he, too, looked out at the trees, the well-shaped Connecticut hardwoods, and the just-risen sun gleaming through the leaves. The morning air was already hot, but it did not make him feel the same disquiet he had felt Friday at the gas station. Instead he had the odd feeling that it was fungible, the air, that he could make of it whatever he wanted—that he could will it into summer heat or winter cool merely by the force of his thought. For a moment that sort of power seemed to hang in front of him, ripe for the taking. Then it was gone, and he remembered that it was Monday morning.

He had never spent a Monday morning with her. It was the most quotidian of occurrences and for that very reason he knew it was extraordinary. He tried to tell himself that Monday didn't matter; after all, it wasn't as if either of them had an office to go to. In Mashantum the days flowed together and he often didn't know which one it was, except that now he was always waiting for the weekend—but here he was, in Connecticut, on a Monday. He did not want to feel out of place. He did not want to think he had any order to fit into, any progression to make. He knew that Callie would be at home waiting for him with her flat hopeless eyes, and he resented that great weight. What if he told Callie about Marcella? Told her what—he couldn't tell her everything—part? But that wouldn't work. The edges would become confusing to him, he would forget what he could say and what he couldn't. He and Marcella would never be ordinary, he would never walk through Mashantum hand-in-hand with her. And he felt the fury again, a discrete thing, an obstacle. Its edges glowed white-hot. He had to turn away again. Turn his back although that way he left himself exposed. You had to try to see what was coming.

He turned to Marcella. "You woke up so early," he forced himself to say. He stood, and took her hand and drew her up to him.

"I am an old woman," she said, with a flick of her fingers. "Sleep isn't as important as it used to be." She looked at him from under her lashes. She rarely flirted. Her lack of guile was one of the things he loved. He didn't want her to do it now.

So he didn't answer her. Instead, he leaned down and took the collar of her filmy bathrobe in his teeth. Slowly, he pulled it off her shoulder. Underneath she was naked, as he had known she would be; still he drew in his breath. He blew on her nipple and watched it harden in the air, and then he cupped the weight of her breast in his hand. Her eyes fluttered closed, and he felt himself stirring, the anger retreating. He licked his forefinger and then circled her nipple, and, softly, she moaned.

He watched her face. He had made her float, she was aloft, there was no morning, no Monday, no sun growing hot above the trees. He needed to keep watching her, to not think, and so he pushed himself, hardening, against her, parting the silky cloth between her legs. She opened her eyes, and as he watched, her focus gradually sharpened and narrowed and came to rest on him. "Don't come back from wher-ever you were," he whispered. "Stay there. I want to come with you." Now it was her turn, though, to say nothing and she only pressed into him.

He felt as he always did, that he wanted to lay her down right there, take her on the floor. He forced himself to breathe slowly. He felt his blood pumping. "Feel what you do to me," he murmured. Her pressing became a grinding; the bathrobe fell off her other shoulder. He leaned down again and licked one nipple, hard, then the other, and she cried out.

Yes, he was floating now too. He untied the robe and it fell to the floor and he lowered himself to his knees and tasted her, softly. Gently he pushed her legs farther apart. Her hands gripped his shoulders, hard. He tasted her, again and again, and he could tell from her trembling that she could barely stand. His tongue was flickering, he was gripping her thighs, he was nearly holding her up and now she was roiling above him, collapsing in a long unbroken series of fluttering cries, and so he did lay her down, on the heap of her robe. Her hands groped for him, pushed his head back down and then her hips rose and shuddered and shuddered again. He held himself to her until she twisted away, moaning, and then finally, finally, he rose up and plunged into her. As soon as he was in her, he was safe.

She was all softness and warmth and her scent was everywhere. He remembered they were on the hard floor, and began to thrust with exquisite slowness. There was no separation between their bodies. He did not want to feel any space at all. He was sweating and was sure the heat was only his but then all at once, as though they had been signaled by his body, the cicadas began wailing their song of late summer. They buzzed up into their impossible pitch as though they were screaming *over, over,* and he caught Marcella's face between his hands and buried his fingers in her hair, and as he pushed himself into her as deep as he could go he whispered what he had been thinking since he walked onto the porch: "I will never get enough of you. I will never have enough. I will never have enough."

FOUR
THE
SMILE

Both Marcella and Cecil loved good food, but on the Cape going to a restaurant together was a risk they did not often take. Even several towns away from Mashantum they worried about bumping into a friend of a friend, although it was not as dangerous as it would have been, say, for Anthony, a resident of Boston and the Cape all his life.

Once, they ventured to the mainland, to a seafood place near Plymouth Rock. It was filled with tourists in shorts and had cartoons of Pilgrims on the menu, but they laughed and ordered anyway. As Marcella picked at her overcooked stuffed flounder, she said, "Someday, darling, I will cook for you. A real meal."

"Please do," Cecil said, his eyes crinkling at the corners in the way she loved. "Rescue me."

"No, I mean it," she said. "We will find a kitchen, and I will cook, and we will have a real dinner together."

As she said it, she realized it was more than a joke, or a dream—it was a need.

They made it happen, finally, in August. Marcella had had to plot and plan and lie to arrange a night away and she was sure that Cecil had too, but they did not discuss these exertions; they never did. She also was trying hard not to tell him that she felt the cooling late-summer days ticking by like she was a condemned woman. Every night she could physically feel that the sun was setting earlier, the world darkening in response to their looming separation. She was having trouble sleeping. Her life had broken and she did not know how to fix it.

Cecil had found a better-than-average motel with kitchenettes, in Sandwich, still on the Cape but far from Mashantum. Marcella had planned an entire menu and shopped for all the supplies. They would bustle about the stove together, they would set the table and eat by candlelight, she would feed him a weekday supper—she had purposely picked dishes that were not too elaborate or fancy, dishes she remembered from the kitchen table of her childhood.

That night in the motel suite they turned on the radio and poured wine into the glasses Marcella had brought. She tried to bustle, to let her usual kitchen rhythms take over. Cecil said he wanted to help and so she set him to chopping an onion, but when she glanced over at him a minute or two later he was still trying to peel it with the tip of his knife. "Go," she said, laughing, taking it from him. "Go sit, you silly man." Cecil, his hands up in surrender, retreated.

"All I really want to do is watch you," he said.

"That is all you are good for," she retorted, smiling, and then turned her back and quickly finished the onion. She felt his eyes on her and all at once wished he would look away, that she could hide, just for a moment, and gather herself together. She couldn't care less that he could not cook—neither could Anthony—but she had handed him a knife and told him to do something he never did, and thus had exposed all the things he normally did do, without her. As she had watched him struggle with the onion, a look of earnest concentration on his face, she had seen him with Betsy, in a kitchen that had been theirs for years and years. She had seen Betsy, in her unassailably competent way, taking care of him. She felt the weight of their routines, the life to which he would soon return. She would not be in it and the weight pressed down, making it hard to breathe.

His hand was on her shoulder. She turned to him and his eyes were so blue and she thought with an unfamiliar ferocity, *They are mine. The only eyes that truly see me.* "Why, Chella," Cecil said. "Chella, what's wrong?"

"It's only the onion." She brushed at her eyes with her free hand. "I am too sensitive." She made herself smile at him and he smiled back and in her head she heard an old voice, her mother's: *Ungrateful girl.* Of course. She told herself, *See, this is what I want. This, here. Enjoy it now. What I wanted is here, I have it, I cannot believe it!*

She cooked the dinner and carefully arranged the plates and they sat down to eat with music playing in the background, but she could not keep hold of the dutiful happiness. The mauve tapestry motel furniture clashed with the bright yellow Provençal placemats and napkins she had brought. They were new, so silly, she had spent too much money in a little gift shop in Mashantum Village. She had wanted something unfamiliar. A false trousseau. In the store, as she was paying for them, she had felt a moment of dizzy joy, but that was now gone. In front of her, the food she had cooked, hot and good, was nevertheless unreal. It did not match the reality of the room, of the synthetic sofa cushions where so many other people had sat, the bed where so many others had slept.

She heard Cecil say, "This is delicious."

She knew there was appreciation, even love, in his voice but she could think only of the things he would never say—what Betsy cooked for him, what they talked about at dinner. How this was simply a duplicate of something he already had. "We are just playing house," she said.

"Please don't cry." He reached out and took her hand.

"It wasn't the onion," she said.

"I know."

She sat with her fork poised foolishly in the air and fought,

fought, as hard as she wanted to—but not as hard as she could. She gave in and whimpered, "I want this."

There was a pause. She never forgot that pause. She was terrified, she had broken a rule, she had spoken of the future and of the ultimate breaking of rules. She wasn't terrified of what Cecil would say—he wouldn't rise from the table, displeased, punitive. He wasn't Anthony. She thought instead that leaden silence would descend, that their connection would be broken, which would be the worst thing of all. She had been ungrateful. She had asked for too much.

Instead Cecil said softly, "I do too." She looked up at him. "I want this too."

She didn't answer and the moment lengthened. She took in the still life of their half-eaten dinner and half-drunk wine. She looked at Cecil's blue eyes full of desire. At, not into. She thought of that later. Not into. Still, he nodded, and she felt the smile rise on her face. She would let herself believe it. This moment was the pivot. The world had changed, everything was different. She would keep breaking rules. She would break all of them.

On Tuesday morning, sitting at the kitchen table, Callie said, "It's August."

Jed got up from the table and poured himself a second cup of coffee from the pot near the sink. "Since when are we paying attention to the calendar?" he said. He had gotten home from Marcella's late the night before. The very strangeness of these mornings was becoming familiar, how he felt yanked out of Marcella's house by some alien force, how he was sleep-deprived, still swimming in the feeling of her body, of the timelessness in her bed. He turned around, his back now to the window, and watched the sun slant in onto the worn linoleum floor.

"I don't want to go back," Callie said.

"No, me neither."

"What do you mean?" Callie said, more alert.

He shrugged. "I mean, I don't want to go back. Maybe we could just stay here." There was silence. "Why not?" he continued, and glanced up at Callie. She was looking at him intently, and he paused, and thought of the sensation that he had with Marcella: all the world falling away, all other people shades, the two of them the only living, dimensional beings. He had spoken without really considering his words, but now the idea was carrying him along by itself. "I mean it, Cal," he said, his voice gathering force. "I'll do whatever you want. I'll move to Connecticut. I'll stay here with you. Say the word." *Here is the answer!* he thought. *So simple! It will keep going, it doesn't have to stop. It doesn't ever have to stop—*

She looked at him hard for another moment, and then her eyes seemed to cloud over and she looked away. She waved her hand vaguely. "All right," she said. "Sure. We'll just stay."

"Callie?" Jed said. "You hear me?" Now he was the one suddenly alert. And that was his father's voice—*You hear me?* Meaning, if you listen, all will be well; if you don't, there will be trouble. It was a voice from a long time ago. "Callie?" But she was looking out the window; she seemed to know he was not really paying attention. *Hear. Here. Not here.*

. . . and when you swing for godsakes don't aim at the house. You hear me? The humor in his father's voice. No, he was not in trouble. Jed was out in the yard, here in Mashantum, right where Callie was looking, the sun in his eyes like now, the yellow August sun—only they were looking the other way, toward the house, it was close to sunset. His father's arms were around him, showing him how to swing a bat. The two of them stood together, his father's body behind his to demonstrate the straightening of the elbows, the twist of the hips. On the bat there were four hands. Jed was safe—no, he was engulfed—but had he felt that then? or was it only now? In his mind the scene played forward. He wrested the bat away and turned on his father—but before he could do what he craved and dreaded his father was gone, a hologram extinguished. And he realized that murderous anger had lessened too, and rearing up new and strong instead was guilt he did not want to feel. His father's warm happy voice. The big hands over his. How long Jed had wanted not to remember those things. "Cal? You hear me," he said. It was no longer a question. "Anything," he said. "We'll stay here. Bar the door. You and me."

He needed her to answer. She needed to say, *What are you talking about? What are you afraid of?* He didn't know what he would tell her. He would surprise himself. She would ask and the truth he didn't yet know would simply fall from his lips—and also the truths he did know: *This is whom I go to see. This is what I know now. This is why I keep escaping. Why I keep leaving you.*

But she didn't say anything, and he realized she wasn't really looking at him anymore. She didn't see his stricken face, the mouth that was declaring his loyalty too loudly. He wouldn't, couldn't, tell her where he went. She had burrowed back down deep within herself, and he would not say *You hear me?* again.

HE CALLED MARCELLA that night. Grace was asleep, and while Callie was putting Jamie down Jed took the cordless phone outside. He didn't think Callie would listen, but he still wanted to be well away. He sat in an Adirondack chair facing the house. Behind him was the pool and the screen of trees between their house and the neighbors'. In the darkening twilight, he could pretend that he was backed by wilderness all around. That he was completely alone.

On the other end of the line Marcella's voice murmured on and he felt desire as always, but somehow it was not blocking out his other thoughts. He wanted to interrupt and say, *Something is wrong with Callie, and I cannot figure it out, and I don't want to.* He wanted to say, *I sit by the pool with your sexy daughter and she isn't you, and I hate her for it*—but of course he couldn't say that. Or what about: *Make the summer stop. I will never get enough of you. Make it stay early August forever, almost over but not quite. Do it!*

But instead he said, "I was thinking I might call the detective. In Atlanta. It's still an open case."

There was a pause and he wondered if this idea frightened her. Finally she said, "*Caro,* what would you say to them?"

"I—I would just see. If they had anything else in there besides Dad. I wouldn't have to say anything about you."

"You could, darling, though," she said. Her voice was stronger now. "It will not hurt me. Darling, I don't see how you could not."

"I don't have to tell them anything. I would just check in. I have the right to do that."

"Oh, *caro,*" she said, and he didn't like her voice, tender and reproachful at once, like she was speaking to a child. "It has been so long," she said. "And what if they find who did it? You would just have a face to hate."

He was stunned with how little she understood. "I *want* a face," he said. "Just one. Don't you see? There's a person out there. Some— *animal*—"

"I know."

"Well, then," he began, but he stopped, overwhelmed by possibility, by how much things could change. If he told the police what he now knew, if it became public, if Marcella was the one in the paper— although surely no one cared anymore. No one but him. He said, "He still could have done it. My father."

"What?"

"He could have hired someone. Or something."

Her voice came like ice. "No."

He had never heard it like that before. There, she had done what he wanted her to do, told him what he already knew in his gut. "But someone did it," he said, like a child.

"Yes."

He was tired, he was not sure if he wanted to keep moving on this path that was beginning to seem more like a circle: you knew nothing, then something, then nothing again, but a new nothing. "I just want you," he said. "I just want to see *you.*"

Marcella said, "Then I will try to make you see me." She knew him, she would do what he wanted. She told him about her garden and the beach that day, and the translation she was working on, and the cold soup she had made for her supper; in her words were pictures, her straight back standing at her counter, her hands chopping vegetables she had picked, the sharp knife flashing. She knew that her house was both a dream and a home to him; he heard her trying to weave the spell. But he was not soothed. Instead of seeing her, he watched his own house. His father's house. As the sky darkened, the light in the windows grew yellow and warm. He saw Callie moving in front of Jamie's window upstairs, pulling the shade, and then the light went off. It should have been homey, comforting, but instead the sight struck him as troubling and false, something prematurely extinguished. A few moments later he saw Callie downstairs, framed in the window above the sink. She stood there turning on the water, picking up dishes, but then stopped and was still for a long time. "Darling?" Marcella said.

"I'm here." He wanted to tell her how the yard around him was going from deep green to blue to black. He wanted to tell her that he could feel the presence of the pool behind him, the undisturbed surface looking almost solid. He wanted to tell her that sometimes he thought of her there, still, at that party by the pool, years before, that the image of her now still had not quite erased the dream of her then; that he did not know what the dream had been, what it still was, even though now he had her. What the yearning was. He felt anger rising. "I want to tell you about this house," he said. "Where I am."

"Do, caro."

"But I won't," he said. "Because you know it already. Don't you."

He heard her hesitate. "A little," she said.

"Do you know it well?"

"No."

"Because you didn't come here. You and Dad."

"Jed."

"Tell me," he said.

"We didn't go there."

"Where did you go?"

"I am not going to say, darling."

"Why not?"

"It will not do anyone any good."

He wanted to unleash the rage now, but he couldn't. He loved her soft voice. The same voice his father had loved. "Goddamnit!" he cried.

"What? What is it?"

"It's no good," he said. "It's no good." He stood up. What if his father had sat in that very chair? What if he had talked to Marcella on the phone while watching the light in his own son's bedroom window? Why could he not get used to these thoughts—and what would happen if he did? "I want to see you," he said. "I want to see you *now*." He wanted her essence, wanted her wrapped around him like air.

"I'll come," she said. "I'll leave in five minutes."

"No."

"I will!"

"You can't. You can't come here."

"I will stay somewhere else."

"No. You can't come here. You know that," he snarled. "You know that perfectly well."

He listened to her crying. "Chella," he said, and waited, not for her but for himself. Let her name hang there, let it be his. Let himself pretend. "I'm sorry. I don't know why I had to do that. I'm sorry," he whispered. "Marcella." And she was a miracle again, the long-limbed creature in the chair by the pool, and he felt utterly lost, so far from her.

He watched Callie at the window. Finally she moved away and he could no longer see her. But he imagined he could feel her impatience, her need, emanating from the house. "I have to go," he said.

"Jed—"

"I'm sorry. I'm sorry. I have to go." His whispering voice shook. He was furious, again, that he could not stop wanting her. *I will never get enough of you.* He heard now what he had really said: *never.*

CALLIE MADE HER WAY through her days with a growing sense of dread that sometimes felt, sickeningly, like anticipation. It was as though she were a citizen of a country that was about to be invaded; she felt hazy denial, yet knew also that escape was futile, that the normalcy of the days as they ticked by was surreal. It was all about to collapse, even though she did not know who the invading forces would be, or even what the battle was. She knew only that even on the most beautiful, the most perfect days—days of blue sky and soft breezes and long naps taken by her children—she felt that the perfection was an evanescent gift she was not entitled to accept.

It was a cloudy day, however, when Grace first smiled.

The air was oppressively muggy and the sky looked like it would break open and pour any minute, only it never did. Every so often there were five-minute sprinklings that barely wet the earth, and when they stopped the air was more humid than ever.

"God," Jed said, sitting at the kitchen table, "this day is constipated. Someone needs to get the mail moving." This was something their grandmother used to say and Callie knew she was supposed to laugh, but she didn't.

Nevertheless, the saying seemed to please Jed. He heaved himself up to begin unloading the dishwasher, and as he rattled plates and stacked cups he began to riff: "Give the weatherman an Ex-Lax brownie," he said. "Give that man a bran muffin."

Toni, who remained wilted at the kitchen table, drinking Diet Coke, said, "Oh, shut up. Jamie will just get going about pooping."

"He doesn't know what a bran muffin *does*," Jed said. But from the family room piped a voice: "Who pooped?"

Jed sighed. "No one, buddy," he called.

Jamie appeared at the door. "But Toni said—"

"She didn't mean to say that."

"She said 'shut up.' "

Jed was silent. Toni's eyes flicked to him and then she said to Jamie, "I shouldn't have said that, sweetie. Those are *very* bad words."

Jed had turned back to the dishwasher. Callie could see his back, rigid; the hostility was there as plain as day, and she shrank from it. "Stop it, you two," she said. There was a catch in her voice that she had not intended. Jed and Toni both glanced at her, surprised, and words failed her—"Oh, you two," she repeated, knowing that what she said made no sense, wondering why she was linking them, knowing it would bother Jed but only vaguely wondering why. Then Grace gurgled in her swing, so serious, always serious, the battery-powered ticking of the swing like a clock, Grace the pendulum, and Callie thought, *Why are three of us here and a machine is holding my child?* and she went over and plucked Grace out of the seat and left.

She went straight to her bedroom and closed the door but she immediately regretted it—it was even more stuffy than the wide-open kitchen and she felt that on the other side of the closed door Jed and Toni would be exchanging accusing looks and Jamie would be about to come after her with his automatic jealousy. But she was not alone, she reminded herself. She laid Grace down on her back on the bed and propped herself up on her elbow beside her. "Oh, Gracie," she said, looking down into her baby's face, expecting nothing in return.

Grace was looking at her very intently, with her dark blue infant eyes that were starting to lighten. *Will she be blue-eyed?* Callie thought. *Is it possible that this baby will end up a lighthearted blue-eyed child?* And she was beginning to feel the oddest piercing dread when the corner of the baby's mouth began to go up and her cheek tightened, a lopsided leer for a moment, and then the sun rose, the most lovely smile, her child *there* as she had never been before, beaming at her.

"*Oh.*" Callie's eyes filled with tears. "Oh, Gracie. Oh, baby"—and yet still the beauty of Grace's smile was hazy, it beat against Callie like a moth softly bumping a screen, did not quite reach her. "Gracie, Gracie," she said, and finally hugged her because she knew she should, and because she could not look any more at her face. "Gracie." Her love must exist and she tried to send it to her child but it seemed a heavy package of too-sharp corners, it would not go; she herself was heavy, helpless, and could not give anything, she sat on the bed and laid Grace back down beside her.

There was a knock at the door. "Cal?" She didn't answer and the door slowly opened. "You decent?" Jed said.

"Yes." She remembered their script. "As I'll ever be."

"What's wrong?"

"She smiled," Callie said. "Finally."

"She did!" Jed swooped down and scooped up the baby. "That's my girl!" He waltzed her around the room, a huge smile on his own face, and then cradled her in front of him. "Do it again! Yes, my girl—there! There she goes." He stopped and was quiet a moment, smiling back at Grace. "She's a genius," he said.

"Yes," Callie said. "A little smiling genius."

"I think she's going to have blue eyes."

"Like Mom."

"Yes," he said. "Like Mom." He did not look at Callie. "Hey. Do you want to take a break? Go for a run? Alone?"

"You're trying to get rid of me?" Callie heard herself say things like this with wonder. A nefarious assistant had taken over her body, one who could imitate her voice, be jaunty and flippant in a way she herself had forgotten. "You just want to get it on with the babysitter," she said.

"As if." He raised Grace to his shoulder.

Callie gave him a wicked smile but she herself was lost, she could not feel her own face, these expressions. "Well, I'm leaving Jamie as chaperone," she said.

"Foiled again." Jed rolled his eyes elaborately, but she could see he was pleased—he just wanted her to joke, to be her old self. It was all anyone had ever wanted, for her to behave. Surely she could remember how. How to keep the engine of herself running and running. As she walked out of the room her knees almost buckled with fatigue, thinking of how she could not ever let herself stop.

CALLIE LEFT AND THEN, to escape from Toni, Jed took the baby and went for a run himself. Grace dozed off in the jogging stroller, as he had hoped she would, and once she was asleep her peaceful silence seemed to cocoon them both. He went a new route, west toward Yarmouth Port, hoping to avoid Callie, even though he wasn't sure which way she had gone. He was just guessing. He didn't see her.

The close muggy air made the sweat stream down his face as he ran. It pleased him. He needed to be alone and to be cleansed.

When he got back, he had a fleeting hope that Toni would have taken Jamie somewhere and the house would be empty—but he heard their voices in the backyard. He almost turned around and ran away again, but he wanted to jump in the pool. He wheeled the stroller down the path to the patio. At first he saw only Toni, spread out on a chair. "Where's Jamie?" he barked. Toni pointed limply to the sandbox just outside the gate. "Oh," Jed said. "Hey, bud, you want to go swimming?" Jamie shook his head.

He put the brake on the stroller. With a little luck Grace would be out for another half hour. He walked to the edge of the pool and looked down into the blue. He shouldn't make a sudden splash, wake the baby—instead he would sink down into the silence, maybe not come up. . . . He slid into the water. It slipped over him like cool silk. He sighed under water, bubbles gushing from his nostrils, and didn't rise to the surface until he couldn't make any more.

Toni had moved to the chair nearest the parked stroller and was sitting up, looking into Grace's little face. "I want to hold her," she murmured.

"Leave her be. She'll wake up soon enough."

Toni shrank a little. She gestured again at Jamie, who was making revving sounds in the sandbox. "He is way into those trucks," she said. "I *asked* him if I could play with him and he said no." She gave a wounded little smile.

Jed didn't answer. He heaved himself out of the pool and lay down on a lounge chair without drying off, the water a temporary shield against the heat. He closed his eyes; he was not going to look, again, at Toni's impossible body. Marcella had never looked like that—she was finer-boned, less sturdy. Less American. If he had met Marcella when she was young—if—not possible—

"I know you think I'm slacking off," Toni said.

He kept his eyes closed. "No. I really don't."

"You do."

"Toni," he said, "you have no idea what I think about anything."

She would be looking back at him openmouthed. He turned over onto his stomach and nestled his head into his folded arms, facing away from her, his eyes still closed. Marcella loved her. They rarely talked of Toni but he had seen Marcella's face, her eyes, go so soft, glowing, when they had. Marcella had told him to turn around, she had sent him away—

Grow up.

Toni said, "Um, what's wrong?"

"Nothing's wrong," he said. "I promise." If only she weren't there. If he just thought it—*go away, go away*—

"Um. Is everything okay with Marcie?"

He laughed, in spite of himself. God. "Everything's fine."

"That's good. I guess—things are getting serious?" His eyes still closed, Jed shrugged. "Oh," she said. "Or not."

There was another long silence. He felt her waiting. Finally Jed turned his head and sneaked a look at Toni from the shelter of his elbow. Her arms were around one folded leg, her cheek resting on her knee. He had seen Marcella sit just that way. He closed his eyes again. "It's not really like that," he said.

"Like what?"

"Serious, or not. I mean it is serious," Jed said, wondering why it felt so good to say it out loud. "It is deadly serious. But it's not going anywhere."

"Why not?"

"Because it can't, that's why."

He felt Toni trying to think of the right question. Finally she said, "How old is she again?"

Jed hesitated. "Twenty-six."

"I thought you said twenty-four."

"I was wrong."

"And she's from where?" Toni said.

"Connecticut."

"I know, but what town?" Toni said, as if this evidence would clar-ify the impossibility of seriousness.

"I don't remember," Jed said. "It doesn't matter. She's in Manhat-tan now."

"But—"

"It's just not going to work." He had never said this out loud either—to whom would he say it? "It can't ever work," he repeated, hearing the hardness in his own voice. "Why are you asking me all this stuff?"

He felt he was dancing on the edge of a cliff, and wanted someone to push him over.

"I don't know," she said. Finally he opened his eyes again. She was looking at him with a strange mixture of fear, determination, and allure. "Why are you letting me?" she said.

Her eyes were more hazel than Marcella's. He did not want to notice this. He could almost hear a voice jeering at the edge of his mind—Billy's, maybe—*You could have had this, getting it on with the babysitter, yah, yah,* but it was like looking at another country through the wrong end of a telescope, eerily familiar yet completely inaccessible. He sat up and swung his legs over the side of the chair. "I guess I'm not," he said, and forced a smile. He would rather have glared. "I'm done. I'm out of here. Lots of things to do. It's my fucking vacation— oops. Scratch that." As soon as he cursed, Toni's eyes flicked reflexively to the sandbox. Then back to him, panic rising. The gate hung open. Jed looked around. "Where is he?"

Everything in him was stopping, the weird excitement, the ugly black swirl of anger, and then Toni was standing, looking past him. "*Stop!*" she shrieked, and then behind him there was a splash.

He turned and knew without question that the howling emptiness at the deep end was where Jamie had been standing, and then he was running, only a few steps, more of a leap, and it was odd but he could only feel his feet, first anchoring him to earth and then flexing, pushing, helping him leave it; then he was under water too, his eyes open, swimming down. Jamie was sinking slowly to the bottom, looking dreamy. Jed grabbed his arm, pulled him in; he had not expected him to be so heavy; meanwhile behind him Jed felt another plunge but he ignored it. He had swum all the way to the bottom, they were nine feet down, and he pushed off, all feet again, his lungs were exploding because he had not taken a deep breath before and Jamie was heavy and he could only kick and he seemed not to be moving—but then he felt the fat hollow metal bar of the ladder and that was earth too, and he held Jamie with one arm and pulled himself up with the other and breathed.

Panting, he collapsed into a chair. He was holding Jamie too tightly. "What were you doing?" he cried. "What were you doing? We tell you all the time not to go to the deep end! We tell you *all the time!*" Jamie was coughing and Jed pounded his back, too hard at first, God, but he had to drive it out of him, any water he had breathed in. He wondered where Callie was and what she would say, and all the things he could not say and could not even think swirled back into a dark seething mass and he shook Jamie and said, "Don't *ever* do that again! *Do you hear me?*"

"Don't talk to him that way!"

Jed whirled around. Toni was coming up the ladder, her clothes clinging to her, her hair hanging wet on either side of her face. Her eyes looked huge. Under her wet shirt her breasts were high and round and perfect, her nipples hard dots, God, all he could feel for a moment was their firmness on his tongue—God, what *was* he? What *was* he? "You were supposed to *watch* him!" he snarled.

"What about *you?*" Her face was affronted, amazed.

He let it out, let it go, he was not stopping anything anymore. "It's your job! It's your *only* job! It's the *only reason you're here!*"

Jamie was crying harder and Toni looked at him and her lip trembled. "Buddy," she crooned, and her arms went out, and to Jed's amazement Jamie leaned toward her. Jed yanked him back. "I think you should leave," he said.

"What?"

"You heard me. We're done here. You can leave. Callie will send you your last check, or whatever. That's it. We're done. Get out."

Over in the stroller, he saw the flail of a little hand, and realized Grace was awake. He would have to pick her up too. But his arms were full of Jamie, and he would not put him down. Toni made a move to the stroller, and it was all Jed could do not to bare his teeth at her. She stepped back. She said, "Callie's my boss. I want to talk to *her*." She lifted her chin and he saw it—Marcella, squaring her shoulders, her face set, the gesture he'd never called pride or stubbornness but rather bravery. It was the same movement and for a moment Toni was Marcella before him and his heart leaped but then she was not.

Grace began to cry, tuning up the way she did when she was hungry. Toni looked toward her, agonized, and Jed saw how easy it would be for him to back down, how quickly Toni would forgive him. But he stood up, clutching Jamie, his wet round head against his cheek. He stepped in front of the stroller, blocking Toni's view, and whispered, "I'm not kidding. Please get out. Please just go."

WHEN MARCELLA HUNG UP she found herself literally counting the days. It was Wednesday, he had left on Monday—would she see him Friday?

But he had fired Toni.

He had been contrite, telling her, but she saw that he assumed forgiveness. And she was about to give it to him, to say, *Darling, I understand*—but then she took a breath, cleared her mind. "You are apologizing to the wrong person," she said.

She felt his moment of surprise. "I know," he said. "But—I can't have her around anymore. I can't."

Marcella didn't answer. She had never been angry at him before, never. It seemed a very long time since she had been angry at anyone. "You were rash," she said. "She did nothing wrong."

"Maybe. But it's done. You don't understand—it's better."

She did not want to think about what he was saying. "I am hanging up now," she said.

She knew she shouldn't call the Mashantum house, she was a bad liar. She picked up the phone.

It was Anthony who smoothed the way—something, she knew, he would have been very surprised to learn. He immediately said, "So, are you calling about our daughter's latest escapade?" She almost said *yes*—oh, she was no good at this. She pressed her lips together. "Marcella? Are you there?"

"Escapade?" she said.

"Apparently," Anthony said, "she almost let the little McClatchey boy drown. Jed McClatchey very sensibly fired her on the spot."

"Oh, now, Anthony, surely she didn't mean—" Marcella stopped herself. She did not want to say too much.

"It doesn't matter what she meant or didn't mean," Anthony said. Marcella imagined the regular, handsome lines of his face. Every time she spoke to him, it confused her, even now—hearing the voice of a person who was once hers, his tones and verbal gestures as familiar as her own clothes. She heard now that he was furious and also somehow fearful, the fear itself making him angrier. "I'm glad she's out of there," Anthony was saying, "do not mistake me. But not this way." There was a silence. *"Marcella?"* he said, impatiently. "Here. Talk to her yourself."

"Hi, Mom," came a small, sullen voice. In the background, Marcella heard footsteps going away, and a door slamming.

"Darling," she began, and was astonished to hear Toni start to cry.

"He's been awful," she said.

"Jed?"

"No, Dad. He said how could I—did he tell you what happened?"

"You tell me," said Marcella, and Toni gave an account remarkably similar to Jed's, repeating over and over, *I should have been watching.* Marcella felt herself relaxing with an unfamiliar pride. She had been afraid—no, sure—that Toni would lie, not accept responsibility—why was that? When had she decided to have no faith in her own child? "Darling, how scary," she said. "But it sounds like nothing. The little boy is all right."

"He—Dad—he said it was unforgivable—but it was only a second—I jumped in too—"

"I know, *cara.*"

"And Jed *was* awful. Do you—do *you* think it's unforgivable? What I did?"

"Of course not. Most things are forgivable," she said.

For a moment she could hear only ragged breathing. "I'm sorry," Toni sobbed.

"Honey, you don't have to apologize to me."

"I mean, that I can't talk—he—Mom, he hates me. Jed hates me. It wasn't just today. That's why he fired me. He can't even stand to be with me."

Fury and guilt crowded Marcella's chest. "He was very unfair. But he couldn't hate you, darling."

"Damnit, Mom, he does! And I don't know why! And I—I guess you knew I didn't hate *him*—" Toni tried to laugh, but it came out as a hiccup. "I can't stop thinking about him."

Marcella heard herself say, "I am coming there."

"Here?"

"Yes. I am coming to see you."

"No—I mean, I could go there—but Dad said I have to go out tomorrow and look for another job—and that's just stupid, he knows that it's, like, *August*—I swear, Mom, sometimes he isn't rational. And he won't let me take the car—"

"*Cara,* I am coming there." She might see Jed. She might see him on the street, on the beach. She would have to turn away. "Right now."

Toni tried again to laugh, this time more successfully. "What, are you coming to beat him up?"

"Your father?"

"Jed. You'd fight him for me, right?"

"Carina," Marcella said, "I'd do anything for you."

It started one day when Callie was standing in the analgesics aisle of the drugstore, Grace beside her on the floor in her carrier. Callie was having trouble remembering what she had come for, but instead of feeling hopeless, as she did these days at the sign of any small failing, she instead felt a blip of strength, almost of comfort, at the sensation of being surrounded by the fruits of modern medicine, something like a book lover would feel standing in the stacks of a library. All the boxes and bottles before her. All the antidotes to pain.

Then she remembered: Jed had asked her to get ibuprofen. She took down a box, but instead of putting it in her shopping basket she held it for a moment. The box was a pleasing shape, like a very small present. It fit well in her hand. She shook it and it rattled slightly, like a toy, muffled by the cotton packing. She tossed it into her basket, and then she saw near it another medicine, one she had seen advertised on TV—a new one that lasted a long time, that was extra strength, revolutionary. It was right in front of her. She looked to her right and her left—she was alone. She took the largest size off the shelf. What would she do with it? It was like a weapon. It was a substitute for the weapons she really wanted, the lethal ones that haunted her dreams like lovers. She knew that this bottle of pills would really do nothing to her, and yet the size of it—five hundred capsules—surely that was worth something? She put this one, also, in her basket. She scanned the aisle and, since she was still alone, chose several more—things she could drink, things she could chew. She knew it all meant nothing and yet she felt a strange, illicit power.

After that, she visited the drugstore often. She accumulated a box of pills that she kept high in her closet, away from Jamie. They seemed as shiny as plastic jewels, treasured, worthless bits that a child might collect—dull nickels, bird feathers, odd-shaped rocks that she could count over and over. She knew, too, that she could accomplish nothing with any of it, that it was a child's solution to a problem. And then one day it struck her, the thing she had known already, that had been waiting patiently to be found. A different thing. There was a bottle in the medicine chest, it had been there all along—pills from the hospital, from her emergency C-section, the ones she hadn't taken because adrenaline had made her impervious, she had thought, to pain. The small brown bottle was still almost full. She took it from its ordinary place and buried it in the box of aspirin and Tylenol and cough syrup like a nugget of gold.

There was something Marcella had to figure out. She did not know what it was, but she could find it only in Mashantum. She had not been there in seven years, since the divorce. Since the last summer with Cecil.

In Connecticut, the heat had broken in the night with a thunderstorm, and when she had woken that morning, before she talked to Jed and then Toni, it had been dank and cold. It felt like fall, or perhaps as if summer had never been. She knew these August changes were temporary and thought the weather would improve as she drove east. But instead it grew rainier and grayer, and when she drove into Mashantum Village, at six o'clock, the sky was twilight-dark.

When she had first come to the Cape as a bride, the low gray-shingled houses and wild meadowy greenness seemed completely of the New World. She had assumed that she was going to a summery resort, and could not reconcile the scrubby vegetation and hunkered-down architecture with her memories of the expansive, sun drenched Italian coast she had gone to as a child. Of course she had gotten used to it, and Connecticut after all was very similar; but driving down Route 6A again she felt she was twenty-two, and everything was strange once more. She felt ghosts all around her, of her former self, of Betsy, of Cecil. She felt his absence as though he had just died. She would not see him walking down the sidewalk. If she went to the beach, he would not be there swimming. He would not be in his whites at Nobscusset. She could not run into him, accidentally on purpose, no matter how hard she tried. It surrounded her, this reality of loss, which she had thought she'd already absorbed. She shouldn't have come. She should have come back years ago.

Once she was in Mashantum proper she drove to the deserted beach, and stayed in her car in the parking lot while the rain drummed on the roof. She left the car running, at first thinking she would leave any minute, but finally gave up and turned off the ignition. It was an effort to lift her hand. Memory was engulfing her, not like thought, but like pungent smell, or sound. It surrounded her, whispered against her skin, transformed her. If she looked in the mirror, surely years would have fallen away; she would have fainter crow's feet, no gray hair; she would glow. She did not look. In front of her, the waves crashed against the seawall. The roar came through the closed windows.

She tried to remember something particular about Cecil, something small, maybe his face in the sun, here on this beach. But instead she thought, *Jed is here*. Instead of Cecil's gentle warmth she felt Jed's heat. That sweet watery contentment had been nothing— she was wrapped in rough cloth now, she was being rubbed awake, she was alive. Jed. God help her, they were so close here, Jed and Cecil, she sat in her car dumbfounded, Jed and Cecil, they were both here—but only one was alive—God, she could not think that. He was close, she could feel him, *it was possible to have him now*, she would only have to go to him—break it all wide open—but then the impossibility of it snapped her straight. She had missed him before, but she had never felt this rebuke, as though he were telegraphing it from his house, a mile away, wanting her. She should not have come.

Another car drove into the lot and she shrank down, looking at it furtively. She did not recognize it or the driver, but someone she knew could drive by any minute. She would see people she knew this week-end. It was inevitable. She would have to smile, be polite. Be only Toni's mother. No one's lover.

Toni. Baby girl, not a baby—Toni was waiting too. By coming here, Marcella was making a gesture, and gestures were important, especially to Toni; as a mother, Marcella had not made enough of them. Hand on the key. Turn it, back up, drive away down the sandy road. She remembered the way to Anthony's family's house. And she knew she should forget everything else. Toni was the only reason she was here.

ANTHONY HAD LAST SEEN MARCELLA the previous spring, at a par-ents' weekend at Toni's college. Marcella had seemed the same to Anthony, the same, that is, as she had been since the divorce: sad, a bit faded. He did not flatter himself that he was the source of her sad-ness. There were moments when he caught the old elegant beauty but they had not made him nostalgic, and he had reflected grimly that this must be recovery, all he could expect of it. He did not let himself consider that grief for his old longing was longing in itself.

But the Marcella who was walking through his door now, on this rainy night, was different. She was vivid. She stood in the kitchen and shook the rain out of her hair—she had not put up an umbrella for the walk from her car to the house. "Let me take your coat," Anthony said.

"Oh, that's all right." Unspoken was that she would take Toni and leave as quickly as she could.

"You're looking well." He did not say that there were still droplets in her hair, that they shone like silver in the bright kitchen light.

"Thank you. And you, Anthony," and her eyes met his and flicked away, around the room. "It is odd to be here," she said.

"You're always welcome. You could have stayed here, you know."

"Oh, no. The motel is fine for me."

"Motel? You're not at the Isaiah Howes?"

"Full," she said.

He wasn't sure he believed her, and thought, *That is a change, if she can dissemble so easily.* Probably she had not wanted to get into conversations at a bed-and-breakfast. She wanted to be anonymous. He stopped himself from asking which motel; he didn't need to know.

"So," he said, "you have come to rescue Toni."

For the first time she met his gaze directly. "And from what does she need to be rescued?" she said, and laughed. A hectic flush rose in her cheeks, and her eyes grew a trifle wild, and then she looked away again, at anything but him. Still her old doelike skittishness—but what was different? Her eyes brighter, her gestures a little more sure? Marcella said, "I just missed her. She is"—her voice dropped conspiratorially—"so sad about this babysitting affair. There are times when you need to see a person in the flesh, the telephone will not do—ah! *Bella!*"

Toni was in the doorway and Marcella was looking at her with undisguised delight. "Hello, love!" she said. Anthony could only watch Marcella's face. Damnit, there it was, that look, she'd had that look since he had met her, it was so rare—that exquisite joy she bestowed on a face she loved. The essence of what he wanted, what he had thought for so long he had: someone who would never stop wanting him.

V

After the summer of Cecil and Marcella's affair, when Marcella returned to Wellesley, she had trouble eating, and even getting out of bed. Yet she felt not gloomy but euphoric. In the mornings after Anthony and Toni had left, she would sit immobile for minutes, even hours, at a time, her coffee cold at her elbow, her mind racing. She was waiting to break the rules.

She was obsessed with images of Cecil. She had never been to Atlanta, and it bothered her tremendously that she had to make things up, that she was not seeing him as he really lived. She imagined a master bedroom, a vast, quiet, carpeted space, and pictured Cecil and Betsy in it—not in bed but in quotidian weekday scenes: Cecil with a fresh shirt half-buttoned in the mornings; Cecil sitting on the edge of a yellow chintz-covered bed with a shoehorn in his hand; Betsy padding across the floor in stocking feet, her hands up, fastening an earring. It took Marcella a while to see that these were the tableaux she had always envisioned for herself. She hadn't realized her dreams were so mundane—merely security, continuity. She supposed—she knew—that there had been intimacy like this in her life with Anthony, but it had not had the depth or the sheen she had always imagined, it had not quieted some fluttering frightened thing in her, and she saw that she had sucked all the meager poetry out of her life as it had existed and given it, in her mind, to another man— her lover—and his wife.

It became impossible for her to distinguish what was hope and illusion and what was actually Cecil. He was very busy with projects that did not involve travel to Boston, and they had not seen each other for weeks. If she heard his voice on the phone, she yearned, but sometimes she was not even sure it was for him. When they talked, she tried to keep her confusion and excitement and nameless fears out of her conversation, and even her tone.

So now she was lying to two men.

Finally, one day in mid-October, sitting in her own kitchen, still in her bathrobe, something in her that had been whirring in endless circles finally stopped. She felt she had been traveling and traveling and had finally come to the edge of a great sea and could not see the other side. She walked outside to her patio and stood in a pool of sunshine, looking around as if she were in a stranger's garden. The asters had seeded themselves everywhere, and now they had taken over, attended by a few late, lazy bees. The day was bright, but she felt that her life was unreal, and what was real instead was Cecil, far away. Cecil who had said he wanted her. She would not wait any longer. She would say she had to see him, would say they had to make plans. She would explain that she was at the edge of this vast, turbulent ocean and she was frightened and he would comfort her. She had not expected to feel so grim. She wanted her elation back.

As if the gods had heard her, she received an invitation to a ladies' weekend in the mountains of North Carolina—the ideal cover. She called Cecil, determined not to sound plaintive, but he in his turn was eager, ardent. "Asheville is just a few hours from here," he said. "I've got business there. Or—I can make business. I'm sorry it's been so long. I can't wait this long again," Cecil said.

"No. It is horrible."

"Chella?" He sounded breathless. "Chella, I'm going to make it so we don't have to wait anymore."

She did not breathe herself, did not even move, at the other end of the line.

"I'm going to fix it," he continued. "Somehow. I don't know how—I don't—but I'll figure out something—I don't know, Chella. But I have to do something. I do."

She whispered only, "Yes. Please."

The next morning at breakfast, Anthony said, "You seem to have snapped out of that mood."

She was standing next to the stove, briskly stirring sugar into her coffee. "What mood?" she said. She tapped the spoon on the edge of her mug, a sharp metallic *clink.*

"Whatever was bothering you. Something was."

She put down the spoon. "It's hard to adjust to the end of summer," she said. She made her voice light.

"Ah, yes. My sun goddess." His voice sounded both sardonic and tender. As he left, he kissed her on the temple. She looked up at him and thought several things at once: *he's handsome, still is.* And, *he saw me. He noticed me.* And, *if he saw I was sad, why didn't he say anything till now?*

And then: *He knows.*

As the door closed behind him, she knew with absolute conviction that he knew. Not who, probably. But the fact of her infidelity—he knew. She stood rock-still, rock-cold. She never would have thought he could take such a thing so lightly.

Surely she was wrong. How would he know? That night, when she told him she was invited away for a weekend, he barely looked up from the papers he was reading. "North Carolina? Why so far?"

"It's her birthday. Her family has a house there. She's flying everyone down." She gave a little laugh. "It is nice to have such money, I'm sure."

He raised an eyebrow, and her composure began to wither. "I didn't realize you were such good friends. Well, have a good time."

She had the strangest impulse to tell him right then. Maybe it was what he wanted. He was trying to confuse her with his nonchalance, to get her unbalanced. She felt herself at the edge of the sea again, the water even stormier, deeper. She was almost afraid to speak but she said carefully, "I am going to bed now. I'm tired." She smiled woodenly at him and left the room.

A journey, she thought, as she climbed the stairs. Movement: that was the important thing. She had never been to North Carolina. She had heard the mountains were beautiful. Mountains, not sea— she was going to the safety of old, old earth. The trees would be flaming yellow and red and orange in their annual, temporary death, but for her and Cecil it would be the beginning of a new life. Yes, she believed that. She had left herself no choice.

CECIL HADN'T MEANT for any of it to happen. That would be clear to anyone who watched him, anyone, that is, who could see into his brain and his heart. At every stage of his affair with Marcella Atkinson he'd thought, *I'm going to end this.* And then he would look at her and think, *Just a little longer! Just a little more!*

But then Marcella had made him that dinner, at the end of the summer, and that brief false domesticity made him realize how he had been holding himself apart from her. He had always felt a little superior, felt that really his marriage was happy while hers was miserable—that she needed him more than he needed her. But sitting at that meal, he had been blindsided by the words that came out of his own mouth: that he wanted a life with her. That he'd meant it. Since then he had been avoiding her—yes, he'd admit that—but only because he was so shaken by this new truth. In an ascetic moment he'd even left the damn bathing suit, his favorite talisman, at the Cape. He'd regretted that more than once.

So he'd meant what he said on the phone, that he couldn't wait so long to see her (even though this waiting had been of his own doing). But he hadn't said the rest. He hadn't said that he couldn't keep waiting while he was *with* her either. Being with her always felt like a fantasy that was too tantalizing, too rich; he realized he was waiting for a life with her that was dependable and real and ordinary. He'd been waiting for his heart to slow down, but instead it felt like it was speeding up and he was growing desperate for some kind of peace. Yes, he had to figure something out.

He did not know for sure what he was going to do until after he had driven into Asheville. If he had been farther south, it might have all been different—if he had not been surrounded by the autumn leaves already past the peak of their color (in Atlanta they were just beginning to turn), if he had just been somewhere familiar, even Mashantum, where he had felt no harm could ever come to him. But here, driving down strange dark mountain roads to the house where they were to meet, it became clear to him that newness and strangeness would not give him peace. Before long he came to a solution, and it was not the one he had anticipated. His extraordinary Marcella was waiting for him, like a rare masterpiece that jolted with its beauty—and he did not want, anymore, to be jolted. He pulled off the highway then, and just sat, in the cold dusk.

Years ago, before he had even met Marcella, it had occurred to him once that marriage was like an elaborate journey—the kind nineteenth-century nobles, say, might take, with multiple, massive trunks, and servants, and first-class trains with dining cars and china and starched tablecloths, and private staterooms with soft beds, where only the gentle clacking underfoot and the moving scenery out the window reminded you that you were on a journey at all. But an affair, he now knew, was a hasty, lean escape. You took only the clothes on your back; you were practically weightless, sleek and swift, a new man. It was exhilarating, at first. But now he wanted to go back to that comfortable way of traveling. The comfort was home. The home he already had.

When he saw her, when he told her, it would feel like he had snuffed out everything wondrous in his life. God, his heart. It hurt, it was breaking, but he had a brain too, one that understood duty. Was he weak to pick duty over desire, or strong? It didn't matter, he didn't have to decide. Duty was comforting that way, he thought, even though he did not feel comforted. But in a few minutes he started the car and got back on the road.

Duty. It meant the decision was already made. The more he thought about this idea, how neat and symmetrical it was, the truer it seemed. Someday, he thought, a long time from now (and it was then that he knew, even in his misery, that he would be all right), he would say this to Betsy. He knew she would agree.

IN A MOMENT OF UNACCUSTOMED BOLDNESS Marcella had—well, not *told* her friend about Cecil. But implied. The friend had immediately understood and had not even been shocked (which in turn shocked Marcella), and as a result Marcella found herself that Friday night not in a hotel but in an empty house that her friend had borrowed on her behalf, an ersatz mountain lodge with massive, rough-hewn beams on the ceiling and cashmere throws on the deep sofas, and enormous chandeliers made of antlers. She knew the place was rather ridiculous but still it pleased her: it looked like a house in a fairy tale. She let herself be giddy and as she waited for Cecil she thought about how she would say this to him and how he would agree and how they would know such a setting was, for the two of them, entirely appropriate.

But when he walked into the house she knew something was

wrong. He kissed her, but she felt something inside him closed and separate. Then he stepped back and looked up at the double-height ceiling and towering fieldstone chimney with a half-smile, but under it his face was pale. Abruptly he sat down on one of the sofas and, not looking at her, began to talk. He told her he was not brave enough. He could not make it, them, work. He had lied.

She said, "You didn't lie."

"I didn't know," he said. "I didn't know until—I just figured it out, Marcella. I didn't want to know. I wanted to believe I could do it."

She almost said, *I am not a challenge! I am not some sort of event!* But she had never said a sarcastic word to him before, and did not want to now. "Cecil," she murmured. "Darling. Don't cry."

He said, "You deserve better."

"Don't say that. Because it is not true."

His face was still averted. "You do."

"I said, don't say that." He looked up in surprise, but she wrapped her arms around herself and walked away from him. She felt completely alone. Always before, even when she was lost in her thoughts, she had imagined that he was somehow with her, thinking just as she did, even if he didn't say so. She wondered now how much of this connection she had manufactured. She was not sure which was worse—if she had made it up, or if it was real, and she was still losing it.

"Marcella," Cecil said softly.

She felt his voice was cradling her. "I love you," she said, her back still to him.

"I'm sorry."

She was about to scream, *Are you sure? Are you sure?* About to cry, *But I am the one you love!* She must not turn around. "Cecil," she whispered. "You have to go."

"I love you too," he said.

She couldn't stand it, she had to turn, she looked and his face was awful. Still she wanted it, him, so much. She stepped back. She wanted to crouch, to shrink. She stayed straight and upright but she had to pretend she was iron; the effort was exhausting. "You have to go," she said again. She just wanted it to be fast, like ripping off a bandage. Only a moment of agony. "Please go," she whispered. "Darling, I am going to begin begging." She did not say that she meant begging him to stay. She closed her eyes.

"Marcella," Cecil said again, and she heard his footsteps coming toward her, and then he was caressing her face, and in spite of herself she was leaning into his touch. After a moment he stepped away and she felt him moving, retreating, and then she heard the door, and only then did she open her eyes and was immediately filled with wild regret. She wanted to see him! She had given it up, that last look! She ran to the window and could see only a shadowy figure lit up for a moment in the car, and then the light went off and the car drove away.

She stepped back from the window like she had been slapped. She was stupid, a fool. Who cared if she had kept her dignity? She wished she had fallen at his feet. She thought of a hundred arguments she could have made. She nearly writhed in regret, waiting for the door to open, for him to be standing there again. But it did not open. She sat on the sofa, then eventually lay down on it. She would stay here tonight alone. She would wait for the briars to grow over the windows, and to go to sleep, and never wake up.

SOMEHOW SHE MADE IT THROUGH the rest of the weekend. After she had rejoined her friends, she claimed sickness and stayed in her room, and if her friends, who were, indeed, not terribly close friends, knew what was going on she didn't care. On Sunday night, when she finally got home, it was already dark. From the driveway she saw a lone light on, in the living room—she could tell it was the one next to Anthony's chair. Should she tell him how she had spent the last forty-eight hours? Suddenly she wanted to. But she wanted only comfort, and how could she be so deluded as to look for it here? She pressed her lips together.

The living room door was closed. That was not usual. She quietly opened it, closed it behind her, and Anthony looked up. She was astonished to see that his eyes were red, and she couldn't help it, she forgot her resolve and went to him, knelt beside his chair. "I'm sorry," she said. "It's—over. I wanted to tell you—" But his shattered expression didn't change. It had been there before she spoke. It did not have to do with her—not entirely. "Anthony," she said, "what is it?"

"You don't know," he said. She shook her head. "I got a phone call," he said. "Yesterday afternoon. From Fred Sprague."

He did not identify them as he normally would have, removed as they now were from summer and the Cape. *The McClatcheys from Atlanta,* he might have said. Or, *from Mashantum.* Neither did he look at her for signs of recognition, or acknowledge that there would be any reason that their acquaintances, the McClatcheys of Atlanta and Mashantum, might already be on her mind. She saw only one quick look, helpless, not accusing, as he told her that there was terrible news about Betsy. Dear God. About what had happened to Betsy.

She couldn't speak. Her brain moved in slow motion: what did it mean? As Anthony gave the few details he knew, she understood that even though she bore, technically, no guilt, she would be bound up in this forever. But then Anthony was pulling her up, they were standing and he was holding her, no, clinging to her, and his mouth was on hers. It seemed he didn't want her to speak, and she thought of herself in the mountains, alone in the strange overscale house dreaming of curling choking vines, and she thought, *Yes. Smother me.* But still, when she was able, she said again, "I'm sorry. I'm sorry."

It was only then that Anthony got a shade of his familiar imperious look. "No!" he cried. He gripped her shoulders and swallowed, lowered his voice. "I don't want to hear it!" he said.

A horrible idea came to her and she tried to pull away, crying, "You don't think that *I* had anything to do with this? That I—"

"Of course not!" He looked wilder than ever. "Please." He framed her face with his hands. "Of course not. Of course not. Not you."

He was holding her too hard. But why was he holding her at all? Wasn't he angry? She could feel every finger pressing into her skull and, crazily, she thought of when they had first met, the beginning of their marriage, when he had sometimes seemed overcome by her, and had held her as though he couldn't believe she was there. This was not the same at all and yet something reminded her. "Beautiful Chella," he was saying. "Marcellina. Don't."

When he took his hands away, there would be white fingerprints on her cheeks. "Anthony," she said, and her tears were rolling down.

"Why are you crying?" he demanded, and then he was kissing her again. He was like her old lover of long ago, eager and hungry—no, he was not, he was more desperate, he was fierce. But how could he want her? His mouth was so rough, he hadn't shaved, his face was scraping her raw. Now his arm was around her waist, supporting her but also commanding, and then he had her on the floor and he was pulling at her clothes. His mouth was on her throat, her breasts, her belly, he drove his tongue deep inside her, and she could not help herself, she cried out, she arched off the floor. "Anthony," she said, and she was begging now, and she wasn't sure what she was begging for. For him to love her, along with wanting her? She had given up on that.

As though he could read her mind, he pulled away. He stood up and she wondered if he was going to leave, and didn't know if she wanted him to or not. She was half-exposed and ashamed there on the floor and she began to curl into herself, and he said, his voice soft again, "Please don't be afraid. Please." He was unbuttoning his shirt, unbuckling his belt. His trousers fell with a soft thud.

Part of her was disgusted because she had wanted to be with Cecil, and even though she hadn't been, wasn't he too close in her mind? *My Cecil, my Cecil,* no longer hers. Betsy was his instead, *Betsy,* it could not be true, she could not believe it, and she knew there was horror on her face and she wanted to explain it but—maybe Anthony understood? He was kneeling now before her; the hair on his chest was gray and she knew it was soft and she wanted to touch it. She had not touched him softly in so long, hadn't wanted to. And then he was on her, inside her, and he started slowly and then he said, "You were all I ever wanted, Chella. All." She didn't answer and then he was moving harder, too hard, he was saying her name and it was as though he wanted to bury himself in the churned-up earth of her. She was afraid now, of him, of everything she had done. "Didn't you care?" he was saying.

"Yes." Oh, how she had cared, and cared, and failed, and ruined it all. She had been sent here for this man right here in her arms, and she had lost him. She had had a task and it was simple, it was only to make a happy life, but she had not known how. And she wanted to tell Anthony but all that came out was sobbing and it didn't matter, because he knew all of her shame, all of it—

"Ah! God!" he cried, as though he could hear her thoughts. His arms were too tight around her, and she thought he wanted to stuff her inside himself, consume her completely, and she thought, *Let him, let him.* Maybe that was what she had been fighting for so long. *Let him.* She thought of Cecil and her mother and her *nonna* and Anthony's glaring parents and all the people she had ever tried to do things for, and then came a thought that utterly surprised her: *No, none of you matter; I will hate you all.* They fell away. There was only Anthony right here. It was her last chance. She would give up all her doubt for him. His face was twisted and he roared into her ear, only breath, no sound, and his breath kept coming and she fought him, they fought together, up and up, she convulsed around him, she offered her cries to him in the cupped palms of her hands.

When finally he was still and heavy on her she couldn't think, not at first. And then her arms went around him again, but gently this time. He seemed to wake up, and then tense. It was as though he were listening to her hands. He moaned, and buried his head in her neck. One of his hands went up and touched her cheek, and his head was shaking silently *no*.

Then the hand went away and he stood up. She caught only a glimpse of his face, ravaged and empty, before he turned and walked to the door, and opened it, and went through, and closed it quietly behind him.

A MONTH LATER, Anthony told her he wanted a divorce.

Toni had just gone upstairs to bed. Marcella and Anthony were in the den, Marcella on the sofa and Anthony in his wing chair by the fire. They were having a drink together, silently. This was their new habit. Marcella would have a glass of wine, which she usually didn't finish. Anthony would have several whiskies, or rum and tonics, or whatever happened to be in the liquor cabinet. By the time Marcella would get up to go to bed, she could tell, by the glassy way he looked at her, that he was drunk. They had not made love since the night he had told her of Betsy's murder. Quite often, he never made it up to the bedroom at all; she didn't know if he slept on the sofa or if he spent his nights, upright and fitful, in the chair. By the time she and Toni got up in the morning, he would be gone.

He spoke to her only perfunctorily and she was too upset by his chilly pain not to answer in the same way. She was waiting for him to say more, or for her own bravery and resolve to come back.

It was two weeks before Christmas. That very day, Marcella had gotten down the boxes of decorations from the attic, and they stood in an unopened stack in the front hall. From where she lay reading, she could just see the corner of the largest box. She had no interest in decorating anything, celebrating anything, but her heart was breaking for Toni, who looked bewildered at the strange, wordless disintegration of her parents. Just the day before, she had asked, in a tentative way that was completely uncharacteristic of her, when they were going to get a tree. Marcella was lying there telling herself that she had to rebuild somehow, could not stay stunned, that the ruins around her were substantial enough to make something strong and new. And then Anthony began to speak.

He said the one sentence. She didn't answer. She didn't know where to begin; she was surprised that she was surprised. She felt as if she could muse on that forever. The silence stretched. Finally he said, "You can have the house. You can have whatever you want."

She said, "I don't want the *house*."

It seemed she should say next, *I just want you.* Had she seen that on TV? In a book? Which book? Her mind wandered, dazed. *I just want you.*

She began, "I had an affair—"

"Please be quiet," he said, with effort.

"Is that why?" He didn't answer. "Because it was wrong. It's over. I ended it—"

"*Please*, Chella—"

"—that weekend! That Friday! *That night!* You knew, didn't you?"

"Jesus! Jesus—"

I just want you. "Please help me!" she cried.

"I can't. I can't help anyone," he said, and he buried his face in his hands. She had never seen him do that before, ever.

She got up from the sofa and knelt beside him, and thought that was what she had done before, that other night, when he had needed her—for the first time in a long time, it seemed. *Did* they need each other? Hadn't they made a pact, long ago, to turn to each other? For some reason she thought of her *nonna,* all in black, the rings, her only jewelry, glittering on her long fingers. *Someday a man will need you,* she had said. Marcella had believed her *nonna* to hold uncanny powers; now she knew that had only been the old knowledge of another generation, but still she wondered, did she mean Anthony? Cecil? Maybe Cecil needed her now. But she couldn't call him. Was even afraid to write more than a sympathy note, stiff and formal, an utter charade—

She was staring into the fire, kneeling at Anthony's feet, thinking of another man. "Oh, Anthony," she whispered.

"Please. Please go away."

"What about Toni?" she whispered.

"I am doing this for Toni!" he cried, and a little of the harshness came back.

"I would never hurt Toni," she said.

At that, Anthony finally looked at her. "You already have, haven't you? You and—" The hard brightness of his gaze blurred. "Everyone else."

That was all he would say.

At the motel, Marcella slept in, or tried to. From six in the morning onward, she tossed and turned, in the grip of dreams that she seemed to be consciously constructing but that still had a disturbing illogic. In all of them, her repeated failure at some minor task became terrifying—either she couldn't dial a phone number, or lace her shoes, or catch up to Toni, who was walking only a few feet ahead.

Finally Marcella woke for good, at nine, anxiety like a dingy film on her skin. The air conditioner was humming, and the room was stale and cold. She got out of bed and switched the air off, and then pulled aside the heavy light-blocking curtain on the window above. Outside, the weather was overcast. Her window looked onto a corner of the parking lot and a patch of scrubby woods. There were scraps of trash under the trees. She wanted to get in her car, drive as fast as she could back to Connecticut, and hide; but instead, she turned on the TV, and the cheerful, bland chatter of a morning talk show warmed the room. She plugged in the room's little coffee pot, and as she fetched water from the bathroom sink she decided that, so far, her visit with Toni had been a success.

The night before they had gone to see a movie, a rather raunchy one, and Marcella had laughed so much she had surprised both of them. Perhaps it had been a sort of hysterical relief. During dinner beforehand, she had made herself ask about the McClatcheys, but

Toni had a new stance of airy dismissal on the topic and didn't want to discuss it. Marcella had known of course that she was putting on an act, with effort, but still she had let it drop. She did not let herself wonder what she would say if—when—the subject of the McClatcheys, of Jed, came up again.

At nine-thirty she called the house and woke Toni, who sounded groggy but cheerful. "Dad is playing tennis," she said. "I guess. He's not here."

"That's too bad," Marcella said automatically. "Maybe he will be back soon, and we could have coffee together."

"You *want* to see him?"

Marcella glanced at the Styrofoam cup and packet of powdered creamer beside her own coffeepot. She felt quite distinctly that she was in a play, that nothing was real, and then for some reason imagined the three of them—she and Anthony and Toni—sitting together in Anthony's kitchen, big smiles on their faces, real mugs in their hands. Anthony would be host, pouring jovially from the old drip pot that Marcella remembered, that she was sure he still used. And then the door would open and Jed would walk in—

"Mom? Are you there?"

She sat down. It was like she was still dreaming, everything sensible and then suddenly turning to horrid fantasy. What was wrong with her? "Of course I'm here," she said. She felt Toni's suspicious silence. "Darling, of course I don't mind seeing your father," she said. She put her free hand up against the side of her head, to steady herself. She felt the strangest dread, as if she were about to lose Toni. But she wouldn't, couldn't, do that—unless Toni found out about Jed. No.

She said, "We are all civilized people, after all."

And Toni said, "Right."

IT WAS A SUNNY MORNING in the Wellesley house. Anthony was sitting at the kitchen table. He was already a visitor. He had moved out weeks before, had, with his customary efficiency, already bought a condo. He was saying now that he had talked to someone at his alma mater—a boarding school that had been all boys in his time, now coed. In the space of a few seconds her mind had wandered, then she had gathered it back and thought *Why is he saying this?* and then, as her heart understood before her brain, the prickling annoyance turned to fear. "It's all arranged," he was saying. "She can go this fall."

Marcella felt as though the floor were dropping away. She held on to the edge of the counter. She said, "Why?"

"She needs consistency. Not one night here, a weekend there. That's no way to live."

"Away from *home* is no way to live! It is the way you die, slowly, day by day!"

"Marcella." Anthony's face had closed tight as a safe, the steel door swung shut, the lock turned.

Marcella knew she was thinking of herself, of the nights that Toni had already been away at Anthony's and she had lain on her bed and sobbed, unable to sleep, unable to get up, the emptiness of the house around her thick and suffocating, Toni's things lying abandoned like artifacts from a massacre. Anthony would say she was exaggerating, he was thinking it now, but it was how she felt—beaten, raw. She whimpered, "Please don't take her."

"I'm not *taking* her. She's *going.*" He took a deep breath and she knew the knife-edge of his voice would soften—this was what she hated, when he cooled himself to ice and could not be argued with. "Children leave, Marcella," he said, so reasonable, as though he were talking to a client.

"You are *making* her leave! Does—does she want to go?"

"It doesn't matter. Things change," he said, and she thought she saw the usual unspoken blame and judgment on his face but then she wasn't sure. If only he would scream at her, if only he would grind her down and say it was all her fault, it would be better than him just sitting there—

And then for one strange moment she thought, *Now. If I reach over to him now. If I tell him I want it to be different, now. Beyond apology—if I look at him, if I see him. The father of my child. The man I loved.*

But she leaned weakly against the counter and stared at the floor instead and let him decide. She really did not think there was any other way. Of course Anthony did not say it, but she believed she had gotten what she deserved.

THEY WENT SHOPPING IN CHATHAM and out to lunch, and then meandered back to Mashantum. Toni wanted to stop at the market. "They have these brownies there," she said. "From some bakery in Brewster. I'm obsessed. I go there practically every day."

Marcella felt more composed than she had the night before. They had seen two different people from the tennis club while they had been walking around Chatham, and it had been all right. Toni of course didn't know that Marcella felt odd, and standing beside her Marcella had found she could better pretend she was at ease. She had hoped to avoid the market, though. It was where you bumped into people.

"They're really good, Mom," Toni said, misinterpreting her silence.

"I'm sure they are," Marcella said. She glanced at Toni, who had one bare foot up on the dashboard, as if they drove around together like this all the time. Her heart gave a glad little flip. "Of course we'll stop," she said. "Why should I resist chocolate?"

The market was almost as weirdly familiar as Anthony's house. The few things that were different stood out to Marcella like neon. "Is that the bakery counter?" she said. "That's new. *Molto alla moda.* In my time you could not find a baguette on the Cape to save your—"

"Oh, my God," Toni muttered. She clutched Marcella's hand.

"What?"

"Jed is over there."

Marcella felt her heart drop like a stone, down, down through her feet, it had left her altogether, she was empty and weightless, no longer attached to the floor. She had known this might happen. She—had wanted it? She should act like an adult. They couldn't run out of the store. "Should we speak to him?" she said.

"No!" Toni whispered frantically.

Of course. *No.* Unthinkingly Marcella pulled Toni closer to her. "Where is he?"

Toni gestured with her head, and then let go of Marcella's hand and slid backward into the aisle they had just left.

The market was not a big place at all and Jed was twelve feet away. He was standing in the crowd at the deli counter, next to the tank of lobsters with their rubber-banded claws. A little blond boy stood beside him. There was an odd dark X on Jed's back and then Marcella realized he was wearing a baby carrier. The baby's head wasn't visible, but she could see the bare legs dangling, mottled with the chill of the store, pink socks on the tiny feet, the most helpless things she had ever seen. If Jed turned just ninety degrees, he would see her.

Toni plucked at her sleeve. *"Mom."*

But Marcella stood mesmerized. The little boy. Jed was holding his hand. As she watched, Jamie tilted his head up, up to look at his uncle, and for a second the fluorescent light shone blindingly on his hair, not blond or white but a brightness beyond color. She was watching what might have been. A little boy with a hand to hold. Jed stood with his other hand curved under the baby carrier. The little legs straightened, and one kicked, and as she watched Jed rolled back the cloth hiding the baby's face and bent his own head down to check on her. Marcella had never seen that look on his face before, whole and relaxed, smile lines at the corners of his eyes like an older man's—the man he would become. What she had never had and what she would not have.

"*Mom,*" Toni hissed again, and yanked at her hand, throwing Marcella off balance. The sudden movement she made as she righted herself caught Jed's eye. He turned to her, and the heart she had felt drop away from her was suddenly inside her again, blooming. She wanted to hold it out to him: *Here it is!* She was losing all caution, not caring, she felt a smile beginning on her face and didn't stop it. *Here is my heart!* But as Jed looked back at her his face never went beyond wooden, except his piercing, burning eyes. Then Jamie said something, looking at her, and Jed bent down to him, and Toni said, "What is *with* you?" and Marcella followed her down the aisle to the register. She glanced behind her once. She knew Jed wouldn't follow them.

"I've never seen the children," she managed to say. "The little boy. He looks like Callie?"

"I guess so." Toni's voice was sullen.

"The baby is so tiny still."

"But she smiles now," Toni said. "She smiled the other day." Her chin wrinkled, her lip began to tremble. The line moved and Toni dropped the container of brownies on the counter. Marcella put her hand gingerly on Toni's back and Toni bit her lip, struggling not to cry.

The checker was a girl about Toni's age, but from a different world, wearing a nose ring, and with deep dark roots at the base of her yellow hair. She looked sidelong at Toni but said nothing as she punched buttons on the register. Marcella tried to catch her attention, wanting suddenly to establish a separate, fleeting connection, something to distract her from thinking of Jed still under the same roof and miserable Toni who might figure things out at any time. But the girl refused to meet her eye, and when Toni did not reach out for the offered bag Marcella finally took it and gently nudged her daughter to the door.

HE HAD SEEN HER, he had seen her, just as he had been expecting, hoping, dreading he would, but it had shocked him still. Marcella had been down one of the narrow familiar aisles with the checkerboard linoleum at her feet, the shallow wooden shelves around her holding—as he had thought as a child—one of everything in the world. She had looked at him, her eyes wide, as if she could feel the heat coming from his gaze. And he had felt guiltier than ever. Trusting Jamie was holding his hand, the weight of Grace's little body was pulling ever so slightly—she was so light!—on his back, tempting him to curve, to clutch and shield her. From himself, he supposed. Because, right then, he gladly would have chucked the baby aside, pushed Jamie out of the way, and gone straight to Marcella and carried her off, a black knight on a black horse. He wanted her so badly he felt himself shaking.

He was able to push the desire far down inside himself until there was nothing but a black, sick feeling in his gut. The butcher had handed him the steaks then, blood-red hidden inside the clean white paper. *They'll be a treat,* he'd told Jamie earlier, when he'd been feeling jaunty. *We're going to grill, just us men.* Now he only nodded at the man behind the counter, turned silently away.

At the checkout there was a line, but Marcella and Toni were not in it.

He had walked to the store with the kids in the double stroller, defiant because rain was predicted, but Callie had objected only half-heartedly before he left. It had been raining off and on for days, it seemed—strange how once the weather changed it was hard to remember that anything else had come before. Outside the market, the air was clammy and the sky was a shifting, luminous gray. Jed put the grocery bag in the basket under the stroller and helped Jamie in, then detached Grace from himself and strapped her in too, the little ball of her, you still had to watch her neck but he could feel her getting stronger—she looked up at him with her newly clear blue eyes and smiled, showing her toothless gums. "Sweetheart," Jed said. "Sweetie, how would you like to go the beach?" He looked at Jamie. "Whaddaya think, pardner?" he said, hoping Jamie would not protest. He badly needed the wide sky, the open sand. He needed the wind and the water stretching out empty, erasing his thoughts. Jamie looked back at him unblinking. "Just for a little while," Jed said. "Then we'll go home and have lunch."

"Will Grace cry?" Jamie said gravely.

Jed had begun noticing moments like this, when Jamie was acting far too old, too responsible. "Nope," he said. "I brought a bottle. But good for you for thinking of Gracie."

When he had left, he'd told Callie he was taking the bottle. Usually she would have refused; she would have said she needed to feed Grace herself. And Jed would have said that she needed a break, and she would have said, her voice rising a little, *No, it's my job, Jed, you don't get it.* Today, though, she had just nodded at him, her eyes tired.

"Here we go, bud. We're going to run. Uncle Jed is turning into a fat slob, he needs some exercise." He slapped his stomach, which was, if anything, too thin.

He thought of Marcella's fingers stroking him, and for the first time felt no sense of comfort.

He kept up a stream of patter, as much as his breath would allow, all the way to the beach, more than a mile. He heard his own voice and felt it was a cloak he had thrown over himself, felt his feet pounding as though they were not part of him. The rage was still lurking. He didn't want to let it out.

At the beach, the sand was pitted from the most recent rain. There were hardly any footprints. It was almost creepy how empty it was, although space was what Jed had wanted; but Jamie, bless him, climbed out of the stroller and ran down the sand as though it were 85 degrees and the gulls overhead were wheeling through a bright blue sky, instead of this strange dank that seemed to belong to no season. Jed followed with the stroller, its big spoked wheels slicing through the sand. Jamie stopped at the remains of someone else's castle. There was a large hole beside it, now dry because the tide was out. "We need to dig for water," he said authoritatively.

Jed got out the sand toys. "You do that," he said. "How about I dig a road? If you don't hit water, then that can be a quarry. You never know if there's going to be water."

"Okay."

The sand was usually therapeutic, even for Jed. The task at hand became all-important, the shoring up of walls and smoothing of streets, the vital organization of castles and bridges. It was an old instinct, a serious play, this urge to build, to complete. But today it was not calming him and he thought how what he had felt in the market was another instinct, an older one: the urge to possess, to declare that Marcella was his, where everyone could see. And then, tensing around Grace, another drive, just as old: to protect. He thought how his father would have been whipsawed by these same desires, and would have known, in the end, how utterly he had failed.

"Uncle Jed, dig."

"Sorry, bud. Slacking off here." He picked up a red plastic hoe and began marking out a wide road. "See, this is my grader. *Rnnnnn, rnnnn.* Now it's backing up—*beep, beep, beep.*" He felt like an automaton, but when he looked up Jamie nodded, satisfied.

He fell to his work and tried to get the road as smooth as he could, tried to see every grain of sand. The strangely intense light and the absence of shadows made it easier. He could be an ant, he thought, bending close, every speck a boulder. Jamie had edged right over next to him. Jed glanced at him and saw that just as he could see individual grains of sand he could also see each one of Jamie's long eyelashes, even where they emerged from his eyelids, could see the minuscule unevenness where the pink of his lips met his pale face. His skin was poreless, incredibly smooth, still so new. *This must be how Callie sees them,* he thought suddenly. *And Billy.* What a parent does. More instincts. Sees every grain of sand. *How my father saw me.*

He stared at Jamie's skin, imagining it rougher. Someday he'd have pimples, someday he'd shave. He looked at the corners of Jamie's eyes and saw that there were the faintest beginnings of smile lines; someday they would be deep grooves—and now Jamie seemed not like his own nephew but a stranger, a specimen who would live to have wrinkles, gray hair. Whose flawless baby skin would someday be grizzled and marked by dozens of inconsequential scars, the dings and blemishes of life. That would be a miracle in itself. Jed hoped for it now like a prayer.

"Dig!"

"I'm just looking at you," Jed said. "You look like your grand-daddy."

"One of my granddaddies is in heaven."

"That's the one I'm talking about."

Of course it was just a lie. It was just something to say. Not that Jed knew for certain that Jamie's features were so different; it could be that he looked just like Jed's father had as a child. Who knew? There was no one who could tell him.

Kneeling there in the sand, Jed could not have even described the father he had known, beyond the generic—balding, blue eyes. Could not have described his face. Couldn't have drawn a picture. Not anymore. All he remembered now was that his vanished, vanquished father was the opposite of Jamie, so new, so full of possibility.

And yet, he had not even been old. He had seemed old to Jed at the time, but now Jed knew that he had died still a young man.

Jed imagined Marcella old. Callie. Jamie and even Grace. His mother—she would have been sturdy and vigorous, her hair silver, still thick. No, older. He saw her: frail, her hands backed with thick blue veins. His father. White hair and stooped back. Belly hanging in front and the rest of him gone thin, bones long and brittle, the flesh loose. Old. All of them—his parents, Callie, himself—their skin growing thin as paper, and then all of them just fading away, no death, no hysteria, just a gradual disintegration. It was the craziest kind of fantasy. No endings, no pain. That was an instinct too, to avoid death, pretend it could be conquered. To fear it.

"Well, well," said a voice. "It looks like we're the only brave souls out here."

Jed looked up into the face of Anthony Atkinson.

He seemed grayer and more heavily lined in the overcast light, and Jed thought for a moment that he was still in his daydream. Anthony's brow furrowed. "Are you all right?" he said.

Jed cleared his throat. "Fine. Nice to see you."

Anthony looked down at Jamie. "Hello, young man. Do you remember me? I'm Toni's dad."

Jamie looked up. "Toni left," he said.

"Yes, she did." Anthony nodded gravely.

"I overreacted to that," Jed said, without thinking.

"No, you didn't. There are consequences for one's actions. Or inactions," Anthony Atkinson said. "She has to learn."

"Yes. Well." Jed was fighting the sudden strange urge to apologize further. He felt a lump of transgression in his throat that could come up at any moment; he wondered what he might say—anything? Everything? It would be a relief, maybe—he wondered suddenly if Anthony could read his mind. *Marcella, Marcella,* he thought, experimentally.

Behind him, in the stroller, Grace began to fuss. He felt a wave of unfamiliar impatience. Of course it had to be now. "Excuse me," he said, and turned and lifted the baby out of her seat, balancing her on one arm while he felt in the stroller's pocket for the bottle.

"She seems healthy. Doing well? After a rough start?" Anthony said.

"Yes, sir." Jed took the cap off the bottle with his teeth.

"Doesn't look like you need help, anyway. You seem to be a natural," Anthony said.

"Thanks," Jed said out of the side of his mouth. Grace was already sucking away. Awkwardly, he reached up with his non-bottle hand, squeezing the baby to him, and took away the cap. "If that's meant as a compliment."

"Of course it is." Their eyes met. Anthony's were unreadable. "Toni's mother is in town this weekend," he said.

Jed didn't look away. "Really?"

"Yes. So"—Anthony laughed and finally glanced away, down the beach—"I am keeping my distance."

"Sounds like a good policy."

"Is it?" Anthony answered, but his eyes did not meet Jed's again. In the emptiness of the beach Jed felt he could hear his own heart, hear it began to accelerate. What if he took Anthony's arm—no, grabbed it—and told him, no, shouted, about Marcella? The fury he had felt in the market began to rise again, redirected. Now he hated Anthony. Or wanted to. Or wanted Anthony to hate him—but his hands were full of Grace and her bottle and Anthony had done nothing to him, he had to calm down. And really he had done nothing to Anthony. No doubt he would not like to hear what his ex-wife had been doing, but the morality of the thing was no longer his concern—

"You're usually away weekends, aren't you?" Anthony said.

"Sometimes."

"Uncle Jed comes back," Jamie said.

Anthony looked down at him with his eyebrows raised in comical surprise, as if a bug down on the ground had started to talk. "Yes, indeed."

"I'm seeing someone," Jed said. His breath was coming too fast.

"Yes," Anthony said. "Toni mentioned it."

Jed remembered Toni leaning over him, over the ankle that had not been sprained, and Anthony watching, watching. "She's all right?" Jed said.

"Doing fine," Anthony said, in a voice of finality.

"Look!" Jamie cried, pointing, and they both turned. To the south, over the dunes, the overcast sky had lowered and turned almost black, the clouds hurtling toward them like ships in a high wind; it looked unreal, like a time-lapse photograph.

As they watched, Jed felt a large drop hit his arm, then another. "We'll have to beat this thing home, won't we, bud?" he said, hearing his own voice going light with relief. He set Grace in the stroller, the bottle beside her, and turned back to find Anthony on his knees in the sand, helping Jamie pick up the toys and put them in the big mesh bag.

In moments the rain was falling steadily and Jed was busy stowing the gear and strapping Jamie in. "Callie will kill me, having the kids out in this," he said.

"Oh, I doubt that."

Jed expected Anthony to follow him up the dunes, but instead he said, over the rising wind, "All right, young James, your Uncle Jed will take care of you," and then he turned and headed back down to the water. Jed ducked his head and ran in the opposite direction, but at the top of the path, panting already from the effort of pushing the stroller uphill, he stopped and turned around. The rain lashed him in the face but he could see Anthony walking down the beach, hunched against the wet, looking like a dark bird blown off course. The fury rose in him again, but now he wasn't sure if it was anger or fear or pure suicidal recklessness. He raised a hand to his mouth, made a path for his voice, and shouted, "There's something you don't know!"

Halfway to the water, Anthony turned. He held his hand to his ear, questioningly.

Or cowardice. Anthony would never hear him. Still Jed took a deep breath and bawled again, *"There's something you don't know!"*

His words were blown away by the wind, bits of wind themselves. Anthony pointed to his ear and shook his head. He waved, turned away, and kept walking.

IT WAS POURING and Marcella was alone in Anthony's house. She and Toni had made lunch but then Toni had a hair appointment, long prearranged, very important, and had disappeared in Anthony's car. Marcella knew she should leave, but told herself she would just wait till the rain slacked off a little. She did not want to think about the motel; she would go shopping, go to the beach, sit in the parking lot again. In just a minute. Outside, the rain was coming down in sheets. She wandered into the living room. There was a phone on the end table by the sofa, as there had always been—an old black phone with a cord. Her cell was in her purse, in the kitchen, but suddenly she couldn't wait one more moment. She sat down and dialed Jed's number.

When he answered he said, "I thought it would be you."

"Are—are you glad?"

"Of course. I saw you."

"I know."

"I wanted to run after you," he said, his voice hard. She didn't answer. "And then I saw Anthony at the beach. In the rain."

"You did?"

"I wanted to tell him."

She looked behind her as though she had heard footsteps, but no one had come in the door. She said, "Of course you did not—"

"No. Of course not. It was funny," he said. Jed's voice did not make it sound funny. "Funny that the idea came to me," he said. "Anthony was almost nice. I wished he hadn't been."

She made an assenting sound. She did not want to talk about Anthony. She looked around the room, so familiar, but not hers—as if it had ever been! She should not have stayed here, but now that she was on the phone she could not leave until Jed became himself again, until he said something that dispelled this fear.

Jed said, his voice low, "I want to see you."

She sighed with relief. "I want to see you too." She huddled into a corner of the sofa.

"I will tell you about it," he said. "When I see you. What I'm going to do." His voice was dropping to a singsong but it was still cold, she had never heard it this way. "Your shirt will button down the front," he said, "and I will unbutton the first one. The second. You're naked underneath. You're so high and tight—"

"Jed," she said, "please." She felt her nipples hardening. "Don't—"

"—I will bend my head down. You'll stay still like I tell you. You're getting wet," he murmured.

"Jed." Her belly swirled. She had never heard him sound so agitated and determined. His eyes would be burning, she felt his tongue on her, felt him deep in the pit of her. She squirmed on the sofa. "Darling," she said softly, "please, you are scaring me."

"What's scary?" he whispered. Then there was a long silence. "I'm sorry," he said, and his voice was his own again. "I just want you. God. When are you going home? I have to see you."

"Why?" she murmured. It was just love talk, just seduction, but suddenly she wondered what he would say. "Why do you have to see me, *caro*?"

"I don't know. When I see you—when I *see* you—I'll know."

"Jed," she whispered, not caring what he said or didn't say, wanting only to hear his name. She knew she shouldn't say it aloud, but it was like a drug, for both of them, she would soothe him, she was the only one who could—

She was nestled on the sofa with her back to the door. All at once, she felt that she should not be sitting this way, exposed. The back of her neck felt so bare. Instead she should turn to the door, ready to ward off—what? She had just said *Jed,* claiming him, needing to, that need briefly eclipsing all sense, and then almost at the same moment—she was never sure if it happened before or after, if she had been prescient or not—she did feel an odd breeze on her neck and heard footsteps. She twisted around, still gripping the phone, and saw Anthony. He was soaked, his hair and jacket plastered to him. His mouth was open, his face white.

She murmured good-bye, hung up—cut him off, her Jed. Then she looked blankly at the wall. She took that small moment. She felt fear but it was different from what she had felt just a moment ago, when Jed had been speaking to her in that voice that was not his. This was a new fear—that she would cower, that she would not remember what was true. That she would not remember she was now herself, alone, and she alone decided what she did. That, mistake or not, what she did was hers.

She turned and faced Anthony. "How long have you been standing there?" she said.

"Long enough," he said.

"You have never been an eavesdropper."

"I've come down in the world." There was a long pause. *"Jed?"* Anthony asked.

She forced herself to keep looking at him. "Yes."

She could see he was waiting for denial or explanation. When none came he said in wonder, "Aren't you ashamed of yourself?"

"Yes. I think I am. For many things."

Anthony walked slowly into the room. She held herself straight, though she was trembling. He sat down on the chair facing her. There were beads of rainwater running down his face like sweat. "You're disgusting," he said. "I had no idea you could be capable of this."

"Neither did I."

"I saw him today on the beach!"

Marcella nodded. "He told me." Anthony stared and she knew that hearing of this ordinary intimacy had made the truth snap into place for him. He sat back in the chair, his hands on his knees, and his eyes roamed the room as hers had done a few minutes before and it struck her as strange that they saw the same things—the same encyclopedia on the shelves, the same candlesticks and ship in a bottle on the mantel that had been there for years. She wondered if those things gave him comfort, or if they looked as newly foreign to him as they did to her.

He said, "Jed McClatchey. That bastard." He paused. "Does he know? About his *father?*"

Marcella felt absurd calm spreading through her, cool water flowing to her fingertips. "Yes."

"Jesus Christ."

She looked at her cold hands folded in her lap and realized she did not need to say anything more. "Have you told Toni?" Anthony spat.

The water turned icy. "No," she said. "But I will if I have to. Maybe that is why I came," she said. "I have been lying, and maybe I need to tell her the truth."

"Don't you dare," Anthony said.

"Why not?" she said. "She will—" Marcella's voice broke. "She will hate me. I know that. *Hate* me . . . but she will get over it, I suppose, eventually . . ." She felt her spine wavering, and bowed her head into her clenched fists. She was surrounded by the past, but now the present was worse than the past. She had done this.

Anthony said, "Do not tell her that filth."

"I would rather tell her before you do." She was crying now.

"I am not going to tell her. God." His voice was now a strangled whisper. "You have no idea. You have no idea what I did for you!"

She did not want to look at him but as the silence stretched she finally did. His own fists were clenched at his sides but this was not like the fights they used to have, when he was all cold surety and would hurl his displeasure at her with complete confidence. He sat stiffly, thinner than she remembered, not trim but diminished. The new, or returned, leanness of his face made him look oddly younger. But the Anthony of twenty years before, the healthy, straight-nosed, jut-chinned, good-looking Anthony, with the hard-driving glint in his eyes and aura of unapologetic self-interest, had seemed to her the hallmark of modernity and plenty and uncomplicated ease of spirit. Now there was nothing easeful about him.

"You're not listening," Anthony snapped. "You never listen. Even face-to-face. Even now."

"I'm listening," Marcella said, quietly. "What is now, Anthony?"

"You have no idea," he repeated.

"Then tell me," she said. "Tell me what I made you do."

ANTHONY HAD GONE TO MASHANTUM unexpectedly on a weekday afternoon and had convinced himself that Marcella would be happy to see him. He was trying harder lately, had been for a while. He took her out for dinner, noticed what she was wearing. He had offered her vacations—he'd suggested Florida, even Italy. When he had said that, though, she had started to cry, and he had felt both powerless and disgusted, whether at her or himself he wasn't sure. All he knew was that even when they made love he felt he did not have her. It made him want her desperately. He wanted her now, and wasn't that what a woman would want too? Romance in the middle of an ordinary day?

But when he got to their driveway he had gone only a few feet up the gentle rise when he saw the car by the barn, a car next to Marcella's—a car he had seen in the dirt parking lot beside the tennis courts. He couldn't place it and he knew its presence meant nothing; Marcella was having some girlfriend over for lunch, there was nothing to stop him from pulling in and parking and going in the front door of his own house and calling out to his wife. But he didn't. He backed down the driveway and parked a little ways up the street. Then he walked back, almost to the base of the driveway, where there was a break in the privet hedge, and stood—not crouched, but *stood*, that detail was important—and waited. Not long.

When Cecil McClatchey came out of the house and Marcella followed him with that look on her face and her mouth tipped up to meet his at an angle that he knew so well, he watched for a moment, then stepped neatly away from the gap in the hedge. He had seen from their lack of hesitation, their matter-of-fact urgency, that this was not the first time, or the second, or possibly even the third or fourth. He walked back around the bend to his car. When he heard Cecil's car drive out and away, he followed.

At the stop sign at 6A he saw Cecil turn left, but when Anthony got to the intersection he turned right. He felt only the instinct to go somewhere safe, and that meant back to Boston. It was an hour and more back, but all he did the whole time was drive, and when he got there he parked his car in the garage at Post Office Square as if he were just arriving at work, and it was not until he followed his own steps to the door of his own building that he realized he could not bear to see anyone he knew. If he had had a best friend he might have called him and asked to meet him in a bar, some manly place where he could curse his wife and lick his wounds and find some steady idea of himself to hold on to, but he had no such friend. He turned and walked blindly away from the building.

He realized a block or so later that he was automatically walking to South Station, but he had his car, he couldn't take the train home. He stopped on the sidewalk and tried to figure out what to do. The problem of his car made him furious. The fact that he had driven it today, that he had gone to Mashantum, that he had not bounded in and beaten Cecil McClatchey until he cried for mercy but had instead driven back like some kind of dumb animal, seared him with shame. He writhed inside to think how long he hadn't known, what signs he had missed. He was outside a bar, one he had never noticed before, and he walked in, still wrapped in disbelief.

It was not the kind of bar that was trying to attract people like him. His was the only tie in the place. The beery darkness and the murmur of cable news on the suspended TVs was democratic, it didn't matter, he'd pay for his drink like anyone else. When the man beside him at the bar started talking, he didn't answer.

"Suit yourself," the man said.

Anthony finished his drink quickly and ordered another. Without comment the man pushed a bowl of pretzels in his direction. Anthony ignored them, but the silence became more companionable, or would have if Anthony had cared. As Anthony was finishing his second drink, the man spoke again. "You look like shit," he said, in a matter-of-fact tone, like he'd known Anthony all his life, and Anthony had no choice but to look at him at least.

"Leave me the hell alone," he said, but once again the man didn't seem to take offense. Anthony had never in his life cursed at a stranger in a bar.

The man had a head of thick dark hair, although Anthony guessed from his deeply creased face that he was past fifty. He had the sort of tan that came not from leisure but from working outdoors. He looked as if he might frequently curse at strangers in bars, and Anthony was frankly surprised that the guy had taken it from him.

He was certain that this was a man who would have beaten Cecil McClatchey senseless, or worse.

Anthony Atkinson had never gotten on well with tradespeople. He did not know how to talk to them, nor did he care to. He had never chatted with the mailman or the plumber and he found it cumbersome to have more than a cursory relationship with his secretary. But he had also never been shocked before as he had been that day, and he had never found himself humiliated to his core, and never felt like a coward. His behavior had always followed strict guidelines, most of which he had inherited rather than originated, standards he aggressively approved of. But now he had no code for himself. He had no plan for being both cuckolded and heartbroken. At the time, he didn't even realize he was the latter. And, later on, he never could remember how he had ended up telling this stranger his most intimate business. Perhaps the man had seemed unreal to him, anonymous, like the bar. Eventually the man had spoken again, as though he had known the part he was supposed to play, and Anthony had told him everything, in a few short sentences. But when the man said he knew someone who could take care of Cecil for him Anthony just laughed, because it was part of this mad nightmare he'd stumbled into.

He left the bar with a phone number in his pocket, a link to a world he had never, ever contemplated entering. "You're insane," he had said to the man in the bar. "What the hell do you think I am? I could go to the police right now."

"You won't do that." The man had looked at him levelly.

All those *never*s. It felt sickening and thrilling and curiously inevitable, like a free fall—exhilarating in the few seconds one had to enjoy it before smashing to the ground.

When he saw Marcella and then Cecil McClatchey that weekend, he could barely contain himself. He saw no way out of it, no way to confront her and have his dignity remain intact. He would not have her leave him. He looked at Cecil's ruddy, oval, handsome face and thinning gray-blond hair and felt nauseated. He looked at Betsy McClatchey, her calm confidence—like his had been, he thought, confidence in a well-built life—and felt pity, as for a weaker being. He had the phone number. He carried it for another week and when he could stand it no more he called and then went to a different bar with a check in his pocket made out to an electrical company, a large check that would go to a different man, whom he would never meet, a check that felt like a live grenade. He had never felt this kind of power. It brought a preternatural calm. He was not only solving a problem but jettisoning all his ideas of who he was—though in fact that had already happened, against his will, when he saw another man coming out of his house with his wife.

It was July, and Anthony told the man to wait until fall. God, no, he didn't want it done at the Cape, near all the people he knew, on a street he knew, in a house he'd entered—with the blue hydrangeas and the sandy soil, the crickets at night, all his things, *his*—God, no, he didn't want it done there. It had to be done somewhere unreal, Cecil McClatchey had to simply disappear, become a forgettable story, the gap he would leave filled in and sodded over by the time Anthony would have occasion to even think of him again. "Atlanta," he said. "In November." The beginning of the end of the year.

He could sleep now with this solution in the future. If his gaze was sometimes inexorably drawn to that spot of approaching chaos on the horizon, then there arose a stubbornness and fury born of this power he believed he had never had before. *Yes, it is unthinkable but it is not. Goddamn it. I have never done the unthinkable. A sin a crime and blood on the ground and on my hands, where whatever else I have done blood has never been*—but my Marcella, *my wife, and goddamn it God damn it God damn it all*—

And except for these moments, he felt himself smoothing out. Marcella seemed very far away to him, but now he could look at her and smile and feel no hatred or anger, only a smug satisfaction which he also tried to push away as unnecessary, a blurring of the absolutes he believed he had invoked. And he waited for November.

But as it approached and he was back in Wellesley and his child, his beautiful daughter, got on the school bus every morning and life proceeded and in the midst of it he saw his wife drift about, a sad shade, her tan fading, leaving her smooth olive skin with a gray tinge of longing, November did not seem far enough away. He wanted it always to be in the distance—the shutting of the door, the resolution. Then one day Marcella seemed different. She seemed a resolution herself. Her back was straighter and she was more beautiful than ever to him, and clearer. The clear autumn light was breaking his heart and he felt they were all hurtling far too fast toward November. Along with the beauty of his wife he seemed to see beauty everywhere like a message, beauty that Cecil, far away, could see too, and along with the beauty, Anthony felt his hatred returning. He realized how happy he had been without it. How much he did not want it, that dark disorder. *I was only trying to get rid of that. I wanted the shut door.*

But he could no longer move lightly and cleanly and he knew he would have to face it, he would have to swim in the muck. The clarity around him would darken, but the infernal storm of November would disappear too. There was that. Yes, he knew what he could and could not do, he knew again who he was. *My God.* He had been insane.

He called the phone number and said, "It's off. Don't do it."

"It's on for"—the voice gave the date.

"No. It's off," Anthony said. There was a pause and he realized why. "Keep the money," he said. "Keep it all. I'll get you the rest anyway. It doesn't matter."

"You're the boss. It's off." Anthony pictured the rough handsome face from the bar. He could almost see the man do a flourish with his hand, a mocking bow, *my liege*.

For some reason, only now he panicked. "Off," he said, "it's off. I do not want this to happen."

"I said you got it, you're the boss."

Anthony heard the contempt dripping. He was ashamed of even noticing the schoolyard dynamics. "Off," he said. "Off," but the man had hung up.

The panic did not leave. He let himself call again the next day. He was going to say *I mean it, I meant it, do you hear me?* The phone rang endlessly, with no answering machine. He called again. The same. He played the conversation over in his mind: he had said *No*, he had said *Don't do it*, right? Had he imagined it? He could no longer believe any of it was real. He could no longer sleep. He had nightmares in which he was ordering the deaths of thousands of people— his own parents, Marcella, Toni—and he would wake up shaking and creep to the phone and call again. There was never any answer. Or had he dreamed it? Had he dreamed the whole thing? It was all he could do not to ask Marcella: *I had a dream, but was it real?* And then she told him she was going away that very November weekend, and it was all he could do not to laugh aloud. He knew she was meeting Cecil. He would not even be in Atlanta. It would not have worked. The whole thing was comedy.

Fred Sprague called that Saturday. Anthony was alone in the house. Toni was at a soccer game and Marcella was in North Carolina with her girlfriends, or maybe she wasn't; he was not past caring but he felt helpless. He heard *stabbed*. He heard *they don't know who* and *surprised a robbery*. "Betsy?" he said. *"Betsy?"*

"Yes. Cecil was out of town on business."

"Betsy? Jesus Christ."

"Can you call a couple of people from the club for me?" Fred Sprague said. "Anthony?"

"Sorry. God. Fred, I don't think I can. I'm sorry."

"You—"

"I'm sorry. I can't do it." Anthony heard the door slam. He heard himself speaking and could not believe he was expressing coherent thoughts. "Toni's home," he said. "Fred, thank you for calling. I have to go now."

He could not sort out what had happened and what had not, what could possibly be his fault and what could not, what he could ever do or say again and what he could not.

"Dad?" Toni came in sucking on a water bottle. Her shin guards made her legs look thick and strong. Her hair was in a ponytail and one loose strand was plastered with sweat to her flushed cheek. She flicked it away with her fingernail. "Who was that?"

If he had had the capacity for any more amazement, he would have been amazed that Toni started to cry when he told her. It·was generic shock, she had never had the experience of a familiar person, even a marginal one, being randomly erased from her life. He had to comfort her, and as he held her and patted her shoulder he had all at once the flashing feeling of being saved. He felt he was casting his gaze, in these few minutes, to every corner of his life and it was only when it alighted on Toni that he had any sense of what to do. A shade of his old imperiousness returned. He had found something unassailable: protecting his daughter. "It's okay," he said.

"It's not okay, Dad!"

"It's okay here. We're okay here."

"Are you going to call Mom?"

He heard himself say, "I'll tell her when she gets back."

"She knew them, right?"

"A little," Anthony said.

Toni wiped her eyes. "I mean, we *saw* them," she said. "We went to their *house*."

"I know," he said, filled with both dread and an immense satisfaction that was at once new and familiar. After a moment he recognized it. In spite of everything else, his daughter was safe.

That night, unable to sleep, he thought over and over again that his only job was to protect his child. He was so grateful for this organizing principle that he began to weep: it was an obligation that blotted out all others. It was so clear and clean that it was a thing of beauty.

"BUT I LOVED YOU MORE THAN EVER. I don't know why," he said to Marcella. His voice was not reproachful. "But—you see—I had my organizing principle—"

She saw him at his desk in his shirtsleeves, surrounded by files and papers, how he was most comfortable: yes, he would have an organizing principle. She was swimming in such shock by that point that she almost smiled.

"And you were extraneous to it," he continued. "You see. Possibly fatal to it."

At the word *fatal* Marcella's flesh crawled. "I don't understand," she said.

"Because I wanted to tell you," Anthony said. "I knew I didn't deserve you anymore—"

"*You* deserve *me!*"

He blinked and she could see that even now interruptions made him impatient. "I sent you away because I was afraid I would tell you," he said. "If I had—you might have gone to the police, you *should* have, there would have been an investigation. Toni would have lost both of us. She would have lost everything. She almost lost everything, because of me."

"But you did not do this thing," Marcella said. Her voice trailed off, and she did not hear what, if anything, Anthony said in response. She sat frozen on the sofa. She was shocked that the room around her had not transformed itself into something new and strange as Anthony had told his story. It was remarkable to Marcella that she could sit here now in this place that was like a time capsule to her, then and now, what was then, what was now—Betsy McClatchey was dead, had been dead, still was, possibly by Marcella's own hand—as good as by her own hand. Marcella herself must have made a fatal mistake, long ago, there must have been some sign she had missed, some hint of how dark things could be under their comfortable surfaces—

Across from her Anthony shifted, just barely, in his chair. She looked at him and it was as though the room had been picked up and shaken and set down again and everything settled back in its place but with the deathly cold sheen gone. She could hear again. "You called it off," she said clearly. He raised his eyes to her, a little surprise in them—she wondered what he had expected her to say—and shrugged, looking more helpless than she had ever seen him. "You did. You told them no. So it was an awful coincidence," she said, and stood up. She had to move. "A coincidence."

"Do you believe that?"

"A coincidence!"

"Do you believe that?" His eyes were hopeless. Nearly.

She stalked to the bookshelves, to the far corner of the room, back, and then rounded on him. "You thought you could take better care of her than I could!" she said shrilly. She would not answer him, she would not! He looked blank. "Of Toni!" she barked. "*Our* Toni!"

"No—I wanted to protect her—from me—"

"You have always wanted her for yourself." But this distracting outrage would not stay. Toni and Cecil and Jed were now jumbled in her mind. She had failed them all, she had taken care of no one. All at once she sat down on the nearest chair. "You did not do it," she whispered. "You told them no. It was a horrible fantasy you had and then you told them no." Her throat was dry. She could barely force out a sound. "Those monsters."

Anthony opened his hands as if he had been clutching sand and was now letting it fall to the floor. "I'm sorry, Chella. I'm sorry I told you. It was selfish of me. I would like to pay my penance," he said. "But that would also be selfish. Do you see?"

He bowed his head. She saw how gray his hair was. She forced the words out. "You can't ask me what is selfish," she said. "Because I want to be punished too."

Marcella called Jed when she left Mashantum on Sunday, and all he said was, "I'm leaving too." She had been home for only fifteen minutes when he opened her door without knocking.

He kissed her as if he wanted to suck all the life out of her and held her as though he wanted to crush her bones to dust. She let him. She let him pull her to the floor. He was flaying her open, digging deep for something that he needed. She let him. He came, agonized, and held her a little more softly and stroked her hair, and then he looked at her and stood and pulled her up with him and led her down the hall to her bed, where he then went over her slowly, thoroughly, in a way that frightened her more, because he was so intent, seemed so determined to expose every cranny of her, he was looking for something and what if he found it? He thrust himself into her, slowly, and carried her up and up, and she fought it but then she was at the top of the peak where he had taken her before and now she was falling, spread-eagled in nothingness; and when she was herself again, clutching him, she felt she was clutching a stone, and the land was barren and craggy and full of hazards.

She could tell him. She could say, *Darling, I know something*. She could give him herself and Anthony, heads on a plate. In the end, though, it would only be more leaden weight for him, it would not solve anything, there would be an investigation as Anthony had said and Toni's life would be shattered and it would still be nothing more than a horrible coincidence. Wouldn't it? It would only make him hate her; she would give him that gladly, though, would welcome the punishment.

She would give him anything, except Toni.

Beside her, Jed rose up on one elbow. He looked down at her and said slowly, "What if you had our baby?"

"*What?*" For the first time, she shrank from him. "Jed."

"Why not?" he said dangerously.

The hope leaping in her had been so brief she almost hadn't felt it. His face was now a stranger's face. "I don't know if it's possible," she said, wondering how she spoke these words so lightly, how she spoke at all. "I'm an old lady."

"You know that? You're sure?"

"Well. No. I don't know it for sure."

"I'm not Anthony. I could get the job done, you know." He was not smiling.

"Stop." She remembered him holding Jamie's hand in the market. How she had longed for that. Then. She had never dreamed he could be cruel to her.

"What would you have done," he said, "if my father had gotten you pregnant?"

"My God!" She pushed herself away from him.

"What would you have done?" he insisted.

"I don't know!"

"Did he?"

"*No!*" And in spite of herself she remembered a long-ago dream, of a child who did not know that his parents had long, complicated histories that preceded him, a chimera of a child who was a new beginning. "My God, Jed, *dio mio,* why are you saying these things?"

His face was hard. She saw that he was pushing himself, going where he did not want to go, where he did not want to even think. She could tell him, now. But instead she eased herself away from him, out of the bed. She stood naked for a moment and then hated herself, her nakedness, her weakness, and went to the chair in the corner, wrapped herself in her robe, curled herself up. From far away, protecting both of them, she said, "Why are you doing this?"

He was no longer looking at her, was instead staring at the ceiling, and when she spoke he turned on his side, away from her. His body was beautiful. The smooth tanned skin was so dark where it met the white sheet. She longed to stroke him. She thought, *So now it begins.* Not touching.

Jed said, his back still to her, "How much did you love him?"

She swallowed. "A great deal."

"But he left you."

"Yes. He did."

On the bed, fury was roaring through Jed's brain, a child with flailing fists. *Mine, mine, she is mine!* Marcella had just said it. His father had left her. *He left us.* The fury howled. It was as though he had been walking and walking down a long corridor, all summer, knowing what was coming, and now he had come out into a roaring arena and was in the ring, his blood racing at almost unbearable speed, and he was trembling, ready. Waiting, again, still, for his father. "Mine," he whispered, so low that even Marcella wouldn't hear him.

But his father wasn't there.

"Marcella," he said to the wall. His voice broke. His hands had been curled into fists. They fell open. "Marcella. Please." There was nothing for several long moments, and then he heard her soft footfalls. He felt the tilt of her weight on the bed. Her arm slid under his and her knees fit against his bent legs, and she held him.

Her bare skin was warm against his back, but for the first time he could remember, he felt no desire. The arena was gone, the ring, he was at the edge of a plain of nothing. His empty hands went to Marcella's, tightened over them.

He loved her. It was true. But the love had been embroidered with hopes and memories and anger and now it was just plain love and it was simple and he was exhausted. It seemed a paltry kernel of a thing to offer her. He had thought of her only as sinning or forgetting but really he had been looking in her for what he had lost, and he had to realize now, once again, finally, that he would not get it back. He burrowed his back into her. He did not want to let go, or to think about what he had to do next.

Behind him, holding him, Marcella felt the pulse of his blood against her cheek. She could tell him. It would be a door closed. She thought of Toni, and tried to hold on to her resolve. *Not yet, not yet.* "You have to forgive him," she said.

And Jed, thinking she meant Cecil, said, "I know."

FIVE
THE
BARRICADE

It bothered Cecil deeply that he had to lie to the police. He was not a person who had ever distrusted the police; on the contrary, he believed that their existence was a sign of a society holding itself together, and he had never felt resentful of their rules or occasional intrusions into his life—a speeding ticket, an inefficient cop directing traffic. They separated the good from the bad, saw the world in clear black and white whereas the rest of life was overrun with gray. It was part of their job to be slate-faced and neutral but when Betsy died he was sure he sensed their grief, especially at the beginning, God, when there was yellow crime-scene tape stretched across his own driveway, when they were in his house with the comfortable things that must have reminded them of their human kinship—the embroidered pillows on the sofa, the cheery family photos on the piano. The basket of clean laundry on the kitchen table, unfolded.

Yes, he trusted the police and their determination. They wanted to find the killer almost as much as he did. More, maybe, because that was what they were trained to do—obsess over this essential lack of order. For them, there was not yet an end to the story, whereas for him his wife was dead and there was nothing further to add. He knew it would be manly to want revenge, but he had no energy for that and was glad to let the police want it for him.

Early on, though, he sensed their suspicion. It wasn't that big a surprise, was it? He was sympathetic to them, he really was, and tried to convey this as well as he could. He wished quite sincerely that he could give them his alibi so they could go pursue other leads, although he didn't know what they might be, and if they even had any they were not telling him. He was a businessman, he wanted to say, he was known for his effectiveness and lack of sentimentality, when necessary. He hated to see them wasting their time.

The very first night they had asked him if he wasn't, by any chance, having an affair. "Are you, Mr. McClatchey?"

"No!" Layered over his numbness he felt a reflexive nausea and disbelief. He did not even feel then that he was lying, because he had never been able to believe it himself. "No! Of course not!"

Before long he realized that it must be a routine question in cases like this. That really it had nothing to do with him at all. Later on they asked again, more than once. *Sorry to bring it up*, they would say. *But, you know, it happens.*

There was one particular detective, a sandy-haired fellow with a weak chin and a military haircut, who liked to use profanity as a way to relax things. Or to provoke him. "There's nobody out there who's pissed at you? No asshole, you know, who wants to pay you back for something?" he had said, at their first meeting. It didn't bother Cecil; it was probably an effective technique. Obediently, he had sat and thought about the man's question. He thought of Anthony Atkinson, of the ferocity of which he was capable, which Marcella had described more than once. But Cecil knew it wasn't physical, that the man had his codes. He thought of Anthony shaking hands on the tennis court once when Cecil had beaten him, the utter correctness of his posture. "No," he had said. He shook his head. "No."

He had looked the man in the eye and regretted very much that he couldn't tell him the truth. But early on, the guilt he had felt all along about Marcella had coalesced into the ironclad conviction that he must keep her name to himself. He had never told Betsy, and to tell someone else now seemed the ultimate betrayal. Patiently, he told his lies once more, instead—that, on the night of Betsy's death, when he had been in North Carolina, he had not been able to sleep, had driven around aimlessly for part of the night, and that when he had come back to the hotel he had lain on the bed without folding down the sheets. A maid had already revealed that his bed had not been slept in; he knew that. But still the repeated questions and the detective's skepticism bounced off of him like arrows off a breastplate, because he began to remember this shadow self like a long-lost twin. He saw himself driving through the night, struggling to stay awake in his cloud of anxiety, of insomnia that quite likely spoke of deeper existential troubles—but what did the police care for that? The sorrow of this phantom and his phantom journey began to seem completely real. If he had suddenly found a confidant, someone he could trust absolutely, even then he would have had difficulty teasing the truth back out of this manufactured memory.

At the same time there was an old arrogance at work, that of a younger, privileged self: he was outraged that his integrity, no, his *humanity*, was being impugned by these suspicions. He refused to believe that such a false accusation could hold up, and indeed, it didn't—he was never close to being indicted, they had no evidence, because of course there was none.

When the detective had left that time, the first of many times, he went into the kitchen and got a glass and some ice. Callie was there but said nothing. However, she followed him into the dining room, where he had gone to the liquor cabinet. "Dad, maybe you should get a lawyer," she said, in a low voice, although there was no one else in the room.

He smiled at her naïveté. "Honey, I've got one. But I don't need him every second."

"What if they twist what you say? What if you say the wrong thing?"

"I don't have any wrong things to say, sweetie." He did not even blush.

It was as if his guilt were balanced by something equally strong: his innocence. Recently he had woken from a dream, a nightmare: Betsy was dead, her body visible somehow in the distance, indistinct but bloody and tattered. He himself was surrounded by iron bars— but it was a cage open to the sky, and now he was atop a pile of kindling, being burned alive like a medieval martyr. He woke up, panicked, and thought, *Did I do it? Did I do it?* and then as the waking world solidified around him in his and Betsy's bed he felt a brief elation. He could believe her death was divine justice. He could believe he had that guilt. But had he held the knife? *No.* Of course not. *At least,* he thought, *I have that.*

It was Monday evening and Billy was there and Jed was not, it was all wrong. Jed had taken off, Callie was not sure when, not sure how long he had been gone. She knew (as though she had read it long ago, in some elemental instruction manual, long since lost) that it shouldn't matter, she should be able to depend on her husband first and foremost, but instead of feeling anchored by Billy's presence she felt she was washing away, being carried out to wild, open ocean, losing sight of land.

And of Billy. Even though he was standing right in front of her, he was turning to a distant speck. He was saying that he thought he'd take Jamie camping. Somewhere real, an actual campground. He knew it was kind of last minute, but it would give her some peace and quiet—

Callie had to squint at his lips to understand what he was saying. To hear the real words. She said, "You're taking Jamie?"

"Camping. Just camping, honey. There's a campground over in Orleans, I already called, they have space for tonight."

"You called?" she said. "You called some place in Orleans? You've planned it already?"

She saw the fear in his eyes. She wanted to step back from herself, join her husband and say, *Isn't she crazy, this babbling woman, who is she anyway?* But instead she turned away from him to the kitchen window. Outside she saw a rabbit, nibbling grass under cover of dusk. As if it sensed her attention, it raised its head, then froze. So stupid! To think it could hide in the middle of the lawn! Maybe she and Billy could say together, *Let's get rid of that woman, chase her away.* Like a scared rabbit, flashing into bushes, down into its hole— *Let's send the fox after her*—let it catch her by the throat, shake her until she's limp, until she couldn't bother them anymore, *that woman*—

She caught her breath with fear. "Please don't take Jamie," she said. The rabbit lowered its head again to the grass, then loped away.

Billy reached forward and turned her to him, took her into his arms. Dear Billy. Hadn't he once been dear? He was saying, "Don't worry, okay? You'll get some sleep. Gracie will be good, I know she will—"

What he did not say was *do you want me to stay* and although her head was full of pleading *stay stay don't take Jamie from me don't leave me here* she could not make herself say it. A short while later, when she hugged Jamie good-bye, she held him too tight and tears rolled down her cheeks, and Jamie, who had been dancing up and down with excitement, grew still and said "Mommy?" and his face was like Billy's, afraid. Ah, she was infecting them all—

"Have a good time!" trilled a voice. Her own and yet not—devious, automatic.

She wiped her tears and if Billy noticed, he said nothing; instead he gave her his cheerful-fearful look and strapped Jamie in his car seat and tossed the tent in the trunk and drove away.

The badness is in me and he knows it, she thought—no, no, he didn't, she had fooled him. *But bring Jamie back to me, bring him back*—no, no, he got him away, good, he had gotten her baby away— no—*bring back my baby*—

In her mind she saw the rabbit, clenched in the mouth of the fox.

She walked into the house and began a circle through the rooms, one then the other, just as she had walked through them in her mind, in the hospital, so long ago. She had come here, hadn't she? But she had thought she would find them, her father and especially her mother, she had thought maybe her mother would have left her a sign, would have let herself be found here in the house she had loved so much if only she, Callie, came and stayed, hunkered down, waited. But she had been waiting all summer, it was August and would soon be September and she finally had to admit that her mother was not here to be found.

And now that Callie was really alone, no Billy, no Jed, there was nothing to stop the badness swirling in her head, rotting it, leaving a ragged hole at her core. It seemed Billy had driven away hours before. He and Jamie had been gone for days. Jamie, oh, *my baby, my baby* and in the other room Grace began to cry. She was not alone. There was the other one. Her baby.

She stood frozen. The other one. What was she supposed to do? She remembered that sometimes the baby's cries went through her like a blade and made her rush and pick her up, anything to stop the crying. That was how it usually happened. But now Callie walked into the living room and stood looking down the little hall at the closed door and felt she had stumbled upon a puzzle. There was some force keeping her from understanding and at some point she would have to fight it, but for now she sat down on the sofa and turned her head numbly to the door and waited. The crying rose and cycled down and rose again and she waited to feel something. She did not know how long it was that she waited. Then there was a long silence and something slid into place with a click of inevitability and she rose and went to the door and opened it.

Grace was lying on her back in her crib. Her face was red and now that Callie had come into the room she could hear her, she was not silent after all, Grace's baby breaths were loud and ragged with hysteria, and Callie felt her breasts hardening and then the front of her shirt was blossoming with milk. She watched Grace, terrified, as she felt the milk dripping, and knew that she should be scooping the baby up and was not, and knew with certainty how horrible she was, how she, Callie, was broken and could not be fixed and how she would infect Grace, too, with this badness, perhaps already had, and there was no cure. She crept closer and Grace quieted, smelling the milk. Then Callie was at the side of the crib. She reached her hand over. She touched her baby's head.

Now you know.

She looked at her hand.

You know what you must do, you have no choice.

She saw how her own hand could encircle Grace's neck, how small the neck was, how soft the bones. But then the hand was in front of her—she looked at it in wonder—it was empty, Grace was still crying, and she knew that was not the way. *You know what you must do* and she knew she was to pick Grace up, go outside to the pool, the surface gleaming in the dark. Pick her up, so light, so heavy. The water outside a live thing calling.

Her mother's dark head breaking the surface of the water, her arm over her head in her beautiful stroke and just as quickly gone, then the other, and she had reached the end.

Grace's cries were longer and quieter now. She was tiring out. *If I just wait, she will stop crying, it will be over, it will be all right,* she begged—

no.

Callie was so tired. She wavered on her feet. It would be a relief, to obey; it was required of her. *Do it.* She realized she had been fighting it for a very long time. So long. She would gather her strength, to do this one last thing. It had been so long since she had been told what to do, since she had not had to decide. She was gathering her strength then   *come here*

in a different voice. A voice like bells. She had never heard it
before—had she? *Come here. Hear.* It washed over her. She took a
step away from the crib. The other voice was shrieking now, her head
was splintering into these voices, it was physically painful; they were
nails and she was the chalkboard, she was being gouged in long
bloody furrows, the only way to make it stop was to do the right thing,
pick Grace up, carry her, far but not far, outside to the water, so easy,
the splash—

but at the farthest, farthest distance like a pinprick of light was
that other voice. She could no longer hear it but even so she took
another step backward and seemed to float or be carried and she was
outside Grace's room and the door was closed.

She had no strength and she leaned against something else strong
that she could not see. She let it hold her up and move her. Across the
room was a hutch, an old, rough thing, made of oak boards from a
barn. It took up half the long dining room wall.

She set her shoulder against it and pushed it across the room to
the hall, on and on to Grace's door, china shattering down.

There was the old pirate chest, even empty it was too heavy to
move, but she let the wind push her again across the room and the
chest came to rest beside the hutch.

The voice was still screaming and she knew that soon her brain
would rip apart. She begged it and then saw the best way to beg was
to keep pushing, moving, lifting, making gashes in the bare wood
floor, crushing china under her shoes. The pile in front of Grace's
door grew higher. Still she waited to hear the other voice again, the
bells, and still there was only the dot of light, and then she remembered her box.

Her box. Of course. Her pretties, her treasure. She had been
thinking of it all along, she had been holding herself from the thought
because it was too delicious, but she couldn't resist anymore and she

went to the shelf in her closet and took the box down. She ignored all the voices and the wind was gone now, and the tiny light flickered and died. Now finally she could go outside, where she was supposed to go, to the smooth water, the liquid glass that would never break.

JED DROVE HOME DEPLETED. He did not turn on the radio. He didn't turn on the air-conditioning either, but instead rolled down the windows and let the air buffet him. He thought about how often he had driven this route and even considered counting the actual journeys, the weekends stacked up in a tall pile, which would not have been hard to do, but instead he made his brain stop and back away because he knew the number didn't matter. It was enormous, endless. He tried to remember Atlanta and his job and his apartment and the life he had left, but they were like things that had happened to him as a child, and now he was an old, old man. He had left them, and in their place he had had Marcella.

The two of them had not said ending words. They had not said much of anything, but for miles and miles his only thought was that whatever he had had with her was almost over. The thought became a physical sensation, whipping him along with the wind.

But as he drove farther from Marcella he rolled up the windows and turned on the air-conditioning and in the new, artificial quiet his drumming mind changed course. He remembered that he had come north not for Marcella, but for Callie and her children. Minutes passed, dark unseen Connecticut flew by, until he admitted to himself that he had come to Callie not because she needed him but because he needed her. In Atlanta, he had lost hope that understanding or contentment would ever come; he had wanted Callie and her routines and resolute practicality to comfort him. But then, almost as soon as he'd arrived, the gallant brother, he'd left again.

He drove in silence, the miles ticking, shame washing over him.

He decided he would tell Callie everything. He owed it to her. He would tell her what their father had done and not done, and before her eyes Cecil McClatchey would shrink from both hero and monster until she, too, saw him clearly, a flawed, adulterous, grief-stricken man who had died of a heart attack, and together they would look at that deflated sad balloon and ache with grief—that would all come back, it plainly had never gone away—but at least they would know more truth than they had known before.

After this he still drove with grim speed and efficiency but his hopelessness had lifted the smallest bit.

When he was approaching the Sagamore Bridge he thought, as he always did, of his father, and how when they were driving north every June he would honk the horn as soon as they had crossed it to announce the news, waking up anyone who happened to be asleep. No one had ever minded. To Jed it had always felt as though they were almost, finally, home, a home at the top of the earth where it was always summer. He had felt it in his body, like an acrobat keeping his balance—they were traveling up the globe, the air was getting thinner, the trees turning to northern evergreens, everything subtly changing. That was when time had been endless in a different way, a child's way, when the future was barely an idea.

It was what he had found again with Marcella—a Saturday afternoon in her bed with the light streaming in had been an eternal present. He had been happiest on Saturdays, not Sundays where the ending tolled—had it been happiness? He did not want to figure out. Instead he thought, stubbornly, that he if had achieved summer endlessness with her, it was the same as happiness.

He was coming into Mashantum now. Route 6A had a few cars and so it did not feel so late; he passed a restaurant and then another that must have had people inside, with the lights bright and the talk loud, but then he turned off the main road toward home and the streets were abruptly deserted. He drove down Whig Street and turned into their driveway and parked next to Callie's car. When he got out, the *thunk* of his closing door was loud in the stillness. It was chilly, the cold that also meant endings. As a child, in August, he had known that he would go back to Atlanta and it would be weeks before the same cold came, and it would be so strange, to think that two places he loved could be so different.

He walked across the gravel to the soft silent lawn, and although he couldn't see it he sensed the swimming pool behind the fence like a living thing, the surface of the water trembling with potential energy. Inside the house, the babies would be sleeping, maybe Callie too. He hoped not. He wanted to talk to her now. He noted that Billy's car was gone and thought how he would have to wait until Billy got back, from the diaper run or the beer run or wherever he had gone, and hoped it would not be too long, because he thought he should tell them together. He would sit them down and say *Let me tell you about Marcie,* and Callie might hate him then, she would scream, be furious, and Billy might say he was sick or loathsome, but in the end Billy would help Callie and they would both understand. He winced a little thinking of how they might hate Marcella, his lovely . . . no, he couldn't think about that, it couldn't be helped. So he walked to the back door.

It was unlocked, as always. The kitchen was a mess—dinner dishes still on the table, two wineglasses with dark red dregs in them. The dishwasher door was open and he closed it with his foot. Lately there were times when Callie would just give up and go to bed without washing every last dish as she usually did. And Billy definitely was not compulsive. No, this mess was explainable. He wanted to call out to her but something about the silent disorder made him hesitate. He didn't hear the TV; he had been right, Billy was out.

But the lights in the living room were on, and through the doorway the slice of it he could see looked askew. He could not say how, exactly, but then he was there, only in the next room, but it was a different country. He stood and stared. The loveseat had been pushed clear across the room and stood upended against a door—Grace's door. And the hutch too. There was a trail of broken china, and chairs and an end table on the pile. He saw the pirate chest on its side, the iron lock dangling. "Callie?" he said, his voice rising. "Billy?" Nothing was missing that he could see, the TV or the stereo, what else . . . "Grace?" he said. He whispered now. *"Grace?"*

He ran past the pile and up the stairs, opened doors, found no one. There was no sound from an awakened Jamie. Jed realized that he was looking for blood. "Callie?" he cried. "Jamie? Billy?" He ran downstairs, bellowing, and then he heard it somehow through his own voice, behind Grace's barricaded door: a cry.

He shoved away the furniture, had to set himself twice against the hutch before he could move it, every muscle stretched, about to tear. The thing ground against the floor and he moved it enough to reach the door handle, to wedge himself in.

She was crying in her crib. There was no blood. She had worked her way out of her swaddling and flailed weakly. She looked younger, shrunken, like the newborn she had been, who hadn't smiled. "Oh, Gracie, baby," he said, and she cried again and then as he picked her up there was a long shuddering pause.

She had been crying for a while. He felt how her cheeks were wet with real tears, how her little back was hot with her effort. He clutched her but she felt loose to him, insecure, and he put her down—she began crying again when he did, heartbroken resigned cries—and he swaddled her quickly the way Callie had taught him and picked her up again, and she stopped. "Gracie, Gracie." He felt fierce, like Callie. He was a lion, he would protect this child. He knew without question that she had been rocking in a sea of danger tonight but he did not know how or why.

The baby began to whimper again and to turn her head and root at his chest. "Sweetheart," he murmured, surprised he could find words, "this calls for some formula," and he carried her into the kitchen and found the emergency stash and shook it up and poured it into a bottle. Usually when he gave her a bottle it was Callie's breast milk, bluish and pale; this stuff was thicker and didn't smell too good, but he tipped the bottle and after a moment found the angle and Grace began sucking without hesitation. "Little girl," he crooned, "little girl, what are we going to do here?" He leaned back against the counter and let his mind go numb, feeling the energy in his arms of Grace's sucking, knowing that in a moment he would have to begin his search again. The window over the sink was behind him. He became aware of it gradually. He didn't know why but he felt he was being watched and finally he turned around and saw Callie sitting by the pool, not looking at him after all but with her back toward him. She was sitting at the deep end, her legs dangling in. She must have been sitting there a long time because as he watched the motion-sensor light went out. He stood and stared, like it was a movie and the film had broken and he was waiting for it to be repaired, and then he was rewarded for his patience, because the light blinked back on and Callie had indeed moved; now she was holding one leg out in front of her, examining her bare foot.

Anger rose in him then and mixed with the fear. He took the bottle out of the baby's mouth and brought her up to his shoulder, patting her back. He felt the air come out and felt her relax, probably she was going to sleep already, and with her still on his shoulder he went to the patio door and opened it with his elbow and walked down the flagstone path.

Ahead of him, the silhouette of Callie was motionless again. She still held her leg stiff in front of her. "Cal?" He came up behind her. "What the hell is going on?"

She lowered her leg into the water slow and graceful as a dancer and turned to him, her head wavering a little. "Hello." Her voice was dreamy.

"Where's Billy? Where's Jamie?"

She turned her gaze back to the pool, and slowly began to shake her head. "Ohh," she moaned softly. "Ohhh."

"Callie? What the hell? Grace was screaming her head off." He squatted down, holding the baby tightly to his shoulder. "I was"—he found he had suddenly lost his voice. He cleared his throat. "You had me scared, there."

Callie was still shaking her head, back and forth, moaning so softly he almost couldn't hear her. "Callie?" he whispered. "Who moved all the furniture?"

Her head stopped. "Mom did," she said.

He went down on his knees. He held the baby and reached to Callie with his free hand, touched her shoulder, and she flinched but it was not a flinch, it was slow, as though she were moving through water. "Cal. Cal, honey." He saw that one hand was curled into her chest. "Cal, what is that? What have you got?" She brought the thing she was holding up to her cheek, caressed it, it was precious. "Callie, honey," he coaxed, "let me see." In the back of his mind a voice said *There was something I was going to tell her,* and he knew it had been big, immeasurable, but he couldn't think about it right now. He reached for her clenched hand and it opened and a little bottle dropped into the water and bobbed away. As it fell, her head lolled to the side and she would have fallen into the pool, too, if he hadn't caught her, and as he held her with one arm and the baby with the other, he knew that whatever it had been, he was not going to tell her for a long time.

SIX
JOURNEYS

In the spring after Betsy died, as soon as the freezer was finally emp-
tied of casseroles (although they still appeared every few weeks), Callie began to cook. Cecil didn't know where or when she had learned
how. He would not have been surprised to find that she was spending
hours in the kitchen with Betsy's cookbooks teaching herself, the way
she would study for a test, and he kept meaning to tell her how proud
he was of her, but then would forget. Most nights, after she and Jed
got back from their classes downtown, she would prepare a main dish
and two sides and dessert and put them on the table with a stern look
like a farm wife who was feeding the hands. But none of them could
ever eat very much, and the leftovers piled up in the fridge. Sometimes, when Callie wasn't looking, Cecil would sneak in and throw
things away.

One evening before dinner, Cecil went into the family room and
sat down to read the paper. He had glanced at the headlines that
morning, but he remembered the old civilized days when his own
father had gotten home at five and sat down with his cocktail and the
evening paper, and he liked every now and then to imitate the old
rhythm.

Inside the Metro section, where he had not seen it earlier, was an
article about the district attorney and his failure to solve some high-
profile cases; Cecil's name was there, a suspect so far having escaped
indictment.

He had seen his name in the paper like this many times before, but there had been a brief lull, and he wasn't prepared for the injustice of this fresh insinuation. His daughter was in the kitchen, cooking dinner—she loved him, for God's sake! He could not believe that people he had known since childhood were now looking at him askance, that his own Atlanta paper, which he had been reading all his life, still could be saying these things. It was unreal. Right after the murder, of course, everything had been unreal and nothing, in the weird upended world, had been unbelievable; his being a suspect was as fantastic as everything else and he had floated along, numbly deflecting the detectives and their questions. But now, suddenly, he couldn't bear it. He got up and walked into the kitchen. Jed was already sitting obediently at the table. "Daddy," Callie said, seeing his face, "what's wrong?"

Cecil waved the folded paper mutely, dropped it, and then sat down. "I can't take it."

Jed picked up the paper and bent his head to read. Callie's lips were pressed together. She set a platter of roast chicken on the table and stepped back, the oven mitts still on her hands. "It's horrible!" she burst out. "Why can't they leave you alone?"

He shook his head. "I don't know what more to do," he said. The knowledge of what he could do—what he could say—seemed irrelevant; there should be no suspicion of him, of all people, none at all.

"I hate them!" Callie cried.

Cecil became aware that Jed had finished reading. He looked at his son's handsome averted face. "You know I didn't do it," he whispered. "You two know that."

He was not even sure if he had said this before.

"Stop it," Callie said.

Had he said it? Early on? Of course it didn't need to be said, but look at his son, so recently a child, you had to explain things to children, they did not understand the most basic processes of the world—why apples fell downward, why the sky was blue. "I didn't do it," he said again. He was looking straight at Jed now.

"My God!" Callie cried. "Of course you didn't!"

Jed began serving plates.

"You don't believe me," Cecil said.

"Yes, we do!" Callie said. "Of course we do! How could you say that? How could we not believe you?"

Jed spooned peas, potatoes. "They're full of shit, Dad," he said, not looking up.

Was this enough? Cecil wondered. "I should have been there," he said.

"It was some crazy person!" Callie cried. "Someone evil! A *murderer*! Why are we *talking* about this!"

Cecil nodded absently. He was remembering being a son. He realized there was no way a son, even a grown one, could see his father broken and not believe he was guilty of something. He rose and hugged Callie for a long moment, so hard he felt a pain in his own chest, but she didn't flinch. "I'm sorry, honey," he said. "I'm sorry." He let her go and sat down, not looking at either of them. "Let's eat this marvelous feast," he said.

But dinner was nearly silent and they picked at their food, and after they had pretended for as long as he could stand it and it became clear that no one was going to eat any more, Cecil said he was going for a drive. "What do you mean?" Callie said. "Where?"

"Just want to clear my head," Cecil said.

They knew he did this. They knew he couldn't sleep. That sometimes he let pointless miles calm him; that that was what he had done, one night in November, in the mountains of North Carolina. He had told them that, and it was true; he did not have to remind Callie, and she did not ask again.

As Cecil drove down the peaceful, dark streets of their neighborhood, the car seemed to steer itself. He felt he was watching himself looking into the rearview mirror, merging into traffic, clicking on the turn signal. He watched his hands on the wheel.

He really was not surprised—how could he be? His children were rational people, they could pursue a thought, from *a* to *b* and onward to its logical conclusion. Logic was the thing, it couldn't be argued with, he had to remember that. If Jed had seen policemen talking to his father, over and over; if he had waited and waited along with the rest of them but had never been given a culprit, a conclusion, why would he not look across the table at his father and accuse him? Why had it even taken so long for Cecil to see? The linearity was unassailable. Cecil pointed his own finger at himself every day. He could not blame his son for doing the same.

An entrance to I-75 was not far from their house and he went there first and in a few miles exited onto I-285, the perimeter. He did this as if he had been programmed. He would not go north to Charlotte or Chattanooga, or east to Augusta, or south to the ocean—or even west, true west, true American escape. Instead, he would keep to an endless circle. There was no escape to be had. He had always had this essential weakness, this secret lack of bravery. He could have asked Betsy about it, she would have said *No, don't be silly,* she would have known him and loved him and made him stronger; but now that she was gone, there was only the Betsy of his mind, who told the truth. She looked at him with steely, blaming eyes. And he bowed his head and did not argue.

So now he drove. He drove west, then south, then east, feeling the directions as though the compass needle were in his gut. And then north, and he was pointing to the place where he had begun. He knew about circles. For the past months he had, more times than he could count, felt he was moving, moving, and then all of a sudden would realize he had gotten nowhere, had only gone once more around a hopeless track. He always ended up in a place where he could do nothing, learn nothing. He seemed to never leave it.

It was an old habit of his to drive in the left lane. He had once had a car that pulled to the right, it had been years ago but he still stayed left to compensate. He did it now even though he was barely driving the speed limit. Cars and trucks flashed their high beams and honked with malevolent exasperation, but he was powerless to change course. He had no idea now how he had managed to get himself on the highway. He didn't know how he would get home. It felt pointless to wonder. Pain pumped through his heart like boiling water.

Another truck bore down on him and, through the pain, he pressed the gas. When the Jersey barriers were somehow suddenly in front of him instead of to his left he thought, *Oh. I see.* He saw his hands on the wheel; he could have turned it back to center, but did not; there was a moment of almost calm regret but then it was over, before he could think what it was that he regretted.

Nancy Hale would keep Grace. Jed had not known at first whom to call; he had seen, with a kind of tangential clarity, how impoverished he and Callie were, how for years now they had not let the people who wanted to help them do it. But there were still a few of them around, these people who, he had thought, belittlingly, were merely well-meaning, not understanding what that meant, how they wove a fabric that kept a person from being completely exposed to the elements of the world. He knew he needed to ponder that someday, when he had time, but for now he had called Nancy Hale and she had come.

She arrived in less than five minutes, looking as she always did, collected and alert, with her iron-gray pageboy and the ever-present bobby pin on either side holding back the rigid curl—some odd decision of style made long ago and never changed. He explained what he had to, what little he knew. He told the truth.

Her brow furrowed and she made a little ticking noise that was almost comical, except that it was a sound of sympathy, not surprise, and for this he was absurdly grateful. The fact that she was not shocked calmed him down in a way he would never have expected. "Go on, Jed," she said. "You need to leave right now. Where's the baby?"

He pointed to her room. "She's asleep," he said. "I just fed her—

a little while ago. The formula is in the kitchen—over here, I'll show you—"

"I'll find it." She shooed him away with her hand. "Go. Oh—where is Billy? And Jamie?"

"I don't know. They—must have gone on some outing. An overnight. Billy's been talking about it."

He said this out of an impulse to make up a story that would make sense to Nancy Hale, although he knew she didn't need one, but when he said it he felt even more of the unaccountable calm. That was when he thought to look for the tent. He needed to go to the hospital, the ambulance had already gone screaming away, but first he went upstairs to look in Jamie's closet, where he kept his special things. The tent wasn't there. He didn't bother to look anywhere else. He had to resist the urge to call down the stairs to Nancy and have her come see for herself: *Look! No tent! Something that makes sense!*

But instead he went back down to the kitchen and said, "They went camping." Although he cared nothing for appearances he was glad, for the moment, that Billy was covered. Glad he was off being a dad, sleeping in the woods with his little boy, maybe with the flashlight still on to scare away bears, coyotes, monsters. Jed knew that later he would scream himself hoarse at Billy, because *Billy had left her,* but he also hoped that Billy and Jamie might stay in some enchanted wood forever and never be hurtled forward into this new present that they did not know existed—

"Jed? I'll wait here for Billy," Nancy said, her voice nudging him forward.

He was remembering the dean at the door of his room, early one November morning. How Callie had been out in the hall too, grayfaced. He had been a junior in college, it was a Saturday, he was hungover but something in their faces made his mind perfectly clear, and he had wanted to close the door and lock it and not hear whatever it was they were going to say, because he knew it would hurl him someplace he did not want to go. Sometimes he still dreamed that he had never let them in.

"Jed, dear?"

He looked·at her bleakly. "Thank you, Mrs. Hale," he said. And he left.

BUT WHEN HE GOT TO THE HOSPITAL Callie was not dead, and after a long time, he was not sure how long, they gave him a room number on another floor, and instead of thinking about what this meant and how the main worry was over, for now, he mutely followed the nurse's directions.

The hall was brightly, institutionally lit, but when Jed eased open the door of Callie's room, it was dim inside. The only light came from a bulb over the desk area and the blinking sensors of various machines. Sitting in a chair next to her was a heavyset woman, her white uniform stretched tight around her thighs. "I'm her brother," Jed said, but the woman only nodded. The nurse had briefed him—this person was the suicide watch: she, or someone, would be with Callie all the time. Jed sat down in a chair on the other side of the bed.

They sat in silence for a few minutes. The presence of the stranger filled Jed's head with a buzzing. "You can take a break if you want," he said.

"I'm not supposed to leave her," the woman said.

"I'm here," Jed said. "I'll push the button—I'll push it for anything." The woman's face was kind, plain, tired. "Have you eaten?" Jed said. "Go eat, I'll be here."

He was not kind, wanted only for her to leave.

The door closed behind her with its pneumatic *whoosh* and as he moved across to the woman's chair, the buzzing went away. Callie's head was slightly turned, he could see her face better here. It was slack. Not peaceful, but blank; there was no richness. The richness of sleep when he watched Marcella. All she had seemed to hold within her. Callie was in between, in shadow. When she woke up it would not be day, with the sun out; it would be dark or at best early, early dawn, they would have to lead her gently hoping not to lose her.

They said she might have wrecked her liver. That was all Percocet did; people didn't know. *And if she had really meant it,* they said, *she would have really done it.* Apparently people who really mean it do the research. They didn't try twice. Jed thought of his father.

A machine beeped in the corner: her heart. The jagged bright line. Its movement was supposed to be a comfort.

This is when the mother is supposed to come, Jed thought. When the soft light should come on, when the hand strokes the forehead. This was when the mother appears and the chaos reorders itself around her and she becomes the sun, with planets revolving in their courses. This was when the polestar should appear in the sky, true north unwavering, all questions quieted.

The machine beeped in the corner. The red line, the mountain range building itself over and over and then the valley. Instead there was that. No polestar, no center; a line instead of a circle. A line going forward, the future always unknown, the line probing on into nothing until it was something, a cliff and then the fall and then again the climb. The mother gone, all that was left was the journey away.

Instead the shadows under Callie's eyes were circles. The globes of her eyes under her closed lids. The roundness of her earlobes, the curve of her chin. The hollow at her throat. She seemed all hollows. Hallowed. The beeping line an incantation. The beating of her heart solemn music he did not understand.

He wanted Marcella there. *What do you make of this?* he would say, pointing at his sister, like an experiment gone amok, in the bed.

What does it mean? And he tried to think of Marcella as stark and cold, as a clean angular figure in this new world he saw of unadorned lines and spikes and valleys. But she blurred, the distinctions in his mind dissolved. *Darling,* she would say. Circles under *her* eyes. Her hand on his brow. *Explain this,* he would say.

He thought of Marcella as a child, the solemn face she had surely had, her first communion, Marcellina kneeling, white veil, little child-bride of God. *Explain this to me.* The white veil turned ghostly. *Explain it!*

He thought of all the explanations he had wanted. He saw instead of Marcella's face his father's, looking at him that last night, before he drove away and did not come back. The agony in his eyes. His father, whom he had not believed—whom he had also loved so badly. Was he, Jed, to blame? For what was he *not* to blame?

The machine continued to beep. He bowed his head to the hard circles of his fists and waited.

CALLIE WAS LOST but she was not floating aimlessly; instead she was anchored in place with the tide lapping at her chin, and only her mind could roam free, her memory. She cruised an endless shadowy landscape, and although her body was trapped she felt a strange leisure in her spirit and from far above, like an eagle, spied a bright place to land. She wheeled down to the blue gleam of a swimming pool set in a green lawn.

A party. She saw herself with a fledgling independence and in-betweenness, and a hard lean body unstretched by childbirth, and a belief that life would only ever be exciting. She was twenty years old. She remembered herself and the light and shadows falling over the pool, the soft rustle of leaves. She remembered her parents as they always had been at parties, gathering the guests into themselves, her

father always the more tense one, louder when they started arriving—
the one who was relieved to be surrounded by people, who liked to
take care of them, put drinks in their hands, to feel that he had woven
a social fabric that had not existed hours before, a particular, palpable
energy.

Her mother was calmer; but sometimes she had a hard sheen
that surprised Callie, that she thought was part of her mother's way of
being efficient, of getting the canapés on the plates, the flowers on
the table. Odd to see her mother retreating into herself, for that was
what it was, a shell she wore, before a party, and sometimes other
times too. That thinnest of veneers, a bright polish that only Callie
sensed, that kept her from burrowing into her mother's secret heart.

She had not known then but knew now, floating both within and
above, that her father had sensed the barrier too, not even realizing
he did, feeling only respect for his pretty capable wife that was also
distance. And that her brother also felt it but that he had loved their
mother for it; maybe he had the same thing himself; Jed saw their
mother and understood the clarity of her outline, that their mother
knew who she was, there were things she would and would not do.
She was a woman who spent little time on doubt. Callie saw that her
brother leaned on her, needing to know only that she would never
fall.

But Callie, being her daughter, needed to understand how she
worked and of what materials she had composed herself, and felt
deflected by this crystalline calm that soothed Jed. That day by the
pool, in the swirling midst of the party and the shifting shadows of the
leaves, she saw that her mother had sat down at the edge, was dangling her legs in, and like a jealous child Callie was drawn to her and
the empty space beside her, wanting to take it before it was taken by
someone else.

Betsy was talking to someone in the water, Larry Stowell, who had been doing cannonballs, splashing everyone and making them feel that they were youthful and carefree. That would have been something her mother appreciated. Stirring things up, just a proper little bit. She was the only woman touching the water, her mother was. She could not be said in any way to be an iconoclast but nevertheless cared little for what other people thought. It was a hot day, after all. After folding a towel to sit on, taking off her white dressy sandals and hiking up her flowered dress, she had situated herself at the edge of the pool and sunk her legs in up to the knee.

And Callie drew next to her and sat down. Betsy continued to talk to Larry but leaned almost imperceptibly toward her daughter, and Callie felt embraced. So how did she feel at the same time deflected? The party drifted slowly around the pool and the patio and on the shaded grass under the trees outside the gate. She saw her father in his madras shorts handing around mint juleps. A thought had flickered past—*Is Dad handsome?*—and then disappeared, since it was a matter of no importance. She saw men grouped around the grill and women by the table of salads picking at them and keeping an eye out for their children who were playing on the lawn. It was not like Callie to sit and watch middle-aged adults so carefully but her friends weren't there yet, they were coming later, and besides she felt attached to her mother, who continued to chat with Larry but who nevertheless held her.

Jed was in the water, he was leaping in the air, catching something, Callie could tell he was showing off. She wondered for whom.

Her mother was beside her and the air was hot and humid like Southern air. The water had been cool and she had been bored and not wanting to talk to anyone either older or younger and feeling abandoned so far by her friends who had said they were coming. They had come eventually, had all left together—maybe that was the night she had made out with Hammy Storer at Mayflower Beach. But at that point she was alone and it was odd, she wanted her mother to herself, she wanted to tug at her elbow, insistent. But she was twenty and an adult, or so she had then believed, and instead she had stretched her leg out in front of her, examining herself to pass the time. She held her leg up straight over the water, flexed her foot, studied her red-painted toes. It was the silent display of one pleased with her young body; it meant nothing.

Larry Stowell swam off with a heavy splash like a sea lion and her mother, freed, looked at her with a smile and instead of saying anything stretched her own leg out also. For a moment, long enough to lodge itself in Callie's mind and now years later float to the surface, they looked at their legs outstretched and Callie saw her foot, a replica of her mother's, saw her leg the same, Betsy's with silk-fine folds of skin above the knee and the twisty blue vein on her calf that was the lasting mark of pregnancy but still a familiar shape, their feet together a single Rorschach blot, the ink their own flesh, revealing two where there had been one, the shape of creation. Then they bent their legs again, they were under water, the vision was gone.

Callie saw it now and understood as she had not then. She understood that the diamond-hard barrier of her mother was meant only to keep Betsy sane—meant not to keep Callie out but to hold her mother up. It had been the scaffolding of her sanity, her way to say *This is who I am,* and if her mother had lived and grown older with Callie the barrier would have crumbled, there would have been no use for it, and one day Callie would have looked at her mother and they would have been on equal footing.

She remembered her mother and remembered also how that day by the pool, feeling suddenly alone, she had wanted to dive into her mother's lap, entwine herself in the being of her mother. But also—she felt this as memory, although it was a shining thing, newly emerged—she had felt herself strong and joyful and separate, because sitting next to her mother, next to her mother's flesh that was her own, she had seen her mother within her. She had seen of what she was made.

Jed, watching her in the dim hospital room, saw the shapes passing over her face, not cloud or shadow but light. He wondered if she dreamed in her artificial sleep. She had almost left him and he knew he could have been furious, but he saw that his fury had become irrelevant, that it had burned itself down to a cinder as weightless as dreams themselves. When the sitter came back and settled herself, without speaking, into a chair in another corner, Jed sat back also, and slept.

When Marcella did not hear from Jed for several days she thought she knew what it meant. She was surprised. She hadn't thought he would simply disappear. She hadn't thought he would act badly, she told herself, in a severe schoolmistress tone. But as hard as she tried, she couldn't manufacture pettiness to cover her grief. She longed for him. And she still hadn't told him about Anthony—or, rather, there still had not come a moment when she said to herself, once and for all, *yes* or *no*.

The heat returned, one last August wave, and this seemed cruel, because if Jed was not coming back to her she wanted the summer to be over, over. On the hottest day, the sky low and oppressive, she spent the entire afternoon in her garden, tearing out the weeds she had let take over, cutting back the overgrown plants that might have flowered again had she taken care of them, but that were now spent. There were split tomatoes, which she hadn't bothered to pick, rotting on the ground. Everything was parched. That day she watered and watered, and at first the moisture simply beaded up over the dust and then made a great muddy mess, but she didn't care. At one point she stood and looked at her longest border, her hands at the small of her back where an ache was beginning. She felt her eyes sting with tears and then thought, unexpectedly, impatiently, *Stop it*. It was a garden, they were plants, and if she'd killed anything, something else would come to take its place, and it was not so hard to restore order, a different order. *Fool!* she thought. It was her *nonna's* voice, and she agreed with it. She turned on her heel and went back into the house.

She was showering when she heard a noise outside the half-open bathroom door. Her body went rigid but she stayed under the spray, rinsing her hair, until it came again, a muffled crash. She knew what it sounded like—what it was: the unmistakable footsteps of an intruder going through her house.

Without thinking, she thrust the faucet off and yanked at the shower curtain. It flew open across the bar with a screech on its metal rings and she stared levelly at the door, naked, dripping, waiting for whoever had come for her to appear. In the sudden silence, she heard only her own breathing. It seemed like a moment she had been waiting for for a long time.

Then the noise came again: thunder.

She felt her face slacken, but did not feel relief so much as surprise. Slowly, she reached for a towel. She wiped the water out of her eyes, and then wrapped the towel around herself without drying off. She glanced at the faucet. Her hand had smacked the lever. Not so long ago, she would have left the water on, cowering against the wet tile, praying, dear God, only that trouble would pass her by.

And she thought, as she had so often lately, of Betsy. Of Betsy opening her own kitchen door and entering her dark house, not knowing what awaited her. She wanted to believe that Betsy had been brave. Betsy the blameless, the innocent. Had she had any time to think? Had she fought the man who had been sent by Anthony—or who had not?

Had she believed this was the final price for a life too easy, for challenges not met, for people not adequately loved?

No, those were Marcella's own sins.

Slowly she left the bathroom and walked down the hall. In the heat, she could not tell if she was merely wet or if she was perspiring again. Never clean—

Fool. Stop it. And she remembered her hand striking the faucet, how strong it had been. She remembered how she had glared at the open door.

She had just put on fresh clothes when the phone rang, for the first time in several days. She knew it could be anyone, not just Jed, but nevertheless she began to shake. *Decide,* she thought, thinking of Betsy in her kitchen. Marcella knew she should be terrified but she hurried to answer anyway and it was Jed and she wanted to sing into the telephone like a girl. She dropped into the nearest chair, her hair still dripping down her back, to listen as hard as she could—*decide, oh, decide*—but in the next instant she heard something in his voice that she knew had nothing to do with her and she said, "What is it?"

He told her. "I should have known. I should have seen. I mean— I did—oh, God, I knew she was bad off. But not that bad. I should have *known*."

"Darling, no, it's so easy not to see," she cried. "And Callie is all right. She is all right. That is the main thing—" She was thinking, *My God, not another one, Cecil, what did we do?*

"I was distracted," Jed was saying. "You know." He laughed a little. "Just a little bit preoccupied. I saw it." He took a deep breath. "I just didn't want to."

"You think that now, darling. But you knew she was tired—you just wanted to assume the best, that is natural." *Not another one. But she is all right, she is all right—*

"You don't have to defend me." She heard the weariness in his voice and also a new, great distance. "It doesn't matter whether it's natural or not."

Marcella didn't answer. She was gripping the phone so tightly her knuckles were white. She remembered when Cecil had called her about Betsy. When she had picked up the phone and heard his voice and been glad in spite of herself, because his voice was all she wanted to hear—even though she had known what he would say, by then, because Anthony had told her. Had told her that Betsy was dead. And she had thought too, waiting for him to speak, that everything would be different; she didn't know how different, she had known she was about to find out. She had said, *Darling, I know, I heard.* She had wanted to spare Cecil having to say it. She'd said, *I know, darling, oh my God—*

and her voice had trailed off to a whimper because she could already feel his agony over the phone, and then a sound had come that she had never heard before from a man, an animal sound, and she knew he had not made that sound before and would not again. In the midst of her disbelief and confusion and weird pain—how to describe it? the death of one's lover's wife? the death of the innocent obstacle?—she had been proud, she never forgot it, *proud* that he gave that unearthly sound of pure pain to her and her alone. She would never stop being sorry that she had felt pride at that moment.

Cecil had begged, *Please don't tell anyone about us.*

Telling. No one telling anything.

But she had told Jed—and that had been right. She had defied Cecil. She had done that one thing.

Jed said, "Marcella?"

And she was back, and it was Jed on the phone, not Cecil, and Jed was alive. "I'm here, *caro,*" she said, more fiercely than she had meant to. "Callie is lucky to have you! You have done nothing wrong!"

What she really wanted to say was, *Enough. Enough. Don't get ideas. You cannot leave me too.*

But a chorus of voices was growing in her head. *Fool, fool.* Who was the fool? Herself? Callie? *But she did not die, her babies still have her.* And, *They are not yours. Callie, Jed, the babies. None of them. They never were.*

"I have to stay here," Jed was saying. "I have to watch the kids. Billy is a mess. And he's threatening to have his mother come up—God." He gave a weak laugh. "I'd call Toni, except I know she hates me."

"You could, darling," she said. *Toni.* Toni's face when she had looked at Jed.

"I—no," he said. "I can't."

She murmured, "I know."

"Chella." His voice broke. "I don't know what to do."

"Darling. It will be all right," she crooned, and she knew that the conversation was slipping away. She knew she hadn't told him, and that she wouldn't, not now. Not because it would hurt him, not because he would hate her, but because she could see Toni, her own child, in her mind's eye as clearly as she could see Jed.

"I don't know if it will be all right. Chella," he whispered. "I want you."

"Oh," she said, "*oh,* I want you too," and it was all she could do not to go on and on, to pull him to her with the rope of her voice. She sat in the hard chair and felt her blood pulsing, her real blood in real veins. Felt her living hands hold the hard plastic of the phone. "But *caro. Carissimo.* We cannot do anything about that."

"In a week or two—when things have calmed down—"

And she knew. "No, darling. Not in a week or two."

"Please—"

"Jed," she whispered.

There was a long, long pause, and then he said, his voice ragged, "I've made so many mistakes."

"No," she said, and her own tears were spilling over. "No. Not you."

"I have. But that's my problem. Marcella?"

"Yes, *caro.*"

There was another pause. "Are you all right?"

His voice was more tender than she had ever heard it. "No," she murmured. "I'm not. But don't worry, darling. Don't worry." There was silence. She would have to tell him. She would have to be the one to do it. "You must go now," she said.

More silence, and then a whisper. "Yes."

She listened to his breathing and his tears but he did not say anything else and she took the phone away from her ear so she would not hear the click. She got up and walked over to the little table and very carefully set the telephone into its base, and then she tiptoed away, as if it were a baby, and she did not want to wake it.

Betsy McClatchey and her friend Shirley Barnes drove, in Shirley's car, down Betsy's dark street. They were dissecting the movie they had just seen and laughing about the leading man and how they thought he was hot (it was Shirley's word, she had fifteen-year-old twin daughters in the house) and how their husbands would be amazed that they thought such things anymore. Betsy skated easily along the surface of this conversation, grateful for her friend and the easy connection, their laughter bright like the stars outside in the chilly sky. It was cold that night, for Atlanta, for November.

Betsy thought her friend would be surprised to learn that under her chatter Betsy was thinking a different set of thoughts entirely, slow and gelid like the water under the surface of a frozen lake. She thought about the empty house to which she was returning, wondered if she had left the back door light on. She stayed at this prosaic thought a moment to steel herself. Then, *Cecil*. One tentative finger touched his name in her mind. It was a wound, and she winced. He was with his mistress. Whoever she was. Betsy knew this.

She and Cecil had always shared a deep understanding, to which Cecil had admitted only long ago, when they were in college and he was not afraid to sound poetic occasionally; but it was still there and what it amounted to now, for her, was a picayune kind of transparency. She could read the set of his shoulders or a motion of his head like an old-fashioned telegram, brief and concise. After enough of these missives—months of guilt and exhilaration and despair, extremes of familiar feeling that she hadn't seen in a long time—she had realized, even without hard evidence, what was going on.

Of course she had felt betrayed, aghast, but she had kept it to herself. Whether she stayed silent out of fear or pride she wasn't sure. Before long, she sensed that the affair was something to do only with Cecil, some mad frenzy he had to spin out like a planet cut loose from its orbit, lost to the order it had always followed. She knew she had only to wait and she knew, too, that when Cecil returned to her he might be different, on an altered path, and maybe she would be too, but she couldn't face that until she knew what she was dealing with.

She had loved her life, that was the truth. She did not stop herself from thinking in the past tense, but neither did she commit to it. Anything could change, anything, even now. She had always known that of course but never before had she bumped up against this strange fear of the future—and then she realized they had come to her house.

Shirley was dropping her off. That had been the plan. But now her friend said, "I'll come in with you. Wasn't there a robbery somewhere last week? Wasn't it nearby?" Betsy waved her hand dismissively. "It looks dark," Shirley said.

"No, no. I think I left the back light on," Betsy said. "Don't worry. The solitude is nice. I admit it." (This was the line she had been taking with herself.)

"I'll just watch you go in—"

"No, no!" Things had not changed so much that she would inconvenience someone. Betsy stood resolute in the driveway and waved until the car pulled away. She felt the house empty behind her. The fear was still there, looming, and now that she was alone she could turn and stare it down. She walked to the back door. She had not left the light on after all.

As she fumbled with her key in the dark, she reflected that for a while she'd been waiting for something to happen. She was so fortunate, there had been so few sadnesses in her life, few inconveniences even. When she began to suspect Cecil it was the first shoe dropping, and she could not shake the notion that she deserved it: she had not had her share of pain. At times the idea of his infidelity didn't seem like a crime against her or their family or a moral issue at all (she told herself) but instead like a small pestilence, an act of nature, a minute slice of the horrors one could read about in a newspaper on any given day.

But as she entered the dark back hall and then her empty kitchen, wondering where Cecil really was and whom he was really with, her calm practicality finally failed her, she felt her heart finally rend, and she gave a little cry.

So what happened next simply seemed like more of the same, the other shoe, a thundering of shoes, a blossoming in her chest that felt like a great weight stamping down upon her. The man came around the corner and she knew immediately that whatever she might say would make no difference. *If I had not cried out.* He was so angry: what had she done? She did not even have time to ask. She heard Boston, the Cape, in his voice: how could that be? Her surprise now was so utter, so total, that it felt like the complete absence of surprise, she was wiped clean, she would believe anything. She had been thinking something about Cecil, it did not matter. In these strange few endless seconds her vision became one of a craggy landscape of peaks and valleys, and clarity such as she had never known, the air thin, becoming nonexistent. She felt herself reaching out but she was not sure her arms were moving. She searched for Cecil, for her children, but she was suspended on points, the land below her was sere and brown, they were not there. Still she reached, she sent herself out to them, her horror and now her own anger became fierce and enormous, *no no no,* her main duty *no,* her main duty, her only, not to leave. She pushed herself through pain and made herself an arrow pointing to him, to her children, and with the last of her strength shot herself through the sky, arcing against the stars, but she had not realized she was forever split from herself and instead of reaching them she was going away, although raging and determined she was diffusing, she was becoming enormous and everywhere. *I love you I love you* she thought, she was. *Oh oh oh*

so this is what it is.

SEVEN

MASHANTUM.

In late September, Anthony called to say he had business in New York and would be driving through nearby. He asked Marcella if she would like to have dinner.

She hesitated, then, to be civil, said yes.

She hung up not at all sure she should have agreed. She had seen him a few weeks before, when he had taken Toni to school and she had met them there with some of Toni's things. She had not been able to meet his gaze; she had been afraid there would be questions in it, or answers, and she had not been prepared for either. She had determinedly kept the conversation light, but whenever her eyes had skated across his face she had felt he was looking at her with particular intensity.

He was due at seven. A little before six, she went to the beach. The day had been gray, and the light would last for less than an hour; the parking lot was deserted. Down at the beach the tide was low, and with the wide expanse of empty sand the light seemed brighter—a flat, colorless light. A wintry cold blew in sharp and hard from the water, and she raised the hood of her jacket and began walking with the wind behind her. It pushed her along. Her way back would be harder, she knew, but beginning in this direction was her routine, and she would not alter it.

With the hood around her ears the world was muffled, and in the quiet she was aware of her body, the grinding of the sand under her feet, her muscles stretching. She thought of the first time at this beach with Jed, how hot it had been, how crowded; how she had longed to touch him, how she had felt she was only body. She waited to miss him, but she had had these same thoughts so many times by now, walking in this direction past these landmarks under this sky, that they felt like part of the beach. The thoughts and the sadness were landmarks themselves. She was used to them, and she knew if they altered, it would be at an almost imperceptible pace.

She had begun to think of moving, although not to get away from memories of Jed. No, that would be a loss. But at some point, she would have to leave the cottage that was, she now saw, her way station. And she would also leave the coast. The sea was journeys, it was wandering, and someday soon she wanted to look out instead at old, old earth, earth soaked with the histories of others, earth that was home. It was time.

"Marcella."

She did not believe anyone could be speaking to her, and kept walking. It had been her own mind—sneaking away, looking for Jed, maybe, wishing he were here, calling for her.

"Marcella!"

And she turned. "Anthony?"

He had been walking fast; he was breathing hard. As he slowed, he put his hands in his pockets. She was so surprised she could think of nothing to say. They stared at each other, his chest heaving, until she had to look away, look down. "You're going to ruin your shoes," she blurted.

"I hope not." He looked down too, at his feet, as if surprised. He was still dressed for work, in a suit and tie, and wearing leather dress oxfords. "I suppose I should take them off," he said, and knelt down.

"You're early," Marcella said.

His head was bent; he didn't look up. "I wanted to beat the traffic," he said.

"I didn't know you knew where this beach was." She almost said *my beach*.

He finished rolling up his trousers and stood, shoes in one hand. "I just went toward the ocean," he said, with a small smile. "You weren't at the house, and I thought you might be here. And I saw your car." He paused, and seemed about to take a step backward. "Do you mind if I walk with you?"

"No. No, of course not."

They walked in silence for several minutes. Inside her hood, she couldn't see him unless she turned her head. She could even pretend she was still alone. But one must be polite. "It was nice of you to call," she began, but even as she spoke her heart clenched and she drew in her breath. "Is something wrong with Toni? Is that why you're here?" *Stupid! Of course!*

"No, no. Everything is fine," he said, and just as quickly she relaxed. She risked a look at him, expecting impatience or even scorn, but instead he was smiling at her ruefully. She found herself smiling back. It was unavoidable, this understanding they had, thinking always of their child.

They passed an American flag on a mast in front of a large gray-shingled house. The shutters on the house were closed for the season. The flag rippled in the wind. "Did Toni tell you she was in another play?" Anthony said.

"Yes."

"I think she has a little talent."

"She doesn't mind the spotlight," Marcella said.

"It's true. We've always known that," Anthony said, and laughed. "She'll be with that same redheaded boy. Now, he might go places."

"Yes," Marcella said again. They walked for several minutes in silence. She could not remember what she had chitchatted about, the last time she had seen him. She could not even remember how to do it now. The beach was too huge and empty to let her dissemble. "We should turn around," she said. "It's going to get dark soon. And you will get cold, with no coat."

"I'm not cold," he said, but she turned without looking at him, and he followed.

There was a line of indigo at the horizon. Now the wind was in their faces, solid and biting. Even in her jacket she shivered. "There's the first star," Anthony said.

She said, "Why are you here?"

She could feel that he wanted her to stop and look at him, but she kept going, her eyes fixed ahead. He said, "I thought it would be nice to—"

"It is not my business to forgive you or not," she said. She had to speak above the wind. "If that's why."

She was walking fast, and he was keeping up. "I know," he said.

They passed three sailboats in a row, shackles dinging rhythmically against the empty masts. It was a sound of departures, of endings. They passed the flag; now the wind was making it heave and snap. "You know that I should tell him," she said, and suddenly Jed was there with her. The memory was so clear she could almost believe that he would be waiting for her atop the next dune. She wanted to say his name over and over, not to invoke him or to taunt Anthony but to keep feeling this way, so alive, aware. "It is the only thing he wants," she said. "To know who killed his mother."

"You haven't—"

"I haven't spoken to him in weeks," she said. "I haven't spoken to him since August." The truth of this hit her harder than the wind and he was no longer with her at all, but instead gone, gone. She stopped and turned, finally looking at Anthony head-on, and repeated, "Why are you here?"

Just as she herself felt uncommonly alert, Anthony, too, looked weirdly vivid, here on the wrong beach. In the rapidly dying light his face seemed drained of color but its outlines were sharper. His eyes were dark and his hair was ruffled by the wind. "I wanted to talk to someone," he said.

"To someone?" He didn't answer. It seemed to her that he had never stood before her so passively, almost obediently. "To me?"

Slowly, he nodded. "You are the only one," he said. "The only one."

Her eyes began to sting. "I have to tell him. I want to tell him—"

"I'm sorry, Marcellina, I'm sorry—"

"—but I don't know what is brave anymore."

"Marcella," Anthony said. "They wouldn't have killed Betsy. I have thought and thought, I have remembered everything." His voice was faster now, urgent. "There was no misunderstanding, it was crystal-clear—do you hear me? They were going to—use a gun, for—" He faltered. He still couldn't say Cecil's name. "But Betsy was—it was, not a gun—"

"*Stop it,*" Marcella hissed. "That is why you came here? To give these excuses?"

"No," he said. "No." His eyes no longer burned at her. "I don't want to give excuses. I don't have any."

The beach was still empty. There were no lights in the houses. She felt a sob rising in her throat, a bolus of love and grief for Betsy, for Cecil, for Jed and Callie and Toni and herself, and for Anthony. He was so close, a foot away, standing stiff and helpless. Waiting. Perhaps he had always been that way. "Oh, *caro,*" she said. "I have caught you in this."

"And I have caught you."

"We are all caught," she whispered, and she reached out and touched his cheek. His hand came up and covered hers. He nodded, his own eyes wet, and she was surprised again, that they understood each other.

It was several weeks after Labor Day, and Callie and Jed were sitting in the living room reading in front of the fire. It was evening; Jamie and Grace were asleep. "I guess it gets cold this early in Connecticut?" said Jed. He thought of Marcella, alone, in front of a fire. But then he made himself stop. Callie was talking. "What?"

"I said, sometimes. Sometimes it's this cold in September." There was a pause, and Jed hoped she was not going to question, again, the need to go home. But she said instead, "Are you sure you want to come back with us? Don't you have to work eventually?"

"Eventually. But yes, I'm sure."

"You're keeping tabs on me," Callie said, looking at him with her new expression—resigned, a little ironic. Jed could see it, sometimes, through the haze of her drugs. Jed wasn't sure if Billy saw, or understood, this look—Billy was a bag of nerves, and he was the one who had asked Jed to go back to Greenwich with them, finally, the following week, and stay for a while. But to Jed, there seemed to be something newly calm at Callie's center, and he did not believe it was because of psychopharmaceuticals. She seemed to have shed some dark weight.

That did not mean he wasn't still afraid.

And that, he told himself, was the reason he was still here. It was true that he could not forget how close Marcella was, and how she would be even closer when he went back with Callie. But he knew, too, that he would feel her, out there, in the world, no matter how close or far away she was. Day by day, the urge to give in and jump into his car was lessening, although it was possible that that would never go away entirely either.

Callie had stretched to her full length on the sofa. "I still say we could winterize the house," she said, but it was an old and half-hearted argument, and he didn't answer. He watched as her eyes traveled thoughtfully around the living room. He had put it all back together, and the only thing different was the china missing from the hutch—big blue willowware platters that had come with the house. In their place he had put some of the regular everyday plates, and he thought now that Callie's gaze lingered there a moment. Then her eyes came back to his, and grew sympathetic. "What's with you?"

"Oh, nothing. Tired."

"Marcie?"

"Maybe. Sort of."

"It's been a while now, Jeddy." Her voice softened. "Maybe this one didn't have to end."

He was surprised to feel a swell of anger. *Don't even suggest it. Don't let me consider it*—and then, just as quickly, the anger subsided. Instead he wanted to say, *I loved her, I loved her, I think I still do.* Callie was looking at him encouragingly, but what he really noticed was that though there were circles under her eyes, her gaze was clear. She was really listening, she would really hear what he had to say. If he said it. "Jed?"

"I'm sure," he said finally. "It wasn't—designed for longevity." He got up and turned his back to her to put more wood on the fire. He tossed in a log and it crunched onto the coals with a shower of sparks. Nothing happened for a moment, and then the edge of a piece of loose bark began to glow, and then burst into flame. "I'm sorry I left every weekend, Cal. I'm sorry I kept escaping."

Callie *humphed.* "I don't blame you."

What if he told her? He never stopped considering this possibility. In his mind he saw the old, valiant Callie, not this new fragile one he had to guard. She would be appalled—scathing, furious—but it wouldn't matter. He would say to her, *Now we know. Now we know for sure.*

That what?

That Dad didn't do it.

And Callie would say, *I already knew that.*

He thought of Grace and Jamie, peaceful in their beds. He wondered if he would ever be like Callie—resting after a long day with children, surrounded by the thick contentment of their sleep. What would he tell them about their grandparents? What would he say to Jamie and Grace, about these people so obviously missing?

He would say, *There are some things we will never know.*

The quiet stretched. The only sound was the gentle crackling of the fire. Then Callie said, in a new, tentative voice, "Jed?"

He turned around. "Yep."

"Tell me again about the furniture."

"Again?" he said, not impatiently.

She flicked her eyes at him, then away again. "Yes. Please."

"You pushed it all against Grace's door," he said. He went back to his armchair and sat down.

"How?"

He shook his head. "I don't know."

"All of it," she said. It was not a question; she was like a child who has heard a story a hundred times, whose fear that there might not be a happy ending is purely for show. "All the furniture," she repeated.

He nodded. "The sofa and the chest. The *hutch*." He laughed. "Some other stuff."

"All the china broke," she said.

"Yes."

"I'm sorry about that. That stuff was probably antique. Valuable."

"It doesn't matter."

"I pushed the furniture against Grace's door," she said.

"Yes," he said. "No one could get in."

"*I* couldn't get in."

"Right."

They sat in silence for a few moments. He stole a look at her. She was smiling, just barely, into the fire.

Then, at the far end of the house, they heard crying begin, insistent but not desperate. Callie glanced at her watch. "Right on schedule," she said.

"Do you want me to get her?" Jed secretly enjoyed feeding Grace, now that he could, since breast-feeding had fallen by the wayside. Giving her a bottle was so simple and concrete. Filling a need that could be filled. But Callie had sat up, and was searching with her feet for her slippers.

"That's okay. I'm awake anyway." Slippers on, she stood up, and started out of the room. But at the beginning of the hallway she stopped, and turned back to him.

"Thank you," she said. "I might need you to tell me that story every now and then." She looked at him steadily. He looked back.

"Any time," he said. "I'm here."

ACKNOWLEDGMENTS

Many, many generous friends, mentors, and colleagues have helped me to arrive at this page. I am especially grateful to the following people:

my agent, Henry Dunow, and my editor, Alison Callahan, both of whom are dreams come true;

the rest of the wonderdul teams at Doubleday, Doubleday Canada, and Anchor, especially Todd Doughty, Jennifer Jackson, Kristin Cochrane, Nita Provost, and Adria Iwasutiak;

Mary Granfield, Karen Leigh Heath, Kathleen Hobson, William Pierce, and Elizabeth Rourke, extraordinary first readers;

Anne Aaron, Jaime Clarke, Tim Egan, Atul Gawande, Dana Gioia, Glee Garard Hoonhout, Amy MacKinnon, Tom Perrotta, Michael Rosovsky, Lara JK Wilson, and Paula Rendino Zaentz, for their encouragement and guidance;

my in-laws and fellow outlaws, readers and cheerleaders all, especially Teresa Masterson Howe, Dodge Thompson, and Lisa and Sam Howe Verhovek; and also the late Sylvia Howe Thompson, James Murray Howe, and Barbara Burleigh Howe, whose love of family and of the Cape lies at the heart of this book;

my parents, for their steady love, patience, and faith in me; my children, for making me laugh and getting me out of my head; and most of all my husband, Peter Howe, who really does know me best. This book would not exist without you.

Meet with Interesting People
Enjoy Stimulating Conversation
Discover Wonderful Books